LACK OF AMBITION

LACK OF AMBITION

PETER A STANKOVIC

Paperback: 978-1-63767-769-8
eBook: 978-1-63767-770-4
Library of Congress Control Number: 2022903505

This is a work of fiction.

Ordering Information:

BookTrail Agency
8838 Sleepy Hollow Rd.
Kansas City, MO 64114

Printed in the United States of America

CHAPTER 1

Day 1

There is nothing quite as satisfying as being in control of others. He smiled as he surveyed the group before briefly focussing on the agenda and his written notes in front of him.

He was sitting in his customary position, at the head of the long board room table. He had been in this chair so many times as the chairman of meetings that it was almost a second home to him, like the comfortable leather chair at his Lindfield residence when he was entertaining guests. At Board Meetings, of course, he gave up the chair to the official Chairman of the Board but those meetings happened only four times a year. He was used to deference and to having the final say. He was used to being in charge in almost any situation. After all he was the well known corporate chief John Franks. The title, his title, of Chief Executive Officer was a much coveted position in any public company. But in this company, Easy Insurance Group Ltd which had won many awards for insurer of the year, it was particularly prestigious.

As he looked up from his papers his heart almost stopped.

Today he was not in charge. He was staring at a Glock22 pistol aimed straight between his eyes. The holder of the weapon was a man wearing a balaclava. The man, a metre and some to his left, held the gun as steady as a professional poker player's gaze, appearing calm and in control.

It was not a great start to the day. The global management meeting had begun on time at 9am. All the regional chiefs were present and had been in fine spirits when proceedings kicked off. It was now 9:47am and Franks' schedule would be derailed, something he disliked intensely. He was a man of routine and planning and he didn't suffer disruptions with his subordinates. His favourite saying was: 'If you don't plan, you plan to fail.'

To Franks' right sat the Group Chief Operating Officer, Doug Vincent, next to him Tim Tennyson the US Operations Chief, then Stephen Burton the European Operations Chief, then David Mittlehouse the combined Australia Asia Pacific Operations Chief, and at the far end Don Neilson the Chief Financial Officer, the one man he disliked. To Franks' immediate left sat a bug eyed George Waites, the Chief Risk Officer, then Jennie Jones the Group Human Resources Officer and finally Mark Hovein the Group Investment Manager. Franks' right side represented the operational men and on the left was his Head Office team, all men except for the Human Resources officer who was the lone female executive in the group.

Another female was also in the room – an attractive leggy bottle blonde near the table on Franks' far right. She was cowering by the coffee and biscuits and, afraid she might emit a peep and draw attention to herself, she placed her hand over her mouth. Just as she did, something caught her eye to her immediate right. Another gunman had somehow materialised. She then saw that there were three men in balaclavas and what was surprising was how quickly and quietly they had emerged. Blondie realised, when later questioned, that they had entered from the side door which was connected to the kitchen. The executives, deep in discussion, had not noticed a thing until it was too late.

Franks said, "What do you want? We don't have any cash in here."

The masked gunman in front of him, one of three fit looking men, said, "I want you all to listen and listen good. No noise or screams otherwise harm will befall the young lass next to the coffee table. As for you leaders, you are to get up and in single file follow the fellow near the door."

"What are you intending to do?" said the Chief Risk Officer. "You'll find out soon enough."

Waites sniggered, "Hardly a proper response."

Nobody moved. Then the masked gunman who was focused on Franks turned, took a step forward, and smacked the Chief Risk Officer on the side of his face with his closed fist. The whack, connecting with the cheekbone and nose, made a loud sound audible to all in the room. Blood streamed from Waites' nose. He yelped in pain. Jennie Jones, sitting next to him, offered him a tissue.

The gunman, whom to all seemed to be the leader, said quietly but with undisguised menace, "Now move and leave your possessions with my colleague near the table." To Waites he said, "Stop fussing or you will get another instalment."

Jennie Jones stood up quickly. The men looked at her and slowly stood up, pushing chairs back, then walked single file behind the gunman by the door. Before moving off, the man who had been closest to the coffee table and the gasping blonde opened a carry bag and waited until the wallets and mobile phones had been emptied into it.

The lead gunman was in the rear. He stopped in front of the woman near the coffee. She was in her early twenties and clearly frightened, looking wide-eyed and vulnerable. She was dressed like many city workers in a white blouse, black skirt and high heels. Despite the addition of heels, she only came up to the lead gunman's shoulder. She waited nervously to see what he was going to do.

"I'm going to have to lock you in the cool room," the gunman said, admiring her legs. Blondie stared at him, defiant. "No."

"Want to join the execs?" the gunman said, noting everyone else had cleared out. "Please, I haven't done anything to you. I won't say anything."

"You'll be able to drink a wine or two until somebody opens the door. No point in screaming either, this floor is isolated. Come along. You know where it is."

Relieved that she was not being forced to go with the others, she brightened but realised she had better not appear too pleased. She stood still.

"Come along," said the gunman.

"We don't have one," she said, faking a quivering voice, hoping her attractiveness will buy her time.

"Don't try to con me. I know you have one and I also know where it is. What's your name?"

"Fiona."

"Lead the way then Fiona," he said following her.

The floor plan of the top level of the city office building was just as he remembered it. She led him to the cool room and waited at the door."

"I'll freeze to death in here. Nobody comes to this floor except for the executives and the cleaners."

"Once we're on our way I'll call someone to let you out." She hesitated.

"Open up Fiona and step inside. You'll come to no harm, I promise."

She did as requested and he shut the door and pushed the latch down. Screaming would be totally ineffective.

On his way back he glanced out the window and admired the view of other buildings in the midst of Sydney's CBD. This, he gathered, was a perk of the high flyers.

He walked to the bank of elevators and pressed the button for the carriage with express transit to the underground car park. Coming up to this floor which was reserved for Board meetings and corporate dining required an identification tag given exclusively to Directors, key management personnel and a few others who had a role on the floor. Auditors also had an ID tag in case they were called to a meeting with the Audit Committee. The gunman had an auditors' ID tag in his pocket.

Downstairs, the large elevator came to a sudden halt. One gunman, at the rear of the carriage, had his gun nestled against John Franks' back and the other gunman, who stood in the front, had his gun pointed at Jennie Jones' chest. The occupants were warned that any attempt to charge them would end in the deaths of these two individuals.

As the elevator doors opened, the first gunman stepped out and held up his hand to the others to wait. He then checked that the basement car park was deserted before he signalled that it was safe to proceed. He stood back whilst the group filed past him. His shorter buddy who had been at the rear walked over to a large rental van and unlocked the back doors. Company personnel were then herded into the rear. They were told to sit on the two benches which faced each other before the doors were closed.

Inside the large van, it was dim with only one bulb working but nobody uttered a word until all had settled onto a seat. Finally Franks said, "Don't worry, they can't be stupid. We're too high profile to be ignored for long. Police will be alerted very soon I imagine."

"What are they after," said Jennie Jones, the HR Chief.

"Money, what else," said Tennyson, the US Chief, "as John says, we're well known and they will want a ransom. Happens in South America all the time. But in Australia! Unbelievable."

David Mittlehouse who sat on the right hand side at the rear of the van yawned. At least he'd be able to avoid an uncomfortable meeting with an angry customer which was scheduled for later in the morning. Next to him was Doug Vincent who was agitated. He faced Tennyson and said, "Kidnappers also kill their captives in South America. I think we should figure out a way to escape. After all there's nine of us and only three of them."

"Any ideas?" said Stephen Burton who sat next to Vincent and across from Franks. Burton had eyebrows raised and wondered what sort of idiot Vincent was. Did he want to commit suicide? He was as impetuous in his business dealings and Burton often wondered how this man had scaled the corporate ladder. But then he remembered he was a personal friend of Franks.

Nielson faced Jennie Jones and despite the grim situation couldn't help admiring her trim figure and muscular legs. She worked out in the gym, he knew, but he had always refrained from commenting on how much he liked the way she looked. Perhaps an opportunity would arise under these circumstances. The only positive in this escapade was missing out on yet another boring meeting Franks loved to hold.

The two gunmen waited until their leader arrived. He faced them and said "Ok, let's get the show on the road. Make sure the mobiles are ditched before we move."

"What about the wallets and watches?"

"Keep them, they could serve a purpose."

One of the men emptied the mobiles onto the ground, stomped on them and then placed the fragments into the large waste bin in the garage.

The gunmen removed their balaclavas. The leader was of medium build and dark haired. He nodded to his two colleagues and they climbed into the front of the van. The leader then drove the vehicle out of the basement garage into Phillip Street, using his current employee pass to exit the garage. Once they reached William Street the leader said, "Corey, has it all been set up at the other end?"

Corey who sat in the middle was a tall, slim man in his mid twenties with messy hair. "Yes boss I checked it myself."

"What happens when we get them there?" asked Dan, the third gunman who had been quiet throughout. He was only twenty and somewhat anxious about the assignment, his first big-time crime.

"Not our problem. We get paid then we leave," said the leader. "That's the part I like," Corey laughed.

The leader who had not known his associates before this job was glad he had not told them anything about himself. These young men could be trouble as they were in it only for the money and already displayed a sense of relief despite the job still being in progress. They weren't the professionals he expected when he contacted Koutslakis for resources.

The van pulled up outside their destination forty three minutes later. From the outside it looked like a building site but in fact it was an abandoned block of units which was under construction. Corey and Dan dropped out of the front and opened the door to the basement car park at the end of a long concrete driveway. The leader reversed the van up onto the driveway which then sloped down until the vehicle was just outside the entrance to the car park. With the main door open it was obvious that the building had a considerable number of car spaces and consequently units. The driver, knowing he would have to back down gently if he wanted to ensure his passengers were not thrown around too much, proceeded with care. The van slid into the underground car park, not unlike a cavernous concrete bunker, and the leader backed the vehicle up against the door which led up into a completely closed off room. The leader got out and nodded to his two assistants to push the van door up to enable access to the inside. Effort had been made to ensure that the entrance possessed a sliding door to a room in the basement cleared of all items and modified specifically for the current purpose. There were no windows in the adjoining room and there was only one exit from the basement into the block. Used previously as a storage facility, the empty room was large and could easily contain nine individuals without appearing over crowded.

Corey moved past a number of car spaces and slammed the garage door shut. It had been unlocked when they'd arrived but now he followed the plan and bolted it from the inside.

The men used the underground car park stairs on the right hand side of the basement to enter the block. Once upstairs, at ground level, the leader asked the men to remain in the foyer whilst he took the stairs to a first floor unit which had been set up as the headquarters of the operation. He retrieved items from a safe and made his way back downstairs, ensuring he had not been followed. He then handed each man an envelope which contained cash. He shook hands with both Corey and Dan who immediately went outside, got into their Toyota Camry and sped off, leaving a trail of rubber.

Inside the van, it was becoming unbearably hot. Now that the vehicle was parked with the engine off, air was no longer circulating. The captives were getting agitated. Suits were not conducive to these conditions. The men had discarded their jackets which were nearly always worn in the Boardroom. Jennie Jones wanted to loosen the buttons on her blouse but knew it wasn't a good idea. She'd hold on a bit longer. She trusted these men only so far.

"What is going on?" said Stephen Burton, the UK CEO," this is insane."

"Let's remain calm," said Franks. He said these words, uncertain himself about events to come. He realised he needed to assume control for the moment. It was his job, after all. He added, "They'll need to negotiate soon."

George Waites was nursing his sore head and remained silent.

"Fuck. I don't think kidnappers negotiate with their victims," said Doug Vincent, the Chief Operational Officer.

Franks said, "I know. What I'm trying to suggest is that they'll need to ensure we're ok so that they can negotiate with the outside world."

"Well I hope they bloody hurry up, "said Mittlehouse, "I'm fucking boiling."

Tim Tennyson slipped off his tie. The stifling conditions were getting to him. He was not a patient man at the best of times but now he really had to maintain self-control. He couldn't vent his frustrations like he did when he was in charge in the New York headquarters. Here it paid to appear calm and controlled. He said, "Let's remain patient and relaxed. We'll soon find out what the story is. How are they going to deal with nine of us at one time? As Doug said before, we outnumber them and we'll just need to wait for an opportunity."

"I'm pleased you're so brave Tim," said Jennie Jones, "I will wait for you to carry out the heroics."

Don Neilson spoke for the first time. "Is there any value in bickering amongst ourselves? Let's see what happens, then formulate a plan of action." He ran a handkerchief across his brow.

Mark Hovein, the Group Investments Manager, decided to assess the position later. As in his job, it paid to obtain the right data before making a decision. This was no different. However, he felt particularly frustrated because he usually called his wife, Daya, each day around eleven o'clock to check on her condition. He couldn't foresee the kidnappers allowing communication. They had confiscated their mobiles before entering the van.

Jennie Jones stood up then collapsed.

CHAPTER 2

The Past

Traffic woke her. Cars riding the overpass, the wretched Syd Einfeld Drive, with horns honking as the earlier and earlier peak hour began always got her up before her alarm. The noise was something she would never get used to. Her flat was along Edgecliff Road closer to Old South Head Road than further down the winding, sloping road to Edgecliff station. She slid out of bed and put her arms around herself. She drew the curtain facing the road and, looking down, noted the line of cars already bumper to bumper. She shuddered.

It was a chilly day in late July, a day in mid winter, a day Madeline would rather have stayed in bed for another few hours. She hated winter and simply wanted to spend the day at home but she was not the type of person to give in to her urges. Others she knew would have taken the day off without a second thought but she couldn't do it.

Madeline was not unattractive but today she didn't consider herself attractive at all. She had nothing to wear she concluded after studying her wardrobe. She was not tall but neither would she be classified as short. She simply did not stand out in the crowd. She could be friendly but rarely displayed this trait during office hours. Maddie as she was known to her friends and work colleagues went to work each day but did not find it a satisfying experience. She was in the Human Resources Department. She found the job dull. She found the people dull. She felt her career going nowhere. She did not know why.

Maddie worked for a large public company but she worked in a small department which was an all female department. This HR section was responsible for head office staff which numbered around

They met at the restaurant, an Italian place in Darlinghurst. Maddie was nervous. It had been a long time since she had had dinner with anyone, let alone a male. She arrived by taxi and wandered to the entrance. She had dithered about what to wear and settled on a simple black outfit, with high heels – whirl black bonbons which she bought for a hundred dollars during lunch time. She removed her coat once inside and told the head waiter that there was a reservation in the name of Johnson.

She was shown to a table towards the back of the restaurant. The place was nearly full. The tables were neat squares with red and white table cloths. The chairs were sturdy but elegant. Quality furniture, understated but without question it screamed expensive decor.

Jordan Johnson smiled when he saw her. "Hi." He stood and pecked her on the cheek.

Although he seemed nice and well mannered there was something which troubled her but she couldn't put her finger on it. "Hello," she said, then sat down.

The dinner went smoothly until coffee arrived. They chatted about nothing much in particular, nothing memorable. About work, about where they lived, how they got to work, the weather. In fact the conversation was dry. Maddie wasn't sure whether to be pleased or concerned. Why waste an evening on nothingness but at least she was out – with another person for a change, rather than by herself at a shopping mall or at the movies.

Jordan seemed content. He ate his food slowly, he spoke quietly and he listened attentively. Jordan didn't say much to show who he was. He exuded little enthusiasm. Maddie wondered whether he thought he would get into her bed by saying nothing to challenge or offend her or reveal something about his personality which she might dislike. Perhaps he was simply dull, she pondered.

Jordan's manner changed when their coffees arrived. "So Maddie, you strike me as a girl who would like to have some fun," he said, looking more animated than previously.

"Why do you say that?"

"It's the way you dress."

Maddie was not sure what he meant. She wasn't dressed unusually, she didn't stand out. Her dress didn't make a statement. What did he mean? She stared at him a moment. Maybe he was joking but his expression remained unmoved. "How do I dress?"

"The black dress and pumps."

"Really. Lots of women wear black."

"Yes, that's right and they usually like to have fun."

Maddie didn't quite know how to respond. Perhaps not fuelling the idea might work. But she had to say something. "That may be but that's not me."

"So you're saying you don't like fun." Jordan leaned back, assessing her.

Maddie finished her cup of coffee. The chocolate mousse sat half eaten beside the cup. She had lost her appetite. She just wanted to go home. She felt his eyes burn into her. "Can you get me a taxi?"

Jordan registered a glimmer of surprise but it was short lived. He pulled out his iphone4 and called a cab. After a few minutes, he received a call and accompanied her outside to the waiting white Combined taxi. He didn't attempt to kiss her and said nothing. As the taxi moved off, she noted he held his hand up to say goodnight.

Now, Monday morning, as Maddie read a report on staff turnover statistics, she wondered whether she had been too hasty. Jordan hadn't complained when she left the restaurant, leaving him alone with a brandy, although he acted the gentleman and saw her out. He seemed quite calm, as though it had happened to him before.

Maddie got up and walked to the kitchen which HR shared with a number of other departments. Walter who worked for the Finance Department, situated at the front of the building, passed her and mouthed hello. He was a serious guy but was always polite to her. Others made fun of him because he was obese and moved awkwardly but Maddie tried not to let that colour her view of him. She'd often wondered why HR was located at the back of the floor where the view from the windows was of the backs of other office buildings.

A man walked into the narrow space and Maddie turned. She said hello to Mark, poured water from the cooler and walked back to her desk, feeling confused. She wanted to run into Jordan to talk about Saturday night, or, she thought, maybe it was best left as is. She dismissed the thought. Setting her water down on her coaster near the in-tray, she returned to the job at hand. But as time passed the feeling of guilt grew. She didn't like being unpleasant or giving that impression.

The day went slowly. Louise chatted to her but Maddie hardly responded. On the dot of five o'clock she gathered her belongings and waited at the elevators. The doors opened and out strode Jordan.

"Hi," he said and walked past her.

That night, at home, in front of the television, Maddie wondered whether her life was going to stay as it now was. The thought depressed her. She tried to turn her attention to the soap opera being played out in front of her but this made things worse. What was she doing watching other people living life? She wasn't old enough to have given up on participating. She went to the fridge and took out a tub of chocolate ice-cream.

The next day she resolved to be more positive. Why couldn't she just go around to Jordan and talk to him? She decided to do something outside her comfort zone for a change. When she arrived in the office, she did a search on the company's intranet, found a familiar name and called. She asked Sarah where Jordan was located and also asked what she thought of him.

"He's relatively new and I haven't spoken with him very much."

"What's that mean?" Maddie persisted.

"He seems okay but I really haven't had much contact with him. He seems a little shy, if anything. Keeps to himself."

"Thanks Sarah."

"Why? Are you interested in him?" There was a note of curiosity in the enquiry.

"No, no. Just gathering information," Maddie was quick to point out. They chatted a little more and she discovered that Jordan Johnson was in the Group Audit Department which explained why he could move freely to different levels within the company. He was relatively new to EIG but had previous experience and currently held a senior position in Audit. He was perceived as pleasant and unassuming by others on the floor the department was situated on. He was handsome and single, she was told, but she already knew this.

Sarah giggled. "He'll never invite you out." Maddie hung up, smiling to herself.

CHAPTER 3

Day 1

Don Neilson was quick to react as the HR boss fell to the floor. He was beside Jennie in a split second and tried to assess whether she had fainted or whether something else had occurred. He loosened her blouse while the others watched.

"Is she alright?" said Franks.

"Let me finish this," Neilson said, checking her pulse. He then placed his index and middle fingers on her neck feeling for the trachea. She seemed fine so he helped her onto the bench.

Jennie appeared confused. "Where am I?" Neilson smiled at her.

Then it all came back to her. "God, it's hot in here."

"It is," agreed Neilson, "just stay calm. I'm sure someone will attend to us soon." Neilson checked her forehead to check her temperature. It wasn't too high.

Jennie said, "Thanks." She liked Neilson. She had had little interaction with him recently as Franks usually dominated her time. He called on her whenever he needed data on people he didn't know. He was not a good people manager despite his ability to engage the senior executives. He was remote from most of the other staff except when he wanted something. Then he asked Jennie for details on this employee so that he could sound like he knew them intimately.

Moments later, whilst all the occupants loosened more clothing, a door slid open and plastic bottles were tossed in. The door slid shut again.

There were nine bottles in total, one for each captive. They soon removed the tops and drank the water greedily.

CHAPTER 4

The Past

It came as no surprise to Jordan Johnson that Maddie had been wary of him because he knew she was wary of men in general. He had asked about her and discovered she was single, shy and did not socialise with work colleagues. He had been deliberate in the way he'd acted as he didn't want her to gain the impression he was interested in her from the outset. That would have made her suspicious of his real intentions.

Jordan Johnson was known as JJ to his friends and he thought of himself as JJ. Once he felt comfortable with someone, he would ask them to call him JJ instead of Jordan. There was no reason other than he felt it was a form of endearment.

JJ was not new to Sydney but he'd been away for around eighteen months prior to working at Easy Insurance Group. He had spent a year working in London and six months travelling through Europe. He had been devastated by his father's death immediately before heading abroad. He needed to get away to forget, to start afresh, to experience adventure.

He liked Sydney. Of all the Australian cities it was the biggest and glitziest and had magnificent skyscrapers as well as marvellous harbour and ocean views. The city also boasted a world famous Harbour, the Sydney Harbour Bridge, an Opera House and Bondi beach, all spectacular. He was currently renting a unit in Bondi, a congested suburb with lots of restaurants, nightclubs and pubs.

When JJ secured the position at the global insurer nine months earlier in the Central Business District, he celebrated with a rare bottle of champagne. He hadn't made any new friends at the time but invited a neighbour to share the bottle. Usually he preferred beer but getting a job at his second attempt yet first choice made him feel great and he wanted to enjoy something a little different.

During a brief stay in Paris, in the company of a female acquaintance who had moved there to work as an office manager for an English bookstore chain, JJ found himself having to confront his past. He had called Liz on the off chance that she would agree to dine with him. She invited him to stay in her tiny one bedroom flat. She was English but spoke French fluently and, with her in tow, the Parisians were friendly and even helpful. One evening after they lay in bed side by side, naked except for a thin sheet covering their legs, Liz asked what he wanted to do with his life. It felt strange to realise he had no answer. Had he thought it sufficient to meander aimlessly for the rest of his days, enjoying some pleasures but unable to focus on a path or a purpose? He shrugged off the question at the time but the next day, sitting by himself in a cafe, whilst Liz was at work, he pondered the question and had to accept he was escaping from something he couldn't quite put his finger on.

On his arrival in Sydney, JJ sent his resume to EIG's Human Resources Department and it was rejected because he was told the company hired personnel through recruitment agencies unless the individuals were referred from an internal source. He then sent his resume to a number of recruiters and emphasised his commerce degree and chartered accounting qualifications, his technical savvy with computers and his insurance company accounting experience in London. He was soon asked to attend an interview at EIG and secured a job in the Internal Audit Department as an interim step to Finance.

David was a man in his early thirties and lived across the hall from him. JJ had met him a couple of times, coming out or going into the block, and he seemed like a laid back kind of guy. He'd been friendly and JJ thought it would be useful to be on good terms with a neighbour so he thought he should make the first move.

The pair drank champagne and nibbled on nuts, making small talk about the block and its inhabitants. David continued, "Sarah in no 6 is nice. And she also works in IT."

"What do you talk about? Hacking into bank accounts?" JJ was slumped in a grey leather chair, holding his glass and looking at the almost empty bottle of Veuve Clicquot.

"Never brought it up. Asked her out but she has a boyfriend."

"Right. Too pretty for you," JJ said.

"Spot on" David drained his glass. "More champers or beer?"

"Beer. Are you interested in hacking?"

"Just curious. Can you do it?"

"Absolutely, piece of cake. Have you something in mind?"

"No, not really. I work as an internal auditor and my company thinks it's totally protected through firewalls etc so if I were to prove that they were wrong, it might be useful. Just a thought. I probably wouldn't do it. I'm sure I'll be fired if I tried such a stunt." JJ smiled, wondering whether David would be so confident about hacking into a company's records without the drink.

After a few more beers David left, saying that if JJ needed help with computers he should call him.

JJ recalled the incident clearly. He awoke and noted how warm it was. The covers were partially removed. There was another body in the bed. Soft flesh against his bare back was the first sensation he felt.

Something snapped him out of his recollections.

He looked up, startled. In front of him was Maddie, actually smiling. He wondered how long she had been standing there and realised it was embarrassing being caught out like this in his office. His memory of the night with his neighbour seemed also to have merged with a daydream because there was definitely no warm body next to him when he woke the following morning. "Hi," he said, sitting up straighter in his ergonomically shaped chair.

"Sorry about the other night," she said, "I wasn't feeling well and I had to get home."

JJ pointed to a chair inviting her to take a seat. His desk was covered with paper and files and pens. He also had a telephone to his left, a desk calendar and an empty coffee mug. A laptop open at a news site occupied the centre of his desk.

He brushed aside a few papers so he had some uncovered area. "How did you find me?"

"I have my ways," she said.

JJ observed her closely. She had changed her hair and it suited her face which was oval shaped centred with a slightly long nose. She had a pleasant smile, revealing strong white even teeth. "Nice of you to pop in," he said," As you can see, I'm swamped."

"I really just wanted you to know I'm not always so rude but I..."

JJ waved aside her apology. "That's okay, no harm done, "he said. "Want to try again?"

"Why not?" They arranged a time and place. Maddie returned to her desk, feeling more than a little satisfied with her efforts.

JJ smiled. He knew she would come around. He stood, stretched and then took the fire stairs outside to take a walk and grab a cappuccino from a stand across the street.

The second date went entirely differently. They went to a restaurant again and the food and wine were similar to what they experienced at the other Italian place but Maddie's attitude was significantly changed. She seemed to be enjoying herself and JJ often caught her with a happy expression, not the worried facade she seemed to normally carry with her.

He found her a pleasant dinner companion. She was attractive enough without being a real beauty but he also thought she was pessimistic about her appearance. Maddie wasn't vain, a sound attribute, he felt, looking back on some of his other relationships. She wasn't expecting confirmation of her physical appearance all the time like many others he had dated but still, an occasional positive remark worked wonders. All women thrived on flattery. It was a condition of their existence.

JJ found himself also enjoying the outing. He decided not to push Maddie into anything after the meal. He would see how the evening developed. He had no specific agenda tonight. He could relax.

"Where are you from?" Maddie said at one point.

"I'm a city boy. I've lived in big cities, Sydney mainly but I've travelled and spent time in London for over a year and New York for a few months. Don't know much about the country or country towns."

"Why's that?"

"My dad. His job kept us in the one place and he didn't like to move much. In fact I can only recall living in Naremburn and later in Rose Bay. He worked all the time for a big corporation which ate away at his soul until it was destroyed. My mum hated what the job did to him but she felt helpless. She loved him and had to watch his deterioration from one year to the next. She even thought of leaving him, she told me once, but she couldn't do that either. She has no saleable skills but also felt a deep sense of duty for my sister and myself. The only positive was that my father earned a decent income."

Time passed and the conversation flowed easily. They discussed family and friends and JJ learned that she had grown up in Coonabarabran, a small New South Wales country town of only a few thousand inhabitants. Her father worked at the Anglo-Australian Telescope the largest optical telescope in Australia and she had been sent to Sydney as a boarder at Kambala, a Sydney girl's college on New South Head Road, Rose Bay.

They ordered dessert and coffee and Maddie seemed to be enjoying his company. With Rose Bay as something they both had in common, they soon discussed some of the local restaurants and other usual meeting places for young people.

JJ wondered whether she would be tempted to invite him back. If she didn't it wouldn't bother him. He was a patient man. He didn't need her for sex.

JJ asked for the bill. While he waited he scrutinised his date more closely and noticed that she had blue eyes flecked with green. She was dressed in a dark blue top which made her blue eyes sparkle. She had put her hair up which suited her. She looked back at him and held his gaze for a moment. The waitress returned and placed the bill on the table.

Walking to his car, JJ took Maddie's hand and, to his surprise, she didn't pull it away. When they reached his silver Ford Mondeo, he opened the door for her and she slid inside. He walked around the back, wondering why Maddie seemed to have changed so much. He got into the car, smiled at her and switched on the ignition.

The ride to Maddie's Bondi Junction flat was smooth. Few words were spoken. The traffic was heavy but it moved easily enough. JJ wondered how she would react when he reached her place. He watched the passing lights and the people wandering the streets. The night was young and the early beginnings of spring weather allowed people to enjoy the walk and the crisp air. JJ slowed the car once he entered Edgecliff Road, watching for a parking spot, and contemplated suggesting a nightcap.

Eventually JJ came upon a space not far from her block of flats and he stopped the car. Maddie turned to him and smiled. "Do you want to come in?" she said, hesitatingly.

"I'd love to, "said JJ. "But not tonight. Maybe another time."

Maddie appeared to sigh with relief. What had she been expecting? Had she figured if she didn't ask that she would not see the young man again? JJ waited.

"Ok. Is anything wrong?" she said.

"Not at all. I have to get up early for a trip up the north coast. Otherwise I wouldn't hesitate." JJ moved his head closer to Maddie's, put his hand up around her neck and gently pulled her to him. He kissed her lips, but didn't linger. "Good night then. See you on Monday."

"Night," she said, smiling. She got out and walked off. She looked back when she reached the front door of the apartment block and waved.

JJ drove off, happy with his performance. He slipped a CD into the player and drove home. He would sleep in Saturday morning. He didn't need to go up north. That was a lie. It was best to create the impression he was interested in her, but not just as a quick turn in the sack. He needed her until he obtained some important information.

Maddie entered her unit in a happy state. Jordan seemed likeable and he was a gentleman as well. She wondered whether this could be the start of something but she refused to entertain this for long. Inside she tossed her handbag onto the floor beside her bed. She undressed and took off her make-

up. She was pleased now that she had been forward enough to see him. Otherwise she would have missed a great opportunity. Perhaps she should be more aggressive in going after what she wanted.

Sleep came easily that night and she woke Saturday morning feeling energised. She did something very uncharacteristic. She went for a walk to a nearby park. The fresh air felt exhilarating. Then she walked to the Bondi Junction shopping centre. To get her breath back, she sat at an outdoor cafe table. Staring into the distance, she saw Jordan.

CHAPTER 5

Day 1

Franks had finished a series of meetings and was feeling exhausted. He was hungry and wanted some relaxing company, someone who would amuse him and not seek a favour or corporate advantage. He was always being courted by individuals, whether subordinates or industry peers, who wanted something from him. He was heartily sick of it, although he loved the power of deciding how much he would give. He sighed. Sometimes he wondered whether it was all worth it.

A knock on the door disrupted his thoughts. His PA was at lunch he imagined so he said, "Come in."

"John, sorry to barge in but I'm afraid I've got some bad news." A tall white haired thick set man entered. He was slightly stooped but had sharp blazing blue eyes.

"Fred, nice to see you again. I'm looking forward to our game on Wednesday."

"That's what I'm here to talk about. Can't make it, John. I've got to take Helen to the hospital."

"Sorry to hear that. Listen, do you have time for lunch? You can fill me in then."

The restaurant was busy and noisy so Franks arranged to have a spot in the corner where they would be able to talk. Franks took his coat off and hung it at the back of his chair. Fred Harrison kept his blue blazer on. He scanned his surroundings. There were many large gatherings, probably office workers enjoying one form of celebration or another. Wooden floors, wooden chairs. No wonder there was lots of noise. Like most Italian restaurants he'd been to.

Their waiter deposited two menus and left hastily. He was busy running back to the bar to get some drinks for another table. Harrison watched with fascination. He might be a director of the company but he rarely stayed in town for lunch. Franks studied the menu for a moment then thrust it aside.

After drinks had been served and the specials had been announced Franks settled back and began the speech he had planned for Wednesday's golf day. "You know the company has to decide on a successor."

"Sure, it's the first agenda item next week." Harrison tested the wine. It wasn't bad. He preferred a red but at lunch it made sense to choose white and this Semillon was unusual.

"Have you any thoughts on the matter?" Franks looked him in the eye.

"I know you prefer Vincent but I believe the UK Head, what's his name, Burton, has the best industry experience and he's a likeable guy, good with people."

Franks nodded. "So you'd rule out the American, Tennyson, who really wants the position?"

"Oh yes. He's aggressive, arrogant...I don't like him and I think he would make changes just for the sake of it."

"You don't want changes." Franks asked as he swallowed another mouthful of wine.

"It's not that but Tennyson is an empire builder and he wants status for himself more than success for the company. I don't think he has the good of the company as his goal, like you do. He's got an ego bigger than Ben Hur."

Franks leant back in his chair, then said, "Interesting you should say that. You're right, of course. I've always thought Tennyson too ambitious but for the wrong reasons. Vincent may not be as smart but he is loyal and has a lot of support amongst his people. He is a true company man."

"Nobody would fight for the company like you. It's your baby, isn't it?"

Franks regarded Harrison before responding. "Yes, I care deeply which is why I would entrust the control to Vincent. He's dedicated and he listens to good advice."

The entrees arrived. The waiter did his thing with the pepper and zoomed off. Harrison liked his efficiency. "So he listens to you?"

Franks smiled. "Yes."

"Well, I'll give it extra thought." Harrison picked up his utensils and studied his dish. "And I take it you don't like Burton?"

"I think Burton could handle the job okay but I have other concerns about him."

"Because he's a pommie?" Harrison looked at Franks with amusement.

"It's not that. I suspect he will move headquarters to London because of certain intell I received from our Internal Audit Manager. He was over in the UK recently."

"Well we can't have that, can we?" Harrison said, examining his oysters.

Franks observed him closely. "Can I count on you? I know you want the best for the organisation. I know you can see that the way to growth, quality growth, lies with the current team."

"So you'll be pulling the strings from the bench?"

"In a few years I hope to be Chairman of the Board. Under the rules I need to be gone for three years but I'll be in the background."

"Well, that changes things. If you're still in control, then I'm happier. How does Vincent feel about this?"

"He's in charge for the day to day stuff already but he always bounces ideas off me. He lacks confidence to make major decisions without input from myself or someone else. That relationship will continue when the roles alter. We've worked closely together for years."

"And that won't happen with any other contender."

"Not as well. They all respect my ability. That's clear. Just look at the share price increase whilst I'm been in charge."

Harrison nodded. He continued eating in silence.

Franks woke. Startled. His recollection had vanished as he cleared his head. He was somewhere foreign. He was tied up, sitting on a chair and peering into a bright light.

"Mr Franks, good afternoon."

"What is this? Release me at once."

The voice continued, "You don't give the orders here. I suggest you keep control of yourself and listen."

"This is outrageous. Whoever you are, you're in deep shit."

"I think it's the other way around, you fucking fruitcake. Now I'm going to ask you some questions."

"What," Franks spluttered, "do you know who I am?"

The light went off. Footsteps receded. A door opened and closed.

John Franks examined his situation. He tried to wriggle free but he was bound securely, much too tightly, with strange cords restricting any movement so that he could barely move more than a few inches.

After a while he recalled the full horror of his situation: being held up by gun toting thugs, being marched out of the boardroom, being tied to a chair. He recalled the three men with weapons. What was going on? He'd lost track of time. He was disoriented like he'd come out of a deep sleep. Had the water they'd finally received been drugged? He remembered being in the back of a truck. And where were the others from the management team? How did he get here, in this chair, in this state, without recalling a thing? There was no other explanation. This now appeared to be more sinister than a simple kidnapping for money. But this was Australia, not Columbia or Mexico or Somalia or some other god forsaken place in South America or Africa.

Franks waited. He was thirsty but he wondered whether yelling for water would be wise. But he needed a drink. "Water, can I have some water please?"

There was no response.

Time passed. He tried to think logically, something he prided himself on. But his thirst was too great.

The door opened but he saw nothing but a shadow briefly. Footsteps sounded. They stopped when they reached him. A bottle was shoved between his lips and it was elevated enough for the contents to flow freely. Water. It poured into him and down his front. He gulped mouthfuls. The bottle was withdrawn. The footsteps retraced their steps to the door.

Later, much later, the light came back on. Franks shook himself awake. He must have dozed off.

The voice said, "Are you ready to proceed?"

Franks considered the proposition. "Ok, ask your damn questions. What time is it?"

"Have an appointment, do we? Don't you concern yourself with time. Just relax. You'll be here until the interview has concluded."

"Ok," said Franks, perspiration flowing down his face, "what do you want to know? How we calculate claims reserves perhaps?"

The voice sniggered. "Nothing as mundane as that. Tell me how you choose your key people."

Franks frowned, puzzled. This question seemed fairly innocuous. "Well, the company has a process in place. HR are tasked to..."

"If I may interrupt. I have no doubt that the majority of people go through a formal hiring process. What I want to know is how you select the people who report to you – the managers, the big guns if you like?"

Franks shifted as much as was possible. The cords cut into his arms. He was very uncomfortable. He was about to suggest they could discuss this better if he were able to sit less constrained but thought better of it. The person he was dealing with was obviously unpredictable and possibly unstable He said, "It takes a lot to get to the level of General Manager. It requires years of solid performances, sound business judgements, good people skills and great communication skills to climb the corporate ladder. The individuals who possess these attributes and achieve the results usually end up reporting to the Group CEO – me."

"I see."

Franks wondered whether the interviewer simply wanted business knowledge and had an unusual approach to acquire it. But Franks had not revealed much on the topic different to what was espoused in many books on the subject.

"That's good," continued the voice. "What I'd like you to reflect on over the next little while is whether you gave special treatment to any of your direct reports and any influence you may have used to help select their direct reports. Would you do that?"

"I don't understand."

"You will and that's why I'm going to give you time to think about it. Understood?"

"Yes." Franks was not going to argue. He had to collect his thoughts.

"Thank you."

The light was turned off rendering the room dark and soulless.

The room had seemed empty from what little Franks could see apart from the spotlight and the chair on which he sat.

Footsteps approached.

CHAPTER 6

The Past

JJ, leaning on one elbow, watched her sleep. Her breathing was like a light purr. She had lovely silky skin. White all over, milky even. She was soft in all the right places. She wasn't experienced, he could tell. But she had a sweet enthusiasm. He liked that. Although he had not considered the prospect, he imagined she would be a loyal and supportive girl friend for any guy who was willing to develop a relationship with her.

Their third date together could almost have been their last. When JJ had invited her out to see a movie, Maddie hesitated and he wondered whether she was going to break it off. But after some more small talk, she said she would make a meal and they could watch a movie on DVD. At her flat, Maddie offered a glass of white wine, a recent vintage Riesling which he did not much care for, and he accepted. Then when they had dispensed with pleasantries, she said she saw him at the Bondi Junction mall on Saturday morning. JJ sipped his wine.

"Yes, that's not unusual," he said noting that she was watching him closely, "What time?"

"Around nine o'clock," she said.

He had to think quickly because he often did visit Bondi Junction to do some shopping. What would seem plausible, he wondered. He smiled then took a chance. He said he needed to collect some supplies before heading off and, after a moment's appraisal; this seemed to satisfy her curiosity.

The evening then progressed without further hitches and he found that after several glasses of wine, she became more than a little amorous and that going to bed was not going to be something he needed to initiate. This was beyond his expectation.

Now, in the middle of another fine day, as he trailed the palm of his free hand up her leg, he noted that she was deep in sleep. Soon he lay down and studied the ceiling. He closed his eyes and drifted off to sleep as well.

"Hi," she said.

JJ smiled. She was sitting up gazing at his eyes. "Been awake long?"

"A few minutes. I enjoyed last night." Maddie pecked his cheek.

"So did I," he said. Not many women, in his experience, commented about sex afterwards.

JJ moved closer and put his arm around her. "Do you think the office will work out that we're together when they find out we're both absent from our desks?"

Maddie pushed into him a little more, cradling his head on her lap. "I don't care. But I doubt it.

We rarely see each other at work, do we? Besides we're in completely different areas."

"That's correct. Nothing to worry about. This feels even better because it's bad, something the company would frown upon."

Maddie loved the thought. An almost illicit act, so unlike her. She was going to make the most of the day. It had taken a while for her to become comfortable with this idea – she wasn't going to squander it.

"Let's go to a nice place for lunch," she said.

JJ and Maddie were seated in a restaurant at the Bondi Pavilion. They had a table near the glass walls and possessed an unimpeded view of the beach as well as of the people casually wandering along the concrete foreshore. It was a fabulous view and being Wednesday there were few people in the spacious establishment. A waitress loitered but she remained a respectable distance from the couple's table. She was trying to let the customers relax but allow them the opportunity to call on her if wanted. It was that kind of place.

"Have you decided?" JJ said.

"Can't make up my mind. The calamari appeals and the lobster looks good."

"We'll get the seafood platter. That has everything."

"It's expensive Jordan. I don't think I can afford it."

"Don't worry, it's on me. And call me JJ, you're a friend."

"I can't let you do that." Maddie was taken aback. She'd rarely been treated by anyone. And she hardly knew this man. "We're more than just friends..."

"Of course."

"I still feel uncomfortable about you paying."

"Relax, let me do this for you."

"You're sweet," she said, smiling. She placed her hand over his.

JJ motioned the waitress over and ordered the seafood platter as well as a bottle of Pinot Grigio. And when she'd taken the order, he said, "I hope you like this white. I find red a little heavy at lunch."

They ate the meal at a leisurely pace, not saying much but exchanging occasional glances. It was during their dessert of gelato that JJ started the topic he had been saving. "You probably get to see all sorts of confidential records about people?"

"I guess. Why?"

"I get to see a lot of financial data. That's also confidential as far as outsiders are concerned but I can share it with certain personnel within the company."

"So?" Maddie sounded quizzical.

"Can you tell me about someone then?"

"Depends what it is I suppose."

JJ sipped his cappuccino. "All I was wondering was who's next in line for the big job. I've heard rumours that Franks will be stepping down soon."

"Nobody knows who his successor is. That's for him to decide."

"Fair enough. That's what I would have expected, kind of. We might be working for a large corporation but they have the same lack of cohesion on important issues as small places do." JJ kept his eyes on Maddie to gauge the reaction.

"EIG has a process. We have documented succession plans and everything. A lot of work goes into it. Doug Vincent is in the plan to succeed John Franks but until the proper steps are taken and approval by the board is given, it's all up in the air."

JJ felt elated. This was what he wanted. He maintained a straight face. He said, "Well I'm sorry, looks like I shot myself in the foot.

Anyway, not that it has anything to do with us." He laughed.

"Then why did you ask?"

"I guess I wanted to understand something about the top knobs. I've been with the company a short time compared to so many people around me."

Maddie nodded. It seemed to make sense.

JJ was pleased. It seemed he had won her trust. It was a start.

CHAPTER 7

The Past

The next day, Thursday, JJ arrived in the office with a renewed sense of purpose. He discovered that Doug Vincent resided on level 15, the head office of the Australian Operations. Although Vincent was the Chief Operations Officer and had an office on the Group floor, he spent most of his time with the Australian operations and consequently also had an office at the Australian Operations Headquarters which occupied the most of level 15. The remaining floor space housed Australian Operations underwriters.

At a few minutes after ten, after completing a spreadsheet on claims discounting, a re- calculation check, JJ stretched his arms then stood up and wandered away from his office. Usually at this time of the morning, he left the building to buy a decent cup of coffee. He disliked the instant coffee freely available in the kitchen and would often wander outside where he would meet other EIG employees for a chat. This also doubled as a key networking strategy, particularly as auditors were rarely invited to other sections for socializing purposes.

When JJ entered the elevator, he pressed the button to level 15. The woman standing inside the lift as he entered looked ahead blankly until level 13 where she strolled out as if in a daze. She had ignored him completely as though he was not a human or any other kind of presence. Was it big companies that made people appear robotic or was the woman simply zonked out? He had no clue but he concluded that large populations in any organisation or city had a lot to learn from smaller friendlier groups. JJ leaned against the back wall and considered his next move.

The doors finally opened at level 15 and he strode out confidently. The security card he possessed denied him access to this floor. This was odd as his card was able to access every other level. He pressed the buzzer on the wall and a moment later the receptionist, inside the glass enclosure, who noted his corporate ID card zapped open the door lock.

"Hi," he said when he stepped up to the reception counter, "where does Roger Trott sit? I'm from Group Audit."

"Oh," she said, looking composed, "I'll call him to let him know you're here. Just take a seat."

JJ sat in one of two leather chairs to the left of the entrance. He picked up the Financial Review newspaper from the low table on his left. He scanned the headlines and began an article on the latest profit season which included positive comments about EIG and which was particularly glowing about the sound management team. If one knew no better it would appear that John Franks and company were the answer to developing successful insurance conglomerates. JJ wondered why the author didn't comment on the favourable weather conditions for the last few years which always helped insurers avoid numerous and highly expensive catastrophe claims.

Roger Trott arrived a few minutes later. Trott was an inch taller than JJ but not as fit, at least if appearance were an indicator. "Good day Jordan. Finally decided to see how the other half lives, huh?" The two men shook hands, then Trott ushered JJ through another security door to the company's local insurance operations headquarters.

Trott introduced JJ to some of the Australian finance team members after leading him to his boss' corner office. The office was arranged with six chairs facing the large mahogany desk occupied by five men and one woman apparently waiting for something to start. Trott walked up to his boss standing near the desk rifling through some papers. "James Wakehurst, have you met Jordan from Group? He's visiting our area for the first time."

"Hi there," said Wakehurst, extending his hand, "How are you settling in?"

"Slowly, I suppose, "JJ said, unable to take his eyes off Wakehurst's impressive moustache, "I had no idea this company was so ginormous."

Wakehurst was a tall man with an affable nature. "Ha ha, yes it is huge and with all the M&A activity the place is growing all the time,"

Wakehurst said, smiling, "Now if you'll excuse me..."

Doug Vincent strode into the office. "Ready, Jim?"

Wakehurst grabbed some papers and bolted after Vincent who didn't stop to talk to the people who were in Wakehurst's office for a finance meeting, Trott explained.

"Friendly sod," said JJ.

"That's normal," said a middle aged man seated near the window, "he's really friendly with superiors but he ignores anyone who he regards as an underling."

Roger Trott added, "You get used to it."

JJ looked around the room, "do any of you remember James Johnston?"

Trott said, "Sure. He was a nice guy. Treated everyone well. Left about two or three years ago."

"Yeah, I remember James. Used to have Jim's job. Doug didn't like him for some reason," said the middle aged guy. "He and I used to have a drink together every now and then."

The finance group, apart from Trott, filed out of the room with one remarking, "Roger, let us know when Jim is back. No point waiting when he's summoned by the chief."

"Sure thing," said Trott.

JJ chatted with Trott a little more, then rode the elevator to the ground level. He walked around for a short time to get a breath of fresh air and finally stopped at his regular barista to buy a large cappuccino.

He had sighted Vincent. That had been his mission today. Now he needed more information on the man. He decided to arrange lunch with Trott for later in the week, to network and with any luck discover more about Vincent.

JJ called Maddie when he returned to his desk. He invited her to dinner that night. She agreed.

Later, in her apartment, she said, "Maybe we should slow down."

"Ok," he said, "Perhaps it's not good to see too much of each other."

"Please don't misunderstand. It's been wonderful. Truly. But I'm not used to so much attention."

"That's ok. I understand. We'll see each other on the weekend, right?"

"Of course." She smiled, came up closer and hugged him. She loved how understanding he was.

JJ left her apartment not long afterwards, satisfied. He didn't want her to suspect he'd been interested in anything other than romance. He was beginning to like her a little more than he should.

Doug Vincent loved his motor car. He'd just bought a new Mazda MX-5 Roadster. This was the final decision after he'd road tested the Peugeot 307CC which retailed for under $50,000 and the Saab 93 turbo charged convertible for around $70,000. He thought that soon, with a new position and a new salary he could convince his wife that they could easily afford the BMW 335i Coupe or the ultimate Porsche Cayman for well in excess of $100,000.

Vincent took every opportunity to drive his car. For that reason he was always happy to take his nine year old son to sport on Saturday mornings. In the winter season he ferried Ben to his soccer games. As usual, as Vincent watched from the sidelines, he was also engaged in conversation with a few other dads.

"Kick it Ben, kick, "Vincent shouted, pointing in the direction of the goal. "Relax Doug," said Geoff, "it's only a game."

"Yeah mate, I know, but these kids don't know how to fuckin' win."

Geoff grinned. He and Vincent had been over this ground many times. Vincent was so competitive. This was probably the reason why he'd soon be CEO of a major public company. Vincent was not backward in announcing his successes.

JJ was watching Vincent. He was well hidden by the masses of people wandering around the soccer fields. He'd doubted whether Vincent would know who he was or remember him from the other day even if he were to eyeball him. He waited patiently until the game was over then followed.

JJ had learned of Vincent's weekend activities by asking about the man from a variety of sources. When JJ asked Trott what sort of man Vincent was, Trott had informed him that Vincent was a car nut. Details regarding Vincent's son who played soccer and that Vincent also played during the week in an over 35s competition came via Wakehurst. Maddie supplied JJ with Vincent's address when he asked her, on the pretext that he needed to check whether it matched with the details stated on shareholder notifications.

As Vincent walked alongside Ben after the match, he ruffled his son's hair. "Good game mate."

"Yeah Dad, can I have a drink from the shop?"

"Sure, what would you like?"

"A Sprite would be nice and can I have some potato crisps too?"

Vincent put his arm around Ben. "You know your mother doesn't like you having junk food.

Maybe this once and it's our secret, ok?"

Ben looked up at his father and smiled. "Sure Dad, our secret."

In the car park, Vincent opened the passenger door for Ben. He didn't notice that someone was taking a photo. Vincent climbed into the MX-5, lovingly caressing the upholstery before turning the ignition to allow the vehicle to roar into life. He took in a whiff of the new car smell and moved cautiously out onto the road but then changed gear and sped up the hill. It was one of life's great feelings, the power under the bonnet, the freedom of the road. Almost as good as sex.

JJ didn't try to pursue him. He knew where Vincent lived. After all he had followed him to the ground. What JJ wanted was a sense of the man who apparently had little loyalty for his office work team. At this stage he didn't know how this research would benefit him but it certainly couldn't hurt to understand the people he was targeting.

CHAPTER 8

Day 1

Detective Inspector Malcolm Donaldson was deep in thought, focussed entirely on the case before him. The documents seemed to be complete, yet something was also missing. His intense concentration was shattered by the phone. He picked up, listened and did not speak until the message had been totally relayed.

A kidnapping. A kidnapping in the Central Business District. A kidnapping in broad daylight. A kidnapping of nine senior executives. Was he hearing it correctly? He waited until his colleague Detective Sergeant Jane Morris had finished before responding. He swivelled his chair and gazed at his cluttered office. Filing cabinets, stacks of paper, visitors' chairs clogged with case files. He needed to clear out some of the junk. But he rarely got enough time to scratch himself, let alone weed out papers which were no longer required.

"Thanks for the info," he said, "I agree you should go there immediately and talk to the woman who raised the alarm. Take some uniforms to ensure the crime scene is secured. I'll join you as soon as I can."

Detective Sergeant Jane Morris was young and energetic and ambitious. She loved her job and had been promoted recently. With an athletic build, modest bosom but possessing sinewy legs from daily gym workouts, Jane Morris received considerable attention from male colleagues. She stood five foot four in her stockings and wore her dark hair short. Her small olive complexioned face prompted many to assume she was Italian. In fact her mother was Spanish whilst her father was English.

On arrival at the corporate head office of the international insurance company, the police contingent was shown the boardroom and the area was checked out and kept secure until the forensics team appeared.

Detective Sergeant Jane Morris was introduced to Fiona McDowell who was sitting quietly at the company's cafeteria having a hot chocolate. She smiled but was too shaken to talk. Morris didn't force the witness to speak and simply kept her company.

Detective Inspector Donaldson joined them twenty minutes later. He ordered coffee for himself and Morris and offered some to Fiona but she declined.

Settled, Donaldson peered at Fiona and wondered whether this was the best approach to gain information. The witness seemed frozen as though the thought of reliving the experience was too overwhelming. But he had to try.

"Ms McDowell," he began, "can you just tell us what you saw?"

Fiona, head bowed, concentrating on the cup in her hands, looked up. "Three men rushed into the Board room and took everyone except me. They locked me in the cold room. It was horrible." Tears welled up. Fiona sobbed.

Donaldson waited. In his experience it was best to allow a witness to get through the crying episode.

Morris fidgeted but realised Donaldson wanted to proceed slowly. She was originally informed by Ruth, the Group CEO's personal assistant, what had happened. Apparently Fiona had been found after a telephone tip off. She had been in the cooler for a couple of hours. It then took her another hour to gather her wits to actually alert the police.

Donaldson looked at Morris. She picked up on the unspoken message and touched Fiona's hand after a while. She seemed to have calmed down. "Can you continue or would you like to accompany Detective Sergeant Morris to the station and you can make your statement in peace."

Fiona nodded and Donaldson let the two women leave together. Meanwhile Donaldson visited the CEO's PA to learn her version of events.

CHAPTER 9

Day 2

Doug Vincent brushed his teeth, his gums, his tongue. He enjoyed this part of his morning ritual. He brushed and scrubbed and rinsed. Then he barred his teeth to the mirror and inspected his work. Great. His mouth was the best thing about him, he felt. He possessed the best set of white teeth of anyone in the executive ranks. He was tall and a little unfit looking, pudgy around the gut area, but he had fantastic teeth.

Vincent inspected himself in the full length bathroom mirror. His suit was elegant, understated and freshly dry-cleaned. His shoes were polished black. He wore lace shoes with leather soles. They had been expensive, almost as much as the $2000 suit. His red tie and white shirt went well with the dark, fine pin striped suit. His hair was greying but short and trim. He had it cut each three weeks, same time, same day, every three weeks with the same hairdresser unless he was travelling.

He flashed his teeth in the mirror one last time before going downstairs to meet the family. They were all in the kitchen. Marion, his wife, of twenty odd years and his two children. Lucinda was heading out the door, running late for the bus to high school. Ben was still finishing his breakfast of rice bubbles with Milo sprinkled on top.

"Bye," called Lucinda from the door. She slammed it shut.

"Why does she have to slam that door? She does it every day. It gives me the fucking hebejebees"

"Language Doug," said Marion. "But..."

"I know darling, it's irritating but so is your constant swearing."

Vincent grunted. He sat down and ate the bacon and eggs Marion had prepared for him. "Any toast?" he asked.

"Sure darling," she said. "Ben, have you had enough to eat?"

"Yes mum, this will keep me going," Ben stood up, kissed his mother on the cheek, punched his father lightly on the shoulder and walked out.

When the couple were by themselves, Marion sat down with her cup of cooled down coffee. "What's happening in your day today?"

"Well it should be an interesting one because the main event will be meeting with the chief.

We're going to work out how to announce my appointment as his successor."

"That is wonderful. Why haven't you said anything before?"

"It's not easy. Politics. And until everybody's on board you never know."

Marion tried her coffee and then screwed up her face. "That's awful, the coffee I'm talking about."

"I've got to run. Let's talk tonight." Vincent pushed his chair back.

"What time?"

"Can't tell. I'll call if it's going to be very late." He pecked Marion on the cheek and raced to the garage. Marion was looking a little tired these days. He wished he could remark upon it but knew that wouldn't help. She'd take it to heart and end up resenting him. He had to find a way to get her to look after herself. Maybe a gym voucher for her birthday which was coming up.

John Franks, CEO of Easy Insurance Group Limited or EIG as it was commonly known, waited at the elevator bank. It was 6am and he was keen to get going on the issues of the day. He had slept like a baby and rose at his usual 4:30am, raring to go. After a light workout, he had showered, got dressed in his Monday suit, ate his regular breakfast of grapefruit juice, bran flakes, toast and marmalade and took his BMW series 5 to the office.

In his large dark panelled office, Franks went through his mail and quickly went through the Financial Review. He always checked whether his company was mentioned and he also wanted to keep abreast with the activities of his competitors.

Ruth, his personal assistant, would provide him with details of any emails directed to him later in the morning. Anything urgent could be done by phone, his preferred mode of communication. He knew others laughed at him for not using a computer but that did not trouble him. They could deal with him the way he liked. He wasn't going to be bullied to conform to the modern obsession with gadgets and Google and Facetime or whatever it was called. He had systems people who were slaves to technology. He wasn't going to have any part of it.

At 9am, his first meeting was scheduled and Ruth, a busy and loyal servant, buzzed him to announce Doug Vincent.

"Show him in," he said, straightening his gold tie.

Vincent walked in and stood by the huge desk until Franks nodded for him to sit down. Franks adjusted his heavy black rimmed spectacles and smiled at Vincent. He knew that his protégé would be happy with today's discussion. It wasn't about growth, it wasn't about reporting, and it wasn't about debtors. It was about succession.

"How's Marion?"

Vincent settled back in his armchair, "Great John. She's going to have a fine week. Lots of gatherings with friends plus her work at the charity."

"Excellent. Now to our main order of business – your appointment as Chief Executive. The majority of directors have been informed and apart from one other potential prospect, the American, there's no problem. Adrian Carter, you know the 'don't rock the boat' director, still believes Tennyson will come round to understanding that you're better qualified, not that it matters if I can persuade at least one more of the directors. We have four definite votes out of nine. And I'm playing golf with Harrison on Wednesday so I'm hoping to convince him."

"I presume the Yank thinks Tennyson deserves it more?" said Vincent.

"It's all about size according to the Americans. EIG has its biggest share of revenue from the USA and he has this idea that Tennyson can handle the next step up because of it."

"Prick. I just wish..." said Vincent.

Franks picked up the buzzing phone, listened, confirmed something, then replaced the receiver and addressed Vincent again.

"The more important issue is the announcement and how to break the news to the other contenders."

Vincent grinned. He felt elated. It wouldn't be long. He'll have the top job, the big money, the status and he'll be the most successful in his set. Yes, finally he'll outgun Alistair, that pompous bastard. "Fantastic," he said, "Can I tell Marion tonight?"

"Not yet. Let's just make sure it's in the bag. We can announce as early as the first day in spring. That's only four weeks off. There's one thing you still need to do."

"The presentation to the Board next week. Yes, it's nearly complete. Do you want to see it?" Franks nodded. "That'd be a good idea but that's not it."

They continued chatting about personal matters for another ten minutes. After all they were friends. Good friends. They often dined with each other. Wives included.

Vincent was jolted back to reality by the voice. He focused. He saw a blinding light and beyond that a shadow. The voice came from the dark space.

"State your name."

"What," Vincent said, totally off guard. How did he get here? He recalled drinking something. He was sitting in a hard chair with his hands bound flat along the arms of the chair. His legs were also bound. He was some kind of prisoner. Why? Then he remembered being led into the back of a van by gunmen.

"Just answer the question," the voice said. "Douglas Vincent."

"Ok, that wasn't too hard, was it? Now tell me what position you hold in the company."

Vincent was rocking the chair, trying to move but he had been tied too well. He wanted to toss the chair at the insolent prick. He'd never been subjected to this sort of treatment and he wasn't going to take it now. "None of your business, you fucking loser. Release me now or you'll really regret it."

Suddenly it went dark. The room had no windows and all lights had been extinguished.

The door opened and all Vincent could see was a figure disappearing.

Time passed. Vincent had no idea how much time had elapsed when the figure returned. It might have been an hour or two. He spent the time thinking. First he was furious and wanted to destroy the person who had put him here. Gradually he came to the realisation that he was in trouble. However much he ranted and swore, the interrogator wasn't going to respond as he wanted. He wasn't an employee he could cajole or bully into compliance. This was a different ball game.

The spotlight flooded on and he was again blinded.

The voice said, "Now Doug, may I call you Doug, can we continue without the hysterics?"

"Sure. What is your name?"

"You can call me Jack. Ok, let's start again. What is the position you hold at EIG?"

Vincent felt extremely uncomfortable. "Chief Operating Officer. May I have some water please?"

"Yes, in a moment. Answer a few more questions first then I'll bring some water and let you into a room where you will be more comfortable. Ok?"

"Ok."

"Good. You were in charge of the Asian division some years ago. Tell me about the management team."

"Why. What do you want?"

"Doug, we've been through this. Do you want some water or not?"

"I'm parched, I can't carry on."

The spotlight went off. Jack disappeared and after some moments returned. A torch shone into Vincent's face and he felt a glass against his mouth. He drank water.

Moments later, the spotlight came back, causing him to shut his eyes again. He realised that Jack was waiting. He said, "There were six of us. Ian who headed up operations, Dan who was the development manager, Jill who was the HR bird, Paul the actuary, James the finance guy and myself."

Vincent waited. Did Jack want more details? Was he after somebody? Why didn't he speak?

He worried when people didn't talk. It was unnatural. "Is there anything else?"

"How was your relationship with these people?"

"Excellent. It was years ago but as far as I recall we all got on really well."

"So you had no favourites?"

Vincent sighed, wondering where this line of enquiry was going. "I played no favourites from a business angle but I got on more with some than others. It's only fucking natural."

A siren sounded and Vincent listened intently to gauge whether the vehicle was going to stop outside. But the siren soon grew fainter as the vehicle sped away.

Jack prompted, "Go on."

Vincent struggled with his binding for a moment but it was useless. "Ian and Dan were my close associates because of their background which was similar to mine – marketing and operations. And I've known Paul for ages so I was mates with him before I joined. So I had a few beers with them. Jill was prissy and a female who was big into women's lib so I left her alone. James, well, I didn't know him well. He attended meetings but didn't seem too ambitious. He was on a different plane to me too. I didn't understand finance too well so the numbers stuff and explanations often went over my head. I got him to report to Paul who understood finance better."

"How would you describe your weakness?' "What is this? A friggin' job interview?" Jack stood up. The light went off.

Vincent heard footsteps. He also felt a needle prick his arm.

Time passed. When Vincent woke he had no idea how much time had elapsed. He found himself in a room which contained two single beds. He was on the bed to the right of the two facing the solitary door. He was alone. Where were the others? He felt angry and crazed. He raised himself but found his head thumping. He finally got up. He surveyed the room. No windows. Brick. He walked to the door. Of course it was locked. He pounded on it but to no avail. He was a damn prisoner in isolation. He cursed and cursed and could hardly contain himself. What was this all about? He sat down, resigned to a boring time.

CHAPTER 10

Day 2

Large coffee cup in hand, she entered the elevator and rode up to level fourteen. She was by herself which suited her just fine. At this hour not many people were at work, just the dedicated and the crazy. She knew she was a member of the latter. As much as possible she wanted to avoid people. Of course, living in a large metropolis made it difficult not to come across other people but it was also a great way to become invisible. She had no friends. And she was estranged from her family.

She stepped out of the elevator and walked to the security door. Juggling her handbag and coffee, she finally found her security pass which she flashed against the door motion monitor. She stepped into the office and as she wandered down to her cubicle, Roddy who was always in popped his head up. "Hey Mona that coffee is almost as tall as you. Want a hand?"

Mona ignored him and placed the cup and handbag on her desk when she eventually arrived at the cubicle which contained four work stations. She would spend the next eight or nine hours here and this depressed her. She walked to the ladies bathroom and began to weep. It was a common occurrence and she didn't know why this happened. There were no special times or triggers which caused this to happen.

She looked at her small frame in the mirror, not a pretty sight. Others may have commented that she looked like a cute doll but she disagreed. She ran her fingers through her shoulder length dark hair and then wiped the tears from her cheeks.

Suddenly the door opened and Samantha said, "What's wrong?"

"Nothing," said Mona.

"You've been crying. Did someone upset you?"

Mona shook her head and left. She didn't want to be interrogated. She logged into her computer and began to check her calendar. Another dreary day was in store, she felt. Other employees began their week and she wished she was dead.

CHAPTER 11

Day 2

Detective Inspector Malcolm Donaldson returned to the premises of Easy Insurance Group Ltd for the second day. He was accompanied by Detective Sergeant Jane Morris. They were in the CEO's office with Fiona McDowell who was dressed in a simple black skirt, a white short sleeved blouse and black heels. She was wringing her hands, seated in the visitors chair in the large office.

"Tell us again what you saw," said Donaldson, his elbows on the big desk in front of him, his face resting on his hands for a moment before he pulled away and sat upright. He didn't want to give the impression he was casual at his job. He had worked late into the previous night and was dog tired.

Fiona bit her lip, looked briefly at the trim female cop who was standing on Donaldson's right, then returned her gaze to the thick set man in front of her. "I told you yesterday and I also told somebody else at the police station who took my statement."

Donaldson was a big man in his early fifties. His grim features suddenly gave way to a smile. She may have forgotten that she was too distressed to give them more than a brief sketch of what had occurred. Today Fiona appeared to be in much better spirits and Donaldson wanted to capitalise on it before depression set in.

As Donaldson had a daughter Fiona's age, he understood the frustration. He looked at her with fondness and said, "I know sweetheart but we need to ask again in case there's anything else you might remember. Please bear with us. We have a number of hysterical families to console and the media haven't made anything easier by making the unfortunate business a headline story."

"Ok, do you want me to start from the beginning?"

Morris spoke for the first time, "That would be appreciated Miss McDowell."

"Well, I was standing near the morning tea table. I had just come in setting it all up and knew they were going to have a break at 10am. So it must have been around ten minutes to ten. The door suddenly opened and three men wearing black balaclavas walked in. They had guns which they pointed at the group sitting at the conference table."

"What were they wearing other than the balaclavas?" Donaldson asked.

Morris, stooped and leaning forward, was taking notes on a small flip back note pad whilst watching Fiona intently.

Fiona continued, "They all wore dark clothes. Black trousers, dark shirts and black shoes. It all happened so quickly and I was frightened. I didn't have time to take much notice."

"Did they all have the same physique?" Donaldson said.

"They were all sort of the same height, just over six foot. Maybe the leader was a fraction shorter and he was a little stockier than the other two but that's all I recall. Oh, I think one was kind of skinny and he was the tallest but not by much."

Donaldson looked at Fiona closely. "Now think a moment. Apart from their general appearance – dark clothed men, apparently fit looking with no specific outstanding characteristics – are you sure none had anything that could separate one from the other?"

Fiona closed her eyes for a moment. She pressed her right hand over her forehead. Finally she said, "One of them had the makings of a tattoo running down his neck but it wasn't obvious."

"Fantastic, Ms McDowell. Can you guess what sort of tattoo?" Donaldson was getting interested but knew from past experience that most leads were red herrings.

"Not really. It was the start or end of something. Like a snake perhaps. But I could be wrong." Morris looked up from her notebook. "It's something more than we had before so that's good."

"Donaldson said, "Ok the men entered the room. Continue."

Fiona shifted in her chair. "Two of them wandered fully into the room and one of them stationed himself near the door which exited out into the corridor. The third man who appeared suddenly was the one who kept an eye on me. What was I going to do, attack them with biscuits?"

"What do you mean - appeared suddenly?" Donaldson pressed.

Fiona waited for a few seconds and she seemed to be attempting to visualise it in her mind. She said, "I was rearranging items on the morning tea table, my back turned away from the execs when I heard a different voice. I turned to find one man in black pointing a gun. I froze. Then I noticed the second man by the door. I didn't know what to do – scream or remain still. Before I could figure out what was best another man came in from the kitchen entrance. He was the one who came up to me and he put a finger to his lips to tell me to be quiet. That's kinda what happened."

Both detectives watched her. They stayed silent.

Fiona repeated what she had told them previously – about the threats and actions, all too vivid in her memory. She also informed them of being locked in the cooler and later freed by dining room staff. At the conclusion she shuddered as if trying to erase the memory from her mind.

Donaldson stood. "Thank you for your patience. Would you show us the room again and lead us to the basement garage. Our forensics team didn't come up with anything apart from finding some blood on the floor and a spot on the table. How did that happen?"

"Oh yes," Fiona said, "I remember. George Waites spoke back to the leader and he was hit in the face by either a fist or the butt of the gun. I think his nose was smashed. It all happened so quickly I can't remember exactly."

"Once we have some DNA, we'll match it with our data bank. Don't know what that might reveal."

Fiona led the two detectives to the boardroom which had been closed off as a crime scene.

Donaldson and Morris went through the room not sure what they were searching for. Morris noted how finely polished the long mahogany table was and inspected the black leather chairs. Donaldson looked around the large square room, counting the paintings hung on the walls. They were impressive and he imagined that there were some originals but all would have cost thousands of dollars each.

Satisfied that nothing struck them as unusual, they then followed Fiona through to the cold room.

"How long were you in here?" said Morris.

"Over an hour," said Fiona. "I was freezing my buns off. Thank god the kidnap boss kept his word"

"What do you mean?" Donaldson said.

"He promised he'd call so that somebody would let me out."

"I see. A kidnapper who keeps his word."

Fiona then led the two detectives down the elevator to the basement garage. "How can a vehicle just come and go? Isn't there security?"

"Yes," said Fiona, "you need a security card to enter or exit."

"Right," said Donaldson, "we'll look at payroll records of all recent employees joining and departing the company."

"Couldn't a security card be stolen?" said Morris.

"Indeed but the company would have a register of users and employees would need to report stolen passes otherwise they'd be prevented from coming to work."

The human resources conference room was on level seven of the building, in the centre of the floor with windows surrounding it, making it like a fish tank for people passing by. Detective Morris was in charge of obtaining the information and was seated at the head of the long rectangular table. On her right were two payroll people with computers in front of them. They retrieved data specified by the detective.

The three had been working for a couple of hours and now they were ready to print a list of all new employees over the past year and employees who had resigned or departed over the past three months. Another report matched employees who had started within the last year and departed within the past three months.

Yvonne, the lead payroll person, stood and walked out to the printer. Her assistant Michelle continued playing with the computer.

Morris said, "Are there many matches?"

Michelle brushed a strand of blonde hair from her face. "A few but not many. We only focussed on Sydney personnel."

"Ok," Morris said.

"Any more coffee?" asked Michelle.

"No, I'm fine. Already had too many. I guess being in an office makes you want to have more coffee breaks."

"I don't know. Are you on the streets a lot?"

Morris was about to respond when the printed reports were popped in front of her by the diligent and no nonsense Yvonne. "What's next?" Yvonne looked like she was not too thrilled with time taken out of her day by someone who could not advance her work.

Morris said, "Thanks. While I'm looking through these, would you like to take a five minute break? I'm going to need your help again soon."

EIG's Sydney CBD office had 87 new starts in the previous 12 months and 65 departures. There were only three who started and left during that period. Morris read the lists but nothing struck her as useful. When Yvonne and Michelle returned, Morris said, "Can you provide me with information on the three individuals who joined and left during the last twelve months?"

Yvonne, the tall brunette sporting very short hair, looked at her computer screen and reflected for a moment. "Janice Newman is a PA and started nine months ago in the Claims Department. She resigned last month saying she had found a better position. I recall because she spoke to me when she left saying she didn't get the type of work she expected when she joined EIG."

Morris said, "Nothing unusual about that. I'm going to cross her off the list. And the others?"

"I don't have any personal experience with either Richard Lysette or John Dupont but I can bring up their personnel files."

Morris stretched in the chair then stood up and flexed her shoulders. "While you're doing that, I'm going to the ladies for a moment."

Later back at her police desk, with more reports included in her satchel, Morris sat back and glanced at the relevant data. Donaldson arranged to meet her at 7:30pm in a conference room. He brought another detective with him. The three detectives made themselves comfortable and Morris nodded hello to her colleague, Max Braxton.

"So what have we got?" Donaldson asked.

Morris explained the process of eliminating many of the new hires and recent departures. She then informed the two other detectives that, including two men who were hired and departed within the year, that there were eight others, five new hires and three departures, that fitted the profile of potential problem maker or information gatherer. In other words they could not be eliminated because their reasons for starting or finishing were not water tight in terms of what one would normally expect.

"Ok," said Donaldson, "I'd like you and Max to head up teams to check out all these people. I want to know everything about them. Once you have all you can get from a variety of sources such as Facebook, bank accounts, school records, previous employment etc, interview them."

Max said, "Wouldn't it be easier to call them. Whoever is not easily available might be the person who is at the location holding the group hostage."

Donaldson stroked his chin, looked up. "Maybe but the ring leader might be someone else and the employee connection might not be part of the kidnapping team. But we need to act quickly before the media get hold of the story that we are investigating an insider as a potential suspect."

"Have any demands been made yet?" asked Max.

"Nothing yet but it's only the day after the incident. We expect that the company will be contacted with a ransom demand within the next day or so. I mean they've kidnapped the entire management team of a top one hundred ASX company. They will probably demand a large sum of money, perhaps as much as ten million dollars or more?"

"Jesus," said Max, "It seems to have been well planned. Hardly any witnesses. I'm surprised they let the young lady live."

Morris chimed in, "This isn't Mexico"

Donaldson said in a gruff tone, "Before we jump to any conclusions, we need to follow up as best we can. The families are going to stay calm only so long. They have agreed to assist us by not reporting this to anyone else for a day or two. But then, who knows."

Braxton said, "Should an official Task Force be organised?"

Donaldson looked at the young man. "The process has already begun. Strike Force Sigma is being put together as we speak. Hostage negotiators, state crime command personnel and some of the local guys are being recruited. Fingerprint and forensic officers have already been at the scene."

CHAPTER 12

Day 2

Jennie Jones came out of her daze and felt the bonds holding her to the chair. She blinked herself awake. Was she in a dream, or more to the point a horrible nightmare? She struggled. She shut her eyes and opened them again. This was real. Then she remembered the men who entered the boardroom. The Easy Insurance management team had been taken away in a truck. This was absurd. She could hardly believe such a thing was possible anywhere let alone in a first world country. Being British, or more specifically English, Jennie had led a sheltered life compared to many of her girl friends. She grew up in Essex and worked in the city of London and never came across the seedier side of England although she had read about it in the tabloid press. And when she was transferred to Sydney by Easy Insurance, she was taken with the wonderfully clean environment and friendly people. But this was totally out of character.

A bright light temporarily blinded her. She shut her eyes. "Ahh, what's going on?" she screamed.

A voice said, "Stay calm, Ms Jones."

"Who are you? What do you want?"

The voice continued, "Ah yes, the typical questions. You are all so predictable."

"This is outrageous. Untie me now or you'll be in serious trouble. I know my rights." The voice said, "You certainly have spirit, I'll say that. Is this how you operate at work?"

"That's none of your concern," Jennie barked.

The light was switched off and the man departed.

"Hang on, don't leave me here." Jennie Jones tried to sound authoritative but inside she was scared. She disliked being confined and she wasn't keen being in the dark.

After a few moments, Jennie assessed the situation. There was no point in being hostile. She was in no position to act in this fashion as it appeared that the kidnappers weren't content with holding the executive team merely for money. They seemed to want something else. Was some disgruntled employee trying to get back at them? She thought about recent terminations. But she soon realised that she was only involved with senior retrenchments and sackings. In the past few months there had only been a handful of those and examining the ones she recalled, none were likely to cause trouble.

Then she recalled the case of Wing Ho Lowe, the Asian manager who was dismissed for fraud. He was stationed in Malaysia and reported to an expatriate in Singapore. An internal investigation, on the basis of a whistle blower's tip off, resulted in the discovery of kick backs from motor repairers. Wing Ho Lowe diverted all motor accident repairs to Ming Ding Repairs, the principal of which happened to play golf with Lowe on a regular basis.

Although Jennie Jones was not directly involved in his dismissal, did he somehow feel aggrieved enough to stage this kidnapping? On reflection, she thought the idea farfetched.

She tried to sit more comfortably but there was no way to alleviate the bonds which dug into her ankles and wrists.

Jennie sat, thinking. She wanted to scream but decided to remain stoic. She didn't want to allow the person who had been interrogating her to feel that he had scored any points. She would resist. Now she regretted not getting to know more about the divisional employees. She had met with HR heads of the various divisions around the globe and loved travelling but she had not taken much interest in individual employees. Her job was to monitor the departmental progress against policies she and the Group CEO had developed. She played a large part in conducting seminars throughout the world to send the message that Head Office wanted its people to abide by the newly developed policies.

Perhaps she was wrong, she thought. This may have nothing to do with a past employee. She reasoned she could only await the questions to determine what was eating these people.

Then it occurred to her that the company would have by now understood what had happened. Surely the police were mounting an investigation and the situation might be resolved shortly, either with intervention or by negotiation. That's why it was important to delay matters. This idea gave her some comfort.

Some time later she was shaken awake. She must have dozed off. A bottle was pushed near her mouth.

"What is it?" she demanded. "Water."

She cautiously opened her mouth and tasted some liquid. It was water. She began to drink with gusto. She was parched.

Soon the light came on. The voice said, "Are we feeling more relaxed?"

Jennie was going to tell this person her thoughts but stopped herself. He might simply walk out again and she doubted that she could stand being bound much longer. "Somewhat," she replied.

"Good. Now let's start with some basic questions?"

"Is this an interview?" said Jennie, exasperated.

"You can think of it like that. What's your full name?"

"Jennie Anne Jones."

The voice said, "Very good. How old are you?"

"Why the hell do you want that?" Jennie Jones was thoroughly confused. She had been taken hostage and the questions being posed were available from the last Annual Report. Was the man mental or did he have a hidden agenda? She counted to five in her head, then said, "I'll be forty-nine in January."

"Correct," the voice said, "now that's how honest I want you to be with the rest of my questions."

"Is there anything you can do about the binding. I think my circulation has been cut off."

"Sure, as soon as we get through a few more questions I will ensure you are made more comfortable."

The room was stuffy. No windows and the ventilation was poor. Apart from the chair she occupied and presumably there was one for the interrogator, there was no furniture in the room. She wondered whether this building was an abandoned warehouse with a few offices. But that didn't make sense. She had been confined in a flat.

"How much are you involved in the setting of salaries?"

Jennie frowned. "It depends. For operational divisions, I ensure the process is operating satisfactorily. For the Head Office employees, I get my people to obtain market data for each job category and ensure that our employees are within the parameters. Do you want to know about the actual procedures?"

"No I don't. Tell me in what instances you recommend salary increases or when no increase should occur."

"I don't recommend salary increases. That's the manager's job. All I do is review market salary ranges and provide the information to the respective managers."

There was silence for a moment. Jennie wondered whether she was being tested for something. Thinking back she couldn't recall any deviation from the set down procedures. Her staff actually gathered the salary ranges and she simply communicated the information to the Head Office managers. Divisional reviews were left to the divisions. She waited.

Finally the voice continued, "Go back three years. You'd been with a company less than six months. Was that procedure in place then?"

"I can't remember that far back but I think this process was introduced last year."

"So the process had changed?"

"Yes, this is only natural for a dynamic corporation. We need to..."

"Save the speech. I understand what corporations do. What I'm trying to understand is the level of your influence in setting salaries, not only recently but also when you arrived at EIG."

"Alright," said Jennie, "when I joined the company had not yet introduced the systems I had experienced elsewhere. That's why I was hired – to help develop human resource strategies and procedures. And yes in the beginning I was asked to have a say in the levels being proposed for different groups of individuals."

"Very good. That's all for today. I'd like you to reflect on those years so that when we next talk, you are able to respond accurately. There is paper and pen in your room so you can jot down information as it comes back to you. Now you may have another drink from my colleague."

The light was turned off. Footsteps approached and Jennie drank more water. However this time she fell asleep within minutes.

Jennie Jones shook her head. She felt drugged and realised that the last drink of water contained a substance which knocked her out. She gazed about and found she was lying on a bed. She noted that she was in a bedroom different to the one she had previously been held in. She stumbled out of bed and saw that an ensuite was attached. What a blessing.

After returning from the bathroom, she looked around and wondered why it felt so stifling. Then she saw that the windows had all been boarded up so no natural light came in. The only light illuminating the room came from the bedside table lamp. There was an overhead light she observed but it had been switched off.

The room was painted a light grey. It had a high ceiling.

She checked the door. It was locked as she had expected. She was too slight to break it down and wondered what was next.

After a moment she opened the drawers in a cabinet to the right of the bed and opposite the window. There she found some clothes which she felt were her size. This had all been thoroughly planned.

She re-entered the bathroom and filled the single glass left there with water. As she drank she viewed herself in the mirror. Her hair, although short, was a mess. Her eyes showed signs of being bloodshot.

In the full length mirror behind the basin she saw that her slim body was covered with crumpled clothing. She took off her skirt and blouse. In her underwear she looked much better. She had nice legs and a tight arse. Men often remarked on her figure which for a woman in her forties was spectacular, some had said.

She found some books in a small bookcase in the corner of the room. Well, she thought, she might as well relax and hoped the male hostages could negotiate with the strange interviewer.

She chose a novel, discarded her bra, and settled between two pillows in the bed and prepared for a long period of reading. Looking at her wrist, she found her watch missing so she had no idea whether it was night or day.

CHAPTER 13

The Past

There was a buzz in the office. Maddie felt it as she walked into her area. Small groups of women were huddled together all around the limited floor space, most of whom were in animated discussion. Some were from the Group HR Department and some were from the Australian Operations HR Department which also included the Payroll section. She put her new black bag away and joined the group of girls in the corner.

"Have you heard?" said Donna, as Maddie approached. Donna was a tall, dark-haired woman of around twenty-five who loved to chat. She seemed to know much of what was happening in the company. As the Personal Assistant to the Australian HR chief, she seemed to think her job was to talk to all the PAs to keep up to date with events and other people's business.

"Heard what?" Maddie wondered what new scandal had hit. Who was sleeping with whom? Or had a father walked out on his kids?

Donna looked directly at Maddie. "Tim Tennyson is being sued for sexual harassment."

"Oh my God. When?"

"Last night our time. Yesterday in New York"

Maddie didn't know what to say. She eyed the other women who were deep in a discussion about Tennyson's family and how terrible everything was. They loved this. This sort of thing spiced up their day.

Maddie said, "I thought Tim was divorced and had no kids."

"Oh," said one of them, "I didn't know. But it's still bad for the company."

"Who's suing?"

"Not sure," said Donna, "Frida from HR in New York just said that Tim is in big trouble."

Maddie walked away, tired of gossip which had no basis in fact. She got her usual cup of weak coffee and returned to her desk.

At 9am, the Group HR Manager, Maddie's boss, Jennie Jones, announced that the gathered women remain calm and to join her in the floor's meeting room which was located in the centre of the floor. "Girls," she began, assuming the head of the table, "you may have heard some rumours about Tim Tennyson...have you?"

"Yes," said Donna.

Wanda, the payroll clerk, nodded. She played with her wedding ring.

"Yes, I thought so. Unfortunately rumours run through this organisation like wildfire." Jennie looked annoyed but continued, "Although it is true that it looks bad for Tim, at this stage it is not clear what occurred. And until the Executive make an official announcement, the company would appreciate it if you would keep the news inside the company at this point. In other words no comment to outsiders, particularly not to reporters."

Wanda nodded again. "Ok."

Donna said, "What about other employees? How are they being controlled?"

Jennie smiled. "A very good question. But each department head has been briefed and it will be taken care of. So we can't help what's been done but we can create a united front from here on in. The HR boys are being briefed this moment by the Australian Operations Chief."

A few minutes later the meeting broke up and the women filed out with Group HR personnel returning to their desks on level 7 and the others to a George Street building which housed the Australian HR team. Maddie sat and stared at her computer screen for some minutes before she commenced the work for the day. Maddie did not know Tim Tennyson apart from his reputation as a tough customer. She couldn't imagine he'd be silly enough to be caught out in this fashion. But then men didn't always act sensibly, did they?

Maddie got up again after ten minutes. She was somewhat disoriented. She needed to talk to someone. It seemed bizarre that the company took this approach. Did they want to control every form of information so that their precious share price would be kept buoyant?

Maddie picked up her telephone to dial. She wanted to call JJ, but hesitated. What would he say? Was he the sort of fellow who would enjoy listening to her perspective? She had found JJ good company but wondered whether she should confide in him. She knew of Tennyson's reputation. He was not only harsh with his people but he held women in contempt. It was not surprising that he would finally be found out. She'd often spoken with staff in the USA personnel department and they all said that Tennyson was arrogant, dictatorial and was renowned for making ugly remarks about women and minorities. She realised that the comments were hearsay but now, with the company taking elaborate precautions, she felt that some of these comments were based on known events.

JJ was jogging along the footpath on New South Head Road, making steady progress on the inconsistent surface. He had woken late and decided to do his miles before breakfast. He would not go into the office today. He had called in sick, his first day off in the new job, figuring he was entitled to a break. Time passed easily as he enjoyed the various water views and Eastern Suburbs architecture. He was feeling strong as he passed Kincoppal Girls School in Rose Bay. The day girls and boarders had one of the best real estate locations in Sydney with its panoramic view of the Harbour and the famous Harbour Bridge in the distance. Soon he was running up a hill at Watsons Bay, moving quite freely. He felt he could enter the City to Surf, Sydney's major annual run event, and do well enough to finish in a respectable time.

He stopped when he reached the beach at Watson's Bay. He breathed in the air and watched a couple of seagulls skimming the water. The sea was inviting despite the temperature still in the low teens. From where he stood the tourist favourite, Doyle's Seafood Restaurant, was visible.

He felt fit and happy. The plan he had envisaged months before joining EIG had now been fully formulated in his mind. He walked along the foreshore until he came to a cafe. He sat at a sidewalk table overlooking the bay and ordered a cappuccino. Just as his coffee arrived, his mobile shrilled.

"Hello," he said hesitantly, wondering whether the office was calling.

"Hi JJ, its Maddie, hope it's ok to call you on your mobile. You didn't answer your extension."

"That's fine. What's up?"

"You're not in a meeting or anything, are you?"

"No. I'm actually in Watsons Bay enjoying a fine cup of coffee. It's a beautiful day, too nice to be inside an air conditioned office. You should be here too. Blue skies, cool atmosphere and crisp air. It's just wonderful. Makes one appreciate being alive."

Maddie laughed. "You're mad. What, you just take a day off because it's a nice day."

"Sure. You should treat yourself occasionally. Life is not something to be postponed, you know."

"You're right, I must change my outlook. I called to see whether you had heard about the scandal in the American office."

"I haven't heard. Did someone come in with a gun?"

"No, no. Tim Tennyson is being sued for sexual harassment."

"Oh. Has he been suspended?"

"Not that I'm aware. The company seems to be siding with him."

JJ smiled, "I see. Do you want to talk about it?" He sensed that Maddie was unhappy and wanted to tell somebody about her sense of outrage.

"Well it's difficult with you being away."

That night JJ came out of the shower and after towelling himself he applied masses of deodorant. Then some L'Homme After Shave. He found a freshly ironed dress shirt and some form fitting trousers. Add new black shoes and he was ready. He glanced at his closely shaven face and closely cropped hair and he knew Maddie would be appreciative. She hadn't said much previously but he got the impression that she thought he was a fine looking man.

Thirty minutes later JJ was standing outside Maddie's new Bondi Junction apartment in Porter Street. She'd decided some time ago that living on a major thoroughfare was unhealthy. She had found this particular apartment weeks ago but had to wait until her lease had expired on the Edgecliff Road flat before moving in.

When Maddie opened the door, JJ was taken aback. She looked fabulous. A new red top exposing a little cleavage, a tight black skirt flattering her round bottom and red high heel slip-on shoes. She also sported a fresh hairdo, short and neat. The overall image was one of a sexy, confident woman, totally different from the girl he first approached. "Wow," he said, "you look stunning. Good enough to eat."

She smiled. "If that's what takes your fancy, you may be in luck. Coming in?"

JJ stepped inside and kissed Maddie on the lips, a long slow kiss. He followed her to the living room which possessed large glass doors leading to a balcony. She led him outside where the table was laid with two glasses, one with white wine and one for him, scotch on the rocks. He sat down once she had lowered herself into a chair facing the street. "This is a very pleasant way to be greeted. Are we celebrating something?"

"Not really. You were so nice to me on the phone that I felt very warm towards you." JJ smiled. They sipped their drinks.

"I'll show you around the new flat when we've had our drink."

"You seem very pleased with it," said JJ.

"I am. I'm generally indecisive but I hated the place on Edgecliff Road. I simply had to move.

Have you decided where we're going?"

"Sure," said JJ, "we'll stay here. We could order some pizza and settle into the new flat."

"Perfect," said Maddie.

CHAPTER 14

Day 2

As she crossed the road, she was convinced that someone was following her. Almost as frightening was the person approaching her – the strange stick like figure getting closer. She began to quicken her steps but all it achieved was to make the person confronting her seem really scary. Then she noticed the mirror she was walking towards at the corner of the building. She stopped before banging into it. The dreadful looking creature was her. She was appalled. Shocked. How could anyone look so emaciated? And still be alive?

She turned around but nobody was there. Perhaps looking the way she did, no one would bother stalking her.

But she noticed many people in the store. She decided to enter. Crowds were good. Here in New York they ignored individuals. She was alone in this huge place. Invisible. She couldn't imagine living anywhere except Manhattan.

It was nearly six o'clock on a flawless Wednesday evening. The appearance of sunshine after five consecutive gray days was welcome and it even managed to lift her spirits slightly.

She scanned the shelves. She chose a variety of items for dinner. Canned chicken soup.

Lettuce. Tomato. Bread roll. Cheese.

Cooking wasn't her thing. She didn't like eating much either so it was a drama. She preferred a cigarette and some wine. She had plenty of both at home. She planned to watch television and drink wine after dinner. That was something to look forward to. Work had been dull. She'd quit the lacklustre job but it didn't require qualifications of any kind and she needed the money. Besides then she would need to look for another job and the thought of interviews terrified her.

In the summer she usually walked to her West side bedsit on thirty-Ninth Street between 8th and 9th avenues. Today she wasn't in the mood. With the one bag of groceries, she got on a bus heading downtown. She found a seat next to a window. She was as happy as she ever got, looking out at the peak hour rush. All these people in haste, rushing. To go home to someone who expected them. To meet someone at some bar. To attend a pre-arranged dinner or family gathering. The next morning they'll be rushing back to their offices. What a life.

At the next stop, a man with a paunch and unruly mouse-brown hair sat next to her. He didn't seem to take any notice of her. She began to relax. She hated men. She kept her eyes focused to the right, watching pedestrians busily cross streets, quickly enter or exit stores or simply stand, waiting, with expressions of wanting to be gone from here.

She felt a touch and flinched. She turned towards the passenger beside her. He was grinning. She slid past him and got off the bus at the next stop. She felt weird, again. She wondered what was wrong with her. She couldn't tolerate the touch of another human, particularly a man. She slowed down as an outdoor seat at a side walk cafe was in prospect. She sat down farthest from the nearest customer. She closed her eyes. The nightmare returned.

Vivid. Gross. Terrifying.

"Miss, can I get you something?"

She opened her eyes. A short dark haired waiter was peering at her. "Coffee, please. A latte."

After the coffee, she walked home. She fed the cat, a fluffy black and wide moggy. She ruffled his fur. She smiled for the first time that day.

Mona was safe.

CHAPTER 15

The Past

The hall was noisy with tables and chairs arranged so that teachers could meet with parents for their annual discussion about their children. People were moving into position and others were leaving. It resembled a train station more than a school assembly. The Northern Beaches private school preferred this approach more than meeting in a classroom with teacher and pupil and parent or parents. The school held traditions sacred and this was a more recent one which was meant to make pupils feel at ease with the sessions and not something to be feared.

JJ sat next to his father who was facing his English teacher. "Would you excuse me a moment," she said, getting up and wandering off.

"Nice of you to come dad, I know you're awfully busy at work," JJ said, turning to look at his grey haired father who usually wore a pained expression.

"Hey, you're my boy. Why wouldn't I come? I'll be returning to work after this anyway."

"You work such long hours dad. Don't you have enough staff?"

"Deadlines are tight and I can't get more staff because of budgetary constraints. Besides there are some things which only I can do."

A mother and son passed the table. She was saying that he should smile during the interview sessions. JJ watched as they took seats towards the front of the huge hall usually reserved for seating an audience assembled for music and theatrical performances. He had performed here as a lead in a musical in both his senior years.

"I hope the company appreciates your commitment," said JJ. He knew that he couldn't convince his father to make any changes to his business arrangements. His mother had been trying for years, but with absolutely no success.

"I'm well paid and I have certain other perks."

"Such as?"

"A few years back I was able to take your mother on a business trip to Hong Kong. She stayed with me for a week and the local personnel really looked after her. She was taken shopping during the day by the Branch Manager's secretary and allowed to join the executives and myself at dinner. And once or twice we went out by ourselves to sight see. She really enjoyed the trip. Hasn't stopped talking about it."

JJ smiled. He knew that on this occasion his dad was only filling in for his mother who was at home ill. It was something he would treasure as years passed.

The English teacher, Mrs. Cutter, returned, apologising profusely. She sat down and looked at JJ's father. "Well I can say Mr Johnston that Jordan is a delightful student to teach. He shows a lot of enthusiasm in class."

"So it's all good," said James Johnston.

"Yes, except that he could do more study on poetry. That's one area where he's below average." Mrs. Cutting continued her talk about Jordan's achievements and James Johnston, uncharacteristically, smiled and looked pleased during the hearing. As a reserved man rarely given to displays of emotion, James Johnston, nonetheless, showed clear signs that he was proud of his boy.

JJ and his father went round to all his other teachers who were mostly full of praise for JJ's efforts. At five o'clock JJ accompanied his father back to the Ford Falcon and they drove home with music from Fleetwood Mac. They didn't say much during the ride but they enjoyed each other's company. For JJ this was a rare occasion and he cherished the opportunity to be with his father.

At home, James Johnston gave his son a friendly hug. "That went well, Jordan. Keep up the good work. When you get in, tell your mother I'll get a bite in the city and that she should not wait up for me."

"Sure dad. Enjoy the work."

JJ watched the car reverse out of the driveway and speed down the street.

CHAPTER 16

Day 2

She seemed to appreciate what he was saying. She was being very attentive and he hoped it was because she thought him handsome, with his winning smile and salt and pepper hair, rather than because he was a key member of the Corporation's management team. In fact, as Group Chief Financial Officer, he was effectively the second in command at the insurance conglomerate.

"What's that Don?" Michelle came closer and even put her hand on his arm for a moment. Was it because she fancied him or was a touch on his jacket nothing suggestive at all? He wasn't sure but didn't care. He would enjoy the moment and make the most of being in the company of an attractive young lady.

They were standing in the courtyard of the Lowenbrau Keller in the Rocks at a company Christmas party and Don Neilson realised he needed to be wary of the situation due to the awkward nature of it with others watching them at a business function. It was okay for her to be flirting with him but he had to act appropriately because of his position. Some of the young guns could get away with touching or hugging a beautiful young woman at a company sponsored function but he needed to be discreet.

Don Neilson looked into her eyes and said, "I said..."

"Don, can I have a word?" It was John Franks at his side.

Don turned to Michelle. "Would you excuse me for a moment?"

Don and John walked away and Franks asked him about a contract the company had entered. Neilson was annoyed. Franks always did this. Talking shop when they were socializing. Almost as if he were trying to impress on everybody how committed he was. Neilson knew it wasn't a show orchestrated by Franks. The man simply could not switch off. He treated the company as his own property and wanted to know every detail of everyone's business. It was a sickness. Neilson wondered how his wife and kids put up with his overwhelming need to get involved with everything the company did. For a considerable period each year Franks was jetting around the world to oversee the global operations. He was more than hands on, he was a micro manager. Virtually every decision needed his approval. It was claustrophobic and Neilson had been tempted on occasion to quit. But the money at EIG was too good to pass up for minor irritations and he opted to stay put and put up with all the shit. He was an endurance player and he would wait until the man retired before stamping his authority on policy.

Neilson explained the details whilst sipping his bottle of Hahn Light. Afterwards he mingled with other employees to ensure that he was seen to be sharing himself around.

Only near midnight did Neilson come back to Michelle. She was drinking with a couple of colleagues inside the tavern which was now reasonably empty as the majority of people had made their way to a taxi or a train station. He approached Michelle's group who were discussing what Christmas had in store for them. Neilson joined in the conversation and when Michelle and he were eventually by themselves he suggested sharing a taxi.

They arrived outside her place in Newtown. She invited him in. And then she turned on the light...

Neilson was startled by the bright spotlight. His wonderful memory of the night he spent at Michelle's place evaporated like his defrosted windshield in early morning. He was somewhere else. He blinked. Then he recalled the situation and realised that he must have been drugged and brought in, tied up and here he was, confused and feeling off colour.

A voice said, "Hello, Mr Neilson, I hope you had a restful slumber."

"I can't remember much. What's going on?"

"You have been unharmed. You may recall the bottle of water you were all given in the van. Each contained a date drug and you as well as all your colleagues have been asleep for varying amounts of time. In your case you've been asleep all night and this is the second day of your stay. It's now your turn to respond to some questions before the next stage."

Don Neilson said, "Can I have some water, uncontaminated preferably."

The voice laughed. "At least you have maintained your sense of humour. You will be provided with a drink soon."

Neilson soon realised he was bound in an uncomfortable chair. "Right."

"How long have you been with the company?"

"A long time. Around fifteen years."

"Good. And do you remember who worked in the division when you first joined, before you were transferred to Group?"

Don Neilson tried to think. It was the early nineties. He knew Ray Hickson who had since retired. "There was Hickson, Cotwood, Jamieson and Johnston."

"Very good. You've earned a bottle of uncontaminated water."

The spotlight turned off. Neilson was given some water. He was then blindfolded, his hands were untied and handcuffs applied. The leg shackles were removed and he was led out the door and into a room. His handcuffs were removed and he was told he could undo the blindfold once he heard the door lock behind him.

Neilson flexed his hands and stretched his legs. Then he pushed the blindfold up. He was in a bedroom it seemed. He wandered around and found a bathroom attached. The place looked civilised. Nothing like the five star accommodation he was used to on international business trips but not too shabby, considering he was a prisoner.

He decided a shower was in order so he stripped and went into the bathroom. Once he was clean with teeth brushed and deodorant applied he felt much better. He hated perspiration and the sticky sensation shirts made after a long day in the office. He figured he had been at work, as it were, for at least umpteen hours already. It was hard to know as all watches and mobile phones had been confiscated.

He found some casual clothes in a drawer and donned a t-shirt and fresh underdaks. He checked the room out to ensure there was no way to escape easily. The door was sturdy and would not yield to a switch kick or two. The room had no windows so he guessed it was in the centre of the building. From the size and appearance of the room, he imagined that this was a flat or serviced apartment of some kind.

Having not discovered any opportunity to depart without attracting attention, Neilson decided to await what was in store for him. At this stage he had no idea of the comparative strength of the enemy. He was puzzled too by the situation as it seemed that money was not the motive for the abduction.

He settled onto the queen sized bed with a business magazine which had been placed on a table. He hoped food would arrive soon. He had not eaten since he couldn't remember when. The lack of meals was probably good for losing weight and for him that meant the few extra pounds around the mid section but he was beginning to feel the pangs of hunger.

Neilson didn't have long to wait. The door opened and three people presented themselves. All wore black clothing and black balaclavas. The female in the trio placed a tray which contained a plate with some sort of filled roll and some juice. He was so appreciative that he almost thanked them but he remembered he was being held without his consent.

CHAPTER 17

The Past

JJ drove the vehicle, pausing when he reached the outside of the set of terraces in Porter Street, but there was no visible parking space so he moved along slowly until he'd reached the end of the street. He turned the silver Audi A4 around and found a spot nearly opposite Maddie's terrace. He climbed out of his new car, a medium sized sedan which he only collected a few days previously. He didn't know whether Maddie was a car person but he wasn't worried if she could not appreciate the smooth drive or internal features of his new acquisition.

He viewed the bank of two storied terraces from the footpath. They looked impressive from the street, all with balconies facing the road and all painted in delightful pastels. He found the right one and proceeded to the door.

JJ sat back in the sofa. He looked at the black and white print of the Harbour Bridge in the 1930s and wondered what fascinated Maddie about it. She lived in Sydney now so why did she need prints of a previous era? He also noticed other smaller prints with scenes of Sydney dotted around the wall. Perhaps collecting photos of old Sydney was a hobby.

Maddie returned from the kitchen with two cups of coffee. She set his down on the coffee table and immersed herself in an armchair opposite him.

"So how did you go?" said JJ, picking up his cup. He tasted the coffee. It was strong. Good.

"I found a file with succession information but it's rough and could change at any time." She had a crease in her black trousers which she smoothed out.

JJ looked at her and waited.

"There are three contenders for the role of Group CEO and I'm not sure that I'm allowed to say."

JJ went over to the serious faced and obviously concerned young woman and, balancing on the soft leather armrest, put his arm around her. "Maddie, don't tell me if it's going to cause grief. I was curious about the place. I wanted to understand more about the personalities in the company, that's all. I see names on documents but don't know how they fit in or how important they are. I guess I just want to succeed and thought that knowing who to be nice to might help." He hugged her.

Maddie relaxed, pleased there was no pressure. He was a nice guy, really, and what harm could come from talking about the people in the company. Her colleagues gossiped all day long. She said, "You're an employee so I'm not giving away any real secrets. Anyway there's Doug Vincent, the prime contender from what Jennie has told us but obviously said in confidence. And Stephen Burton and Tim Tennyson are also possibilities."

JJ squeezed tighter. "Ok, so they're the big wigs and I'll try not to offend them too much." He laughed. "As you said, that could change, depending on how long the current boss wants to stay in power."

"I think John Franks wants to go on but maybe he's made a commitment. He just lives for the company. I don't know how he does it. "

"Fame and fortune, I'd say," said JJ returning to the sofa. He finished his coffee. "He has dedicated his life to that place. He's just so passionate."

From her expression and tone, JJ could not figure out whether she admired Franks or felt pity for him. Of course he was successful and earned the praise of business types who were largely driven by business success but he wondered whether others found this trait admirable. He didn't wish to dwell on the topic, so changed the subject.

"I didn't visit to talk shop all night. Are you ready for the movies?" They rose and Maddie put her arms around him. She exuded warmth.

As they drove away, JJ thought about the contenders for overall boss and realised it was difficult to narrow down responsibility for what had gone on in the past. Vincent and Tennyson might be possible suspects. There had to be a way to obtain accurate information. He reflected how this might affect his plan and remained quiet for the bulk of the journey.

Nick Koutslakis was a man in his fifties. He was short but powerfully built and he sported a goatee. He eyed JJ cautiously after he had held him close and slapped his back hello. He released the young man and looked him up and down as though it were a surprise to see him so tall.

"Sit, please sit," he said. They were in his office, upstairs at Koutslakis' notorious Kings Cross club which was vibrating with loud disco music. "You're all grown up. I can't believe it. How's your dad?"

JJ settled back in the plush leather seat, crossed his legs and said, "Dad passed away. He always liked you, you know."

"I liked him too. In fact we were like brothers at one time. He set me up in business and helped me go through some tough times." Koutslakis lit a cigarette. "What are you doing with yourself?"

"Nothing much. Working." JJ fell silent. He did not know how to approach the topic he had in mind.

"That's great. Do you remember Tony and Angela? You used to play with them as a kid."

"Sure. I remember them. Angela must be about twenty five now."

Koutslakis laughed, got up and poured JJ some scotch. He handed him the glass. "Twenty six only last week. You were sweet on her years ago. You two should catch up. I'll arrange it."

"Fine. I'd love to see her again." JJ tasted the scotch. It wasn't bad. JJ recalled Angela when she was sixteen. Nick had come over to visit and brought Angela with him. Whilst the two older men went into a separate room to talk, JJ was left to entertain Angela in the living room. She was a beauty with striking dark features and a curvaceous figure. JJ wondered whether he could arrange a date without appearing gauche. But as time passed and as the conversation flowed easily about many topics, he learned that she was seeing somebody. He felt uncomfortable trying to suggest an outing and decided she was far too attractive for the likes of him. There was no point in courting rejection.

Koutslakis leant back and put his feet on the desk. “I presume this isn’t a social visit. What’s on your mind?”

JJ took another sip of his scotch. “I have a plan and I need some help.”

“Ok. I owe your father so much. Whatever it is, I’ll help. But first, tell me about what you’ve been up to.”

JJ briefed him on his London working experience and travel around Europe and how he managed to land a job with EIG.

“Wow,” said Koutslakis, “you’ve been real busy. Angela was wondering why you never called her. She said that you two got on really well last time you were together.”

“I didn’t think she’d be interested in me.”

“That’s where you’re wrong kiddo. She’s had some boyfriends but nothing solid. Who knows what the future holds.” Koutslakis laughed. “Let’s hear your plan.”

CHAPTER 18

Day 3

Tim Tennyson was a short squat man with thinning hair, an unsmiling face and a huge ego. This was the way Joe Mantel regarded him, Tennyson knew because he had overheard him one day. Joe was sitting opposite him in a hard backed chair listening to him rant. And he had good reason; the man wasn't performing. Tennyson was known for his quick temper and his pettiness. He seemed to revel in reprimanding and criticising employees. All this Tennyson was aware of but he didn't care how he was perceived. He had an important position and with it came responsibility. He wasn't here to win a popularity contest. He explained in great detail the targets missed in gross revenue and net operating profit of the section Mandel headed.

"You're the Senior Vice President, Health," Tennyson raged," and I expect a better performance from you and your team. Do you understand?"

Mantel nodded. "Loud and clear. I suppose it's of no value to explain the department is short staffed and that conditions are working against us."

"Don't give me excuses." Tennyson was not a listener. He was a talker and a bully and he needed everyone to realise he was the boss. And he hated this self-serving son-of-a-bitch.

The phone rang. Tennyson picked up. "What is it," he said through clenched teeth," you know I'm in a meeting. OK, sure, put him on."

"John, how are you? And how's your lovely wife? Good, good. How can I help?" He was quiet for a while, then with much enthusiasm, he said, "yes, can do. Fantastic." He replaced the phone with some flourish.

Tennyson noted that Mantel watched him closely. Let the loser watch because he suddenly felt energised and he didn't much care what this man who would soon be without a pay packet thought. He smiled. He looked up and said, "Right Joe, where were we? Oh yes. We'll review the results again next month. I expect them to be much improved. Keep up the good work."

Tennyson imagined Mantel as he walked slowly back down the corridor to his office, far away from the corner office, wondering what was going on. "Keep up the good work!" He'd think -what was all that about. It would be the first time he'd heard those words uttered by the American CEO in his presence. Tennyson liked to keep his employees guessing. Mantel was taller and fitter looking than Tennyson but he savoured the vision when he would inform the Vice President, Health his services were no longer required. He made a note to himself to fire the smug prick next month, on Mantel's fortieth birthday. That would give him something to celebrate.

Tennyson arrived at Kennedy airport an hour earlier than necessary. He was excited. He'd received a personal invitation from Franks to attend a conference in Australia. He hadn't had a chance to look at his calendar and he didn't care. Everything else could wait. For John Franks to personally invite him 'down under' meant something entirely different to a routine management get together. Franks was not a sentimental man. He was all business. And to be summoned like this could only mean he must be in the running for the top job.

Tennyson got through immigration without much fuss as the usually long lines seemed not so daunting today and he soon entered United Airlines' first class lounge. As he showed his ticket to the Airline Club's receptionist he wondered whether he should have mentioned to Franks that he was no longer with his wife. The fact that Franks had suggested she should accompany him made it awkward for him. He said she had plans she felt she had to honour. Bringing his wife probably meant that celebrations would occur. Perhaps he could advise the Executive Group once he was appointed the future Group CEO that his wife had left him. Although Franks was keen for family men to run the businesses, it was not unprecedented for wives or husbands to abandon their spouse in corporate America. Other executives at EIG had also been divorced but none at his level. Should he try to have his ex-wife get back together with him? But really, what was more important - his career or his relationships?

Tennyson strolled through the lounge until he found an empty table and chair. He dumped his coat and hand luggage. After inspecting the catered offerings, he settled on cheese, biscuits and scotch on the rocks. He sat back in the armchair and pondered the immediate future. He was feeling extremely positive. The American Operations had produced good numbers for the past two years. Without his wife, he was free to explore his desires. Once he had the top job, the world would be his. Nothing would hold him back.

When the United Airlines flight landed in Sydney, Tennyson collected his hand luggage and took his time getting off. A beautiful young hostess had captured his imagination and he hung back until the other first class passengers had moved out. He paused in front of the diminutive dark haired woman and asked whether she would join him for dinner if she was staying on in Sydney. The name badge showed 'Samantha' and as she smiled, he felt uplifted but it was a false dawn. She declined politely saying she had to meet friends.

The rejection soured Tennyson's view of matters as he stood near the conveyer belt. Waiting for his luggage now made him curse, particularly as even economy passengers were collecting their dinghy bags. In fact he got to the point where he was convinced that his two Victorinox premium luggage bags had been lost until finally they appeared on the dark grey carousel.

He pulled the bags off the carousel and onto his trolley with care and as he pushed towards customs he saw Samantha, a tiny figure next to a tall male co-worker, walking ahead through a special exit area. His heart sank. She would have been so delicious.

Despite his earlier disappointment, Tennyson looked forward to The Four Seasons hotel which possessed one of the finest restaurants in Sydney. Fun nights ahead beckoned.

John Franks was pacing. He was at his inner city residence preparing for a dinner outing. He had already called the Four Seasons three times and each time he had been informed that Tim Tennyson had not checked in. Franks wondered what was going on. Perhaps Tim was caught up in traffic. The plane had been only a few minutes late so he was puzzled by the delay.

"Rose," Franks called, "how are you getting along?"

"Only a few more minutes darling."

When Rose stepped out of the ensuite, Franks didn't comment on her new dress or hairdo. He rushed her to the car and drove off without a word. He was angry that Tennyson hadn't called and that his mobile was switched off. There was no excuse for this behaviour in business.

Franks didn't enjoy the night. They had reached the hotel restaurant, Kable's, and after a long twenty minutes, began ordering dinner, Franks furious but not prepared to deny his wife some respite. His mind was racing. He had no idea why Tennyson hadn't called. He was meant to check in at some time. He looked up and saw that Rose was bored. "Rosey, I'm not much company tonight. I apologise. But I need to find out why Tim is not communicating."

"Alright John. Make your calls."

"I won't be long. I'll go outside so I can talk. In the meantime, why don't you order dessert?"

Finally Tim responded. "Sorry John. There was an accident on the roads and we were stuck in a tunnel with no signal but I'm close to the hotel now."

"Ok, that's good mate. Look forward to seeing you. I'll see you in the restaurant."

Tennyson was a little put out. His boss hadn't even asked him whether he'd like to clean up first and he seemed totally unconcerned by his wellbeing after such a long flight. New York to Sydney was not a fucking bus ride. Tennyson was still steaming when he entered the lobby of one of the finest hotels in Sydney. Then the spotlight hit him.

Tennyson recalled the incident and Franks' story explaining his impatience and agitation. The intense bright light brought him back to the present.

"What the fuck is going on?"

A voice said, "I ask the questions here, my friend."

Tennyson squirmed, fighting the constraints but it was no use. "Listen buddy whoever you are, when I get out of this you are going to pay."

Silence for a moment.

Tennyson growled. "Untie me now."

"What makes you imagine you'll even be freed?" The voice said these words calmly, then the light switched off and footsteps receded. A door opened and closed.

Tennyson finally decided to curb his temper. There was nobody to vent against. The situation became clearer suddenly. He was amongst a group forcibly taken to an unknown location. God. What did this maniac want? Ransom? And why had he left the room?

CHAPTER 19

Day 3

Mona had made it home without incident. Inside her flat she breathed a sigh of relief and felt the anxiety lift. Back against the door which had locked with the five locks she used when home, she surveyed the small place she had gotten comfortable with. She went over to her sleeping cat, Rufus, and stroked him. He woke, stretched and meowed. Mona fed him.

Not much later there was a knock on the door. She froze. Another knock. She waited. Who knew where she lived? The knock came again, this time louder. She moved slowly to the door and peered through the peephole. A man in a suit and he was accompanied by a woman. They seemed to be holding some magazines.

Mona waited until they left before she felt able to move around the flat again.

After a modest TV dinner and a cigarette, Mona went to bed and watched some television.

She fell asleep during one program but was startled awake by the nightmare, the same one she experienced most nights.

CHAPTER 20

Day 3

John Franks was furious. He was in his office at 7am after having sped in from his home in Hunters Hill. He paced the floor after having tried Tennyson's mobile a dozen times. He was tempted to smash something but he clenched his teeth in exasperation.

Franks turned when he heard rustling. It came from outside. He walked to the door, opened it and found his PA putting objects into a paper bag.

"Hi Ruth, what are you doing here this time of day?"

"I hope I haven't disturbed you. I'm just clearing out junk." Franks smiled. He liked diligent employees. "Not urgent, is it?"

"Oh no but I know it's a big day for you. Thought I'd clean everything up so that I can make myself available for anything that comes my way. I know you have a meeting with a number of overseas visitors."

"Good. Can you try Tim for me? He's been out of contact all morning."

"He might be in the shower. I'll keep on it until he answers." Despite being a large woman Ruth moved quickly and quietly.

"Great." Franks slid back into his office leaving the door ajar. Tim had dropped a bombshell. He'd left a message saying that they needed to fire a senior employee but had given no further details.

Ruth popped her head in a moment later. "Tim's on the phone," she said.

Franks took a deep breath. He didn't want to sound exasperated or out of control. It was not an image he wished to cultivate. Tennyson had such a reputation, of being loud and angry, and it was detrimental to his standing with some of the directors. He picked up the phone, "Yes Tim?"

"Ruth just called, said you were trying to get in touch."

"That's right. Just curious about the message you left."

"Right. Might be best if we discuss this face to face. It's sensitive."

Franks fought between his need to know and his need to appear calm. "Sure, why don't we meet for breakfast? Can you get down to the breakfast room in twenty minutes?"

"Certainly. See you then."

Franks cleared his desk which was usually free of clutter as he liked a clean appearance for visitors. The only item left was a telephone. He did not have a computer as he considered others could carry out anything which required such equipment. His role was to lead, to meet internal and external key personnel, to make decisions, to appear at conferences, to talk to major shareholders. It was not to sit in front of a screen. Besides he loathed this technology. He had grown up in a period of hand written ledgers and normal mail which one posted. He had no time for email or Facebook or twitter.

After he had made his office immaculate, he donned his suit jacket and walked up to Ruth, explaining he had a breakfast meeting. He also asked her to polish his desk whilst he was away. She nodded and smiled pleasantly as though it was not necessary to ask something which she would perform instinctively and automatically. He smiled back and reminded himself to thank her for her loyalty when others were in her presence. He then took a brisk walk to the Four Seasons Hotel in George Street.

John Franks was drinking coffee when Tennyson came into the hotel's main dining room. Tennyson looked refreshed and brimming with energy. He wore a tailor made suit, white shirt and red silk tie with an interesting swirling design. He sat down opposite Franks after shaking his hand. He nodded to the waiter to pour coffee.

"Good sleep?" asked Franks.

"Not long enough. I'll never get used to the jetlag."

"So what's the problem?"

"Straight into it? Could I have some breakfast first?"

Franks was beginning to seethe. This man was pushing all the wrong buttons. However he remained calm. "Sure but I have an appointment at nine."

Tennyson chose the buffet and piled scrambled eggs, bacon, sausages, tomato and an omelette onto a plate as well as orange juice. Franks settled for coffee and pastries.

They ate mostly in silence with some chitchat about past flights and current wives. Tennyson was in the process of raising the divorce matter but decided to remain quiet about this. At the conclusion of his omelette, Tennyson pushed his plate aside and drained his fourth cup of coffee.

"It's Johnston," he said.

Franks raised his eyebrows. "What about him?"

"His investigation into my operation is unauthorised. He doesn't understand our business and I want him to never again set foot on American soil."

"That's a strong statement. What happened?"

"He went into areas which he shouldn't have and if his report is distributed the company may be in a heap of shit."

Franks woke up in a cold sweat. The dream faded and he sat up rigid. Then he remembered where he was. He groaned then slowly got out of bed. He stretched his arms, strolled into the bathroom and splashed his face with cold water. How was it possible for so many people, his team, to be under the physical control of a few thugs? If only the management team were together, the management team that ran a multi-billion dollar organisation, the management team which resolved issues and problems. They would soon work out a plan, then execute ...

A knock on the door stopped him pondering what might be. Franks returned to the bedroom which also doubled for a living room. The unit or holiday accommodation had an unusual layout, he felt. The only door opened to a large room which contained a bed, a table, a bookcase and some chairs. It was connected to an open plan kitchen with a refrigerator, a stove and a dividing bench at which one could eat. The bathroom was the only other room. The flat contained no television, telephone or electronics of any kind. Franks suspected all such gear had been intentionally removed.

A woman, dressed in tight trousers and a balaclava, entered and dropped a tray of food and drink on a table to the side of the room.

At the door a man who also wore a balaclava stood, watching.

"Listen here," Franks said, "you can't keep us imprisoned." The couple left without a word.

After breakfast the door opened again and two men in black, heads covered, stood in the doorway. One came towards Franks with a glass of water which Franks thought might be drugged. He shook his head. The other hooded man then produced a syringe. Franks accepted the water.

The light in his eyes was as painful as on the first occasion in this torture room. Franks said, "Is this necessary?"

The voice said, "This is the way it's going to be for the present."

Franks closed his eyes and prayed that the police were close to tracking them. Surely a hire truck would be easy to trace. "What do you want?"

"Just some answers to simple questions."

"Fire away."

"What do you know about James Johnston?"

"I know of him. He used to work in one of the company's divisions as Head of Finance. That was some years ago."

"So what happened to him?"

"He left. I don't get involved with that. There are too many employees at EIG."

"He was a key part of management. You would have had dealings with him on a regular basis," the voice prompted.

Franks decided he would not be pressured. Nobody could force him to talk. "Yes he was but that doesn't mean I understood what happened between him and the division's CEO."

"That was Vincent, wasn't it?"

Franks said in his authoritative voice, "If you know so much, why are you asking me?"

The light was switched off. The voice continued. "I'll come back when you're ready to discuss matters intelligently and calmly." The only door to the room opened and the interrogator was gone.

Franks pondered his position. Why was this so important? Johnston was merely a past employee. And then he thought: what did it matter if he told this guy that Johnston was fired. Nobody would really know the truth; that was between him and Tennyson.

An hour must have passed. Franks was extremely uncomfortable. What was happening was nothing less than torture, psychological torture. These people would get a long sentence. Then he wondered whether the executive team would be killed, murdered by these punks before rescuers arrived. Where were the cops?

More time passed and now Franks was very thirsty. This was inhumane. And where were the others? Surely they could overpower the kidnappers. He wasn't thinking rationally. He had no idea how many masked men there were. He didn't know what weapons they had apart from the guns they used to wave around or keep in sight as they entered the rooms.

Finally the door opened and after a brief pause the light came on again. Silence for a while.

Franks said, "What are you doing, talk."

"The question is, are you ready to talk?"

"Yes. Why are you so interested in this James Johnston? What's it got to do with you?"

"That's not something you need to know. However what I have been asking has more to do with the treatment of your people. I'm using this name as an example as I know he left under mysterious circumstances."

"That's not true. What makes you say that?" Franks was running out of breath. "Can I have a drink? It's so hot in here."

Minutes went by as the man switched off the light, returned with a bottle of water, helped Franks swallow some liquid and then return to his place and switch the spotlight on again.

The voice said, "I have my sources so don't play games with me. In fact if I find you lying or misleading me, you will earn a punishment and the ordeal you've been through so far you will regard as a picnic in comparison." Silence loomed for a moment before the voice said," Go on."

Franks realised he needed to be careful how he worded his responses. But he didn't believe that the kidnappers would extend their torture without then attracting significant punishment from the authorities. The man was bluffing. "What I can tell you is that

Johnston went beyond his line of authority."

"I see. In what way?" There was an amused note in the tone.

"I don't know the full details but it had to do with his visit to New York some years ago."

"Why did he go there if he was Head of Finance for Asia and the Pacific?"

"He was seconded for a period whilst the US Operations were looking for a replacement for their CFO. They had lost too many senior members in their Finance team and as the Asia Pacific region was our smallest and had good people, Johnston could be spared."

"So when he returned Vincent thought he had carried out work outside his brief."

"Yes, I guess that was the grist of it after he had discussed the matter with the American CEO, but as I said the details are now blurred. He was not a heavyweight in the organisation so I didn't delve too deeply."

"You're sure?"

Franks thought a moment and added, "But it was not only that. I do recall the Asia Pacific CEO saying that he lacked the necessary ambition for the job and it was appropriate to find someone more dedicated."

"Do you get rid of all employees who lack ambition?"

"Of course not. We wouldn't have many employees working if that were the case but at the senior levels it's expected. That's why the company is so successful and why others in the industry aspire to be like us."

The spotlight was switched off. The voice said, "Instead of drugging you we can place a hood over your head and lead you back to your room if you'd rather."

"Yes, I'd prefer that."

"Ok, but bear in mind that should you try anything foolish, you will be severely dealt with."

When Franks was returned to his room he pulled off the hood and looked around. How long were they intending to question him and the others? He wondered whether all his key people were being interrogated. He still had no idea what this was all about.

He needed to get a message to Tennyson because they might ask him about Johnston too and discover that he was dismissed because he uncovered something in the North American organisation which they couldn't allow to be revealed. But then he thought that only Vincent would be asked about Johnston as Tennyson had no real day to day connection with him. Vincent did not know what was behind his sacking. He breathed a sigh of relief.

Franks lay on his bed and closed his eyes. He was exhausted. All he could do was await police intervention. As all their wallets had been confiscated, he felt sure they would have attempted to use some of their cards and the banks would be alerted. They would slip up sooner or later, that was a certainty.

He pondered the Johnston affair and wondered whether more questions about him would be forthcoming. James Johnston had been hired by the Asia Pacific HR department before Vincent had assumed the Head of Division role. Johnston had been a good team leader and competent finance man but he did not know his place. At times he would contradict Franks on how to report items in the management accounts. Franks who was a qualified accountant himself didn't appreciate this interference because he needed to restate each Division's management accounts for bonus setting purposes. Only he knew what deals had been struck and he didn't need some nosey accountant to query his perspective.

Once Vincent took on the job as Asia Pacific CEO difficulties emerged. Vincent knew little about finance or accounting and didn't trust Johnston and asked Franks whether he could be replaced. This was awkward as Johnston had not done anything to warrant dismissal and Franks did not wish to risk an unfair dismissal law suit. So they bided their time until an opportunity arose.

CHAPTER 21

Day 3

It was 8 o'clock in the morning on a cool cloudy Sydney day. The room was buzzing. Twenty one people were standing around or sitting on desks and benches. The talk consisted of what had happened to them the night before or speculating about the reason they were gathered in the conference room at police headquarters.

Detective Inspector Donaldson strode into the room and silence descended. He walked to the front of the room and took in the landscape. Men and women in plain clothes were arranged in a haphazard way around the room.

"Ladies and gentlemen, please take a seat."

He waited while they rearranged themselves in the ergonomically designed chairs. He noted they formed in clusters of friends or from the same station or department.

"Right," he said," you've been asked to help in a most puzzling crime. You would undoubtedly have read about a kidnapping in the CBD in broad daylight, a kidnapping not of a single person but of an entire team of people. Brazen, crazy, bizarre. But it has happened and what is most puzzling after around three days is that no contact has been made by the kidnappers to either the company or any family member of any of the individuals taken hostage. In other words we have no idea why the abductions took place or what the perpetrators want." Donaldson paused to allow the message to sink in and to observe the reaction around the room.

Finally a young man said," Surely there were witnesses to this."

"One woman was a witness to the actual abduction and she has been questioned, "Detective Sergeant Morris informed him, turning to address the man, a muscular fair haired sort with lively eyes. She was seated to the right of Donaldson and facing him, in the front row. "We have also reviewed the company's human resources records to find whether someone internally might be responsible."

Donaldson continued. "Thanks Jane. That's where you come in. We have to get some traction quickly or it may be too late. A list of ex-employees who might fall into the category of potential abductor has been drawn up. We need each one of you to visit someone on the list to determine their likely involvement. You will be split into pairs and only Jane and I will not be going along. We have already spoken to a few people over the phone but now we need to eliminate all on the list."

A buzz went around the room.

Donaldson held up his hand. "Now the two detectives to my right will arrange which teams go where. Let's meet up again tomorrow for a debrief. Should anyone come across vital information I want to know immediately. Ok ladies and gentlemen, let's make this count."

Donaldson walked off. He knew his two key assistants, Morris and Braxton, would set up an efficient process. He only hoped something positive would ensue. They had little to go on and as the whole abduction seemed so out of character they needed some useful material to work with. He grabbed some coffee from the kitchen and went back to his office.

His calendar showed his next meeting was at 10 o'clock with the Deputy Commissioner. This case was attracting a lot of interest.

Donaldson decided to review the news headlines online while he was having his coffee. He knew that once the meetings began he would get little chance to do anything constructive.

CITY KIDNAPPING A MYSTERY screamed one newspaper. EASY INSURANCE DIRECTORS DEMAND ACTION said another. And a third wrote NO RANSOM DEMAND YET.

Donaldson didn't bother reading any of the articles because they were all speculation. He could imagine how the news was affecting the families, none of whom had to date been able to point to any enemies which would account for this kind of action. All the families had been either visited or, if abroad, called to enquire of personal animosities, business jealousies or potential nut cases they were aware of. Apart from a few business rivals and corporate enemies being mentioned, nothing came to light. It was only natural for large corporations to have competitors who would enjoy disruption to their chief rival's business but it was rare for this kind of criminal activity to be orchestrated in a first world country.

Donaldson had to concede this case was completely baffling. No motive, no suspects, no nothing. He was not looking forward to his meeting with the Deputy Commissioner.

Donaldson rubbed his hand over his partially bald head, rose slowly from his chair and air boxed, pretending the target, the kidnapper, was at the receiving end. He donned his suit jacket and marched out with a thin file of what had transpired so far. He expected to be grilled and he also knew he would be expected to demonstrate he had a solid plan in place.

CHAPTER 22

Day 4

She screamed but he wouldn't release her. He ripped off her flimsy blouse, then the skirt and finally her panties. He was already naked. He was rough, grabbing her hair while he thrust his ugly fat body against her. He was a ghastly white and he pushed her down onto the bed. Then he got on top of her. She struggled but he was far too strong for her, a mere five foot and weighing less than a hundred pounds. He pushed her legs apart and his erect appendage penetrated. She woke in a sweat, bolting upright. The same nightmare, over and over, plagued her. It had been years since it happened yet still she couldn't erase the images. The incident was all too graphic.

Mona should have gone to the police those many years ago but she had been so embarrassed. The thought still infuriated, disgusted and reviled her. Her very own hairy uncle attacking the thirteen year old happy girl she had been. He had destroyed any innocence she possessed and subsequently her life.

Who would have believed it? She mentioned the episode to her mother some time later.

At first her mother didn't believe her. Then, after insisting it was true for days, her mother's attitude changed and she said not to cause a fuss. She said she would have a word to him but it never eventuated.

Mona slumped out of bed, exhausted. She bowed her head and placed her face in her hands and sobbed. She was distraught. Her life was horrible. She again contemplated suicide. But she had a cat. She couldn't do it to Rufus.

After another few minutes, she went into the bathroom and prepared herself for another day. When she reached the front door, she hesitated. Did she really want to go to work? She'd call in sick.

She turned the knob. Released it. She stood by the door paralysed with indecision for minutes. Finally she decided to buy some wine and retreat back into her small apartment.

Coming out of the drugstore she saw the headlines about the kidnapping in Australia involving a US victim but thought little of it.

Back in her apartment, Mona started her computer and logged onto the internet and decided to look at the news across the world.

That's when she came across one article on the kidnapping in Sydney which listed the victims. One of the abductees was her uncle, Tim Tennyson.

Mona's initial reaction of unexpected surprise, like accepting the winning of an enormous lottery prize, turned to euphoria, then noisy jubilation. She could hardly contain herself and she frightened the cat.

CHAPTER 23

Day 4

When George Waites awoke from his drugged sleep and looked into the dazzling light, he immediately felt paralysed. At first he felt totally disoriented. He recalled a situation at school where he couldn't read the writing on the bright white board. That was the moment he realised his eyes were at fault and after tests he obtained a prescription for spectacles. His parents were pleased as they had wondered why he had difficulty identifying certain objects in the distance.

His eyes had deteriorated now to the extent where he needed glasses just to see properly over a short distance. His spectacles had been taken from him and he wondered what was now in store for him. His face still ached from the blow he received a day or so ago. He'd lost all concept of time as well. All watches, jewellery and valuables had been confiscated. All he knew was that he had been couped up in a small room for a very long time and that he had slept for a significant portion of that time.

"What's going on?" he said.

A voice came from afar. "Good to see that you're awake. Just relax, I have some questions and then you'll be back in your room."

"I don't want to return to that soulless room. I want to be released. I have a wife and two small children and they must be worried."

"I'm sure they are. But let's not play games otherwise the session will be longer than anticipated."

"What makes you think I will tell you anything?"

"Well George you are the Risk Officer of the company. What risk do you think you're taking if you refuse to co-operate?"

Waites remembered only too well the pain when the fist which felt like the butt of the pistol smashed into his face. There was a time to show courage but this was not one of them. There was nobody around to witness bravery or any other position he might take. It was best to play along. "What do you need to know?"

"That's better. First tell me how you acquired the job at Easy Insurance."

Waites wondered whether this was a trick question. What could he say? He reflected on the past when the previous female Group Financial Controller and his wife were friends. Often they would have dinner parties at home, or out at a restaurant with a group of acquaintances. He was working at a small reinsurance company which was in trouble financially and he knew his wife had mentioned to her friend that he was a good finance executive. So one day, he heard that a senior finance executive had upset the CEO and that the company was looking for a replacement. He got the nod on the basis of the referral from his wife's friend. But how did this impact on the current situation?

Waites swallowed and squinted into the light. "I was interviewed by the Asia Pacific CEO some years ago."

"You mean Vincent?"

"Yes, that's correct." Waites became wary. How did he know that Vincent was previously the head of the Asia Pacific division? Either he had done his homework or he was informed by an insider.

"Go on," said the voice. "Well I got the job."

"Explain the process. How many interviews, with whom, the other candidates, your qualifications etc. You know the drill."

Waites was caught off guard. This guy obviously knew a lot more than he was prepared to say and Waites was worried he would get violent if he lied. He said, "I was the only candidate and Vincent hired me after one interview. But I had been recommended by the Group Financial Controller and the CEO trusted her. I mean I was the right choice."

"I'm sure you believe that but doesn't it strike you as peculiar that the gruelling process of executive interviews became so easy and so instant?"

"I've never thought about it."

The voice continued, "Did you meet with your predecessor?"

Waites thought for a moment. He had met him once socially when his wife was still working at the company. James Johnston. He remembered that he was quite pleasant but couldn't recall much else. His wife had said he was not liked by her friend, the Group Financial Controller, as Johnston would not always agree readily with her proposals. He gained the impression that they would be happy if he were gone, simply to make life easier for the small group controlling the way things were reported. Waites said, "Socially I think but I don't recall much. What I do know is that the meeting was not at the company's offices."

"That's all for now. You will be escorted back without being sedated unless you cause trouble."

"I'll behave. Can I have my glasses back?"

"They'll be in your room."

When Waites was back safely in his room, he was puzzled. There had been no request for information about his wealth or anything connected with money. Questions had been asked but they too seemed quite innocent. Nothing at all to do with the company's secrets or finances. Everything about the abduction was strange and the longer into their capture, the more bizarre it appeared. Being incarcerated in what was, in reality, a holiday flat was far better than being tied and gagged as he had anticipated. From what he'd read about these situations, hostages were normally treated poorly with little sustenance. But these people had provided proper food and drink. Yet he still felt threatened. Was the worst yet to come?

He went to bed. He would sleep, something he needed to catch up on in any event. He had been working long hours to ensure he was ahead of the game. He was ambitious and now that he had an opportunity at a large corporation, he would do everything he could to rise through the ranks. He even coveted the main prize, that of Group CEO. He had already been promoted from his divisional finance role to the Group Risk Officer and so was in the inner circle of knowing the company's plans. He had done very well and his wife was very proud of him.

He closed his eyes and dreamed of future glory. He did not expect to be in captivity for long. He hadn't been mistreated since arriving at this destination and he suspected the kidnappers were out of their depth. If only he knew what they wanted. He couldn't imagine that his colleagues would have suffered if they also co-operated so he guessed it was a waiting game. He began to feel better.

Sometime later he rose in a sweat. He had been dreaming of his meeting with Johnston. Some days prior to Johnston's dismissal, Waites had been invited by Vincent to the Asia Pacific conference room. Johnston arrived after Vincent phoned him using the internal telephone system. Johnston was an elegant looking man with salt and pepper hair and penetrating eyes. He shook Waites' hand, a firm handshake, and sat opposite him. Vincent addressed Johnston informing him that Waites was an accountant from a reinsurer that EIG used. He then suggested that Johnston show him how EIG prepared its claims tables split by underwriting years.

Waites slid out of bed and went into the bathroom. Did the kidnapper want to know how much information had been passed onto him? Was this relevant? For the next few hours Waites was unable to sleep.

CHAPTER 24

The Past

Nick Koutslakis was a businessman. He owned real estate in many Sydney suburbs, both residential and commercial as well as two restaurants and one nightclub. He called himself a property developer but the police suspected he had become wealthy in part because of criminal activity and primarily from drug distribution. Koutslakis denied this to all and sundry as he had left behind that part of his persona when he reached thirty. Now in his fifties he saw himself as a respectable businessman and he became quite indignant if one of his associates referred to his early rise to notoriety and wealth creation.

James Johnston had helped Nick on many occasions and advised him how he could turn substantial funds into legitimate money making investments. Many of these investments attracted a healthy rate of return. For this reason Koutslakis had no problem in providing Johnston's son, Jordan Johnson, with a block of units he owned in the Eastern suburbs, at least until redevelopment work could begin. This block had been recently acquired and was situated close to the beach in Arden Street, Coogee. Koutslakis did not experience problems with the tenants as the block was essentially holiday accommodation and hence all leases were short term. Consequently time was not an issue in ridding the block of tenants and it had been vacated quickly with no new lets made.

It was in this holiday flat complex that JJ had driven the hostages. Not only had Koutslakis allowed him this property but Nick had also let JJ use two of his boys for whatever he had in mind. Angela Koutslakis also volunteered to help JJ. She needed something interesting to do and when she was reintroduced to JJ she felt excited. She had been fascinated by the young man since their early days when they'd first met and the timing for a relationship had been wrong. Although she knew little of what JJ had planned when he discussed matters with her father, she wanted to be part of this experience.

Koutslakis met with JJ at his home in Elizabeth Bay. Angela who had been out in the early part of the evening knocked on the door of her family home at around nine o'clock, just after dinner concluded with a glass of dessert wine. Nick Koutslakis thanked his third wife, Cathy, who had prepared a wonderful lamb dish before he and JJ moved to the lounge which overlooked the bay. Koutslakis was pouring some Galliano when Angela entered. She kissed her father on the cheek and caught sight of JJ out of the corner of her eye.

"Hello Jordan," she said, "I haven't seen you for years. What are you doing here?"

"I'm enjoying your father's hospitality," JJ said. "You look wonderful," he also blurted, unable to stop himself. He was genuinely pleased to see Angela who still made his pulse beat faster.

Angela turned back to her father. "Am I interrupting?"

"We'll be done soon, darling, then you and Jordan can catch up."

After JJ and Nick Koutslakis ended their business discussions, he joined Angela who was enjoying a wine on the balcony. At first they simply sat quietly on the balcony chairs, taking in the view and savouring each other's presence. JJ couldn't believe that Angela was more breathtaking than previously and felt the magic would dissipate if he spoke. But eventually they looked at each other and began to chat.

Angela agreed to JJ's invitation to dinner. He had waited until the very last minute to ask her, having already stood up to go. It was almost an afterthought, she felt and agreed before he could change his mind.

They met at Dish a Restaurant in Darling Harbour the following Saturday night. It was located within the Novotel Sydney and JJ who had made the reservation arrived first. He ordered a Heineken beer and was appreciating the spectacular views of the city's skyline when Angela walked over. She kissed him on the cheek and took her seat at right angles to him.

"Sorry I'm late," she said, "the baby shower went on longer than I anticipated and then I had trouble finding a cab."

JJ smiled and the hovering waiter came near, asking Angela whether she'd like a drink.

"I'll have a margarita," she said and turning to JJ added, "Just as well I'm not driving tonight.

I've already had enough alcohol to fail a breathalyser."

The couple talked and laughed and marvelled at the fine cuisine. The offerings were interesting although JJ's tastes did not extend to the exotic but he hoped that Angela would appreciate the effort he'd made. Angela ordered Goats Cheese Stuffed Tempura Zucchini Flowers, Spring Chicken Fillet while JJ stuck with favourites Sydney Rock Oysters and Black Angus Sirloin steak. They washed this down with a Montana Reserve Pinot Gris and then shared a Honey and Coconut Bavarois for dessert.

Afterwards JJ drove her to his Bondi Beach unit and explained what he had in mind. She had no reservations with his plans and said she would do the catering and other chores associated with the assignment.

Angela studied JJ's bachelor apartment and commented how it didn't meet the usual criteria of soiled clothes and dirty dishes being on display. In fact, she said she rather liked the sparse appearance. A kitchen and bathroom with the usual items but they looked clean. The living room contained a large sofa, one comfortable chair, a large screen television, a stereo and a cabinet with books, DVDs and CDs. The bedroom had a king size bed, storage for clothes and a laptop computer lying on a desk on the right side of the room.

That night JJ and Angela made love for the first time. JJ was standing in the bedroom watching Angela examine the room as she had insisted on being taken on a tour of the one bedroom apartment, apparently totally refurbished inside to give it a modern atmosphere. Outside the block looked old and worn out and one which any respectable burglar would ignore.

Angela smiled, "You have no paintings or prints or artefacts or ornaments. Who lives like this?"

"I'm in the process of buying some prints for the walls but I don't like ornaments much. This place also has storeroom where I keep sporting equipment and other stuff."

"I couldn't live without plants and pretty things...," she said.

JJ moved closer and placed his arm around her. "You're the only pretty thing I need."

She turned into him, put her right hand behind his neck, pulling him gently forward and kissed him. A moment later she started unbuttoning his shirt. From there it was not long before they were both naked and exploring each other's contours.

JJ felt on top of the world. Not only had he often lusted over Angela, considering her out of his class, but it seemed she actually liked him as he was. As a bonus she wanted to help him with a plan which would have made many women nervous. She did not think him a nutcase because of his desire to address a past wrong by engaging in an extreme form of revenge. Instead she listened attentively and even came up with a few suggestions.

Angela was a university drop out and she had not gained a job except to help her father every now and then. Not that she had any financial worries with Nick lavishing her with a fully paid pad and motor vehicle. She was beautiful but possessed a build somewhat curvier than some of her friends. At school she had never been popular with the boys who found her slimmer friends more appealing. Marisa and Elizabeth, her best friends, had not changed much since school and now looked less than extraordinary. Angela, on the other hand, had transformed from a slightly chubby girl into a stunning woman with proportions that made some men drool.

Over the next few weeks, JJ and Angela were inseparable. It was hard for JJ to comprehend why they got on so well. They had a few things in common, such as reading and films, but there were also many things about which they had no common ground. Angela loved theatre and ballet and tending a garden. JJ loved sport and nightclubs.

The relationship between JJ and Maddie had ended but JJ wanted to maintain a friendly connection. Maddie felt betrayed and avoided him as much as possible.

CHAPTER 25

Day 5

The white clouds formed an intriguing pattern, as though a painter had used his brush in circular motions to create swirls of cotton white against blue. JJ jogged along the beach letting the light breeze brush against his face. It was a little after seven o'clock and he expected to be back at the Arden Street vacant block in thirty minutes.

On his return JJ showered in a unit which he and Angela used as their base. After checking that his hair was properly brushed back, he met with the team in a separate first level unit used as the gang's control room. This had been fitted with room monitors and other electronic equipment to ensure the success of their enterprise. Again Nick Koutslakis had people with the necessary expertise to prepare the special requirements in the nominated unit. Freshly dressed in the uniform adopted by the team of black trousers and black shirt, JJ walked into the control room kitchen and poured coffee into his mug.

Although JJ would not allow himself to be seen by the hostages as they would recognise him, he wanted to instil a sense of discipline into his team so that when they visited units for any reason they would only be seen with black clothing and black balaclavas.

Coffee finished, JJ summoned Angela and his assistants Jack and Tony, two of Koutslakis' main muscle men, for a meeting. He impressed upon them how important it was to take no risks and follow the procedures which had previously been strictly outlined. He praised them for their work to date but informed them there was a long way to go and warned them not to become complacent. Mistakes or accidents might occur, he said, but that risk would be reduced if the laid down protocols were observed.

At the end of his talk, JJ asked whether they had any questions. He looked at each in turn.

Jack, the more senior of the two men, shook his head. He was a powerfully built man who didn't spend much time talking.

Tony, an Italian Australian with chiselled features, said, "No problem boss." Finally JJ eyed Angela who simply smiled and said they had work to get on with.

Angela had arranged deli style sandwiches from the local centre. This was a treat. Usually the food was basic and just adequate for the hostages to remain healthy. Trays were arranged and deliveries were made to each room. Angela carried the tray in and Jack or Tony accompanied her. Each had a gun in the event trouble arose. But nothing had occurred so far. No person had shown any inclination to force their way out. But JJ suspected it would happen at some stage. He realised that the longer the hostages were held the higher the risk that something would go wrong.

When the round of deliveries was finished, JJ waited for all to settle into a chair for a drink, then asked," Have any of you got any comments on what we're doing with these people?"Although his team seemed comfortable with the day to day duties they performed, he knew that they all had feelings about the people they encountered and he needed to make sure they aired any concerns or misgivings about that side of the equation.

Tony shook his head.

Jack said, "Nick has asked us to help out and we will do whatever needs doing. He's paying us pretty good so it's just another job."

"What about you, Angie?"

"I'm good. I don't have any questions at the moment. They've all been well behaved...surprisingly!"

JJ began a ham, camembert and salad whole grain sandwich. "They're probably all confident they will be ransomed off or found. Some will begin to crack once it dawns on them they could be locked up for some time. So I want you to monitor their behaviour as well and report anything unusual to me."

"Sure boss," said Tony, scratching the back of his buzz cut head.

"And I also want you to let me know if the job starts to get too hard, emotionally, or in any other way, anything at all..." JJ stopped. He was getting too carried away with this soft approach.

Jack and Angela nodded.

"Did you get some cappuccinos Angie?"

"Absolutely. I know how you like to get your daily fix." She opened another box and handed out the coffees. "This is from my second trip from the corner cafe."

JJ took a sip of coffee and murmured agreeably. He looked at Jack with his strong features and healthy build. "When does Nick want to pull this place down and rebuild?"

"There's no hurry," Angela interrupted, "Another six months, maybe more. Dad's got a lot of projects on the go so I don't think you need to worry."

"We'll be done well before then." JJ sat back. Although Nick was financing this enterprise, JJ knew that with all the information available to them that the cost could easily be retrieved by Koutslakis' experts, should they believe the risk was warranted. In any event Koutslakis was a very rich man and he did as he pleased.

Later JJ walked through the complex, up stairs and then down again. The block of units was only seven levels, a neat and relatively small building but showing signs of wear. It had been constructed in the 1920s and was on prime land overlooking the ocean, but on a street a block away. There were four units on each level above basement level which was atop the garage level. The basement was windowless and consisted of a large room in which the interviews were being conducted. An elevator ran from ground level to the top level. Steps joined the basement to the ground level. It was a perfect setup for the plan which JJ had worked on for a considerable time.

When JJ returned to the control room, he wandered over to Angela and hinted they should go back to their unit on the top level. The captives were contained in the lower three levels. Angela took JJ's arm and appeared content with the world. The operation was going to require patience because JJ believed he would not obtain useful information until the hostages' will had been broken. Elapsed time and isolation would help.

Inside JJ's and Angela's unit, the windows were unobscured and the view was breath taking. JJ often just stood by the window and watched the distant waves. He stripped and when Angela did likewise he stared at her naked body a moment before moving towards her. He took her in his arms and kissed her passionately. He showered her neck with light kisses, then let his mouth and tongue ride down to her large breasts. Soon they were on the bed and slowly savouring the experience many couples only enjoy on holiday after many years doing their day to day jobs. The leisurely sensuous session was in stark contrast to the controlled and measured approach JJ took during the interviews with the hostages. By now all the management team had at least one sitting, some done merely to impress upon them that they were expected to supply information.

"Angie," JJ said when they were holding each other after their love-making, their energy spent, "what do you think of me?"

"That's an odd question. I love you. You must know that."

"Well I'm crazy about you too but that's not what I meant. Do you think what I'm doing is evil?"

Angela rolled around to face JJ. She placed her leg over his torso and looked him in the eye. "From what you've told me you have good reason to do what you're doing. In fact, I admire your restraint."

They kissed.

"What about your dad? Do you know what he does?" Angela jabbed him playfully in the ribs.

"Hey," he said, "what's that for?"

She said, "You bastard. My dad has his bad points but I still love him. He has done stuff in his past which mum told me about but basically he's a loyal man who looks after his own. It was hard for him to get a start and he did some questionable deals and may have been involved in some rough stuff but I don't think he hurt anybody who didn't deserve it."

"I just needed to know where you stood. Whether you had any reservations? My dad knew your father well and he admired him although he conceded that, in certain circumstances, he took matters into his own hands rather than have the authorities deal with it. You see my dad was always straight and would never dream of doing anything beyond what the rules allowed. In that sense he was naive –

he just didn't see what certain bastards would do for money or power. As a result he died prematurely and I have decided that is not the path I'm going to follow."

"I know and I respect you for it."

"Ok. So we know where we stand. The next few days could be gruelling and I want everyone to be on board."

JJ leaned closer and kissed Angela on her neck, cheek and lips. She hugged him harder and returned his kiss.

After another few minutes JJ untangled himself from her limbs and dressed in his customary black jeans and black shirt. "You stay and rest," he said as he admired her naked body," I've got things to research."

CHAPTER 26

Day 5

Detective Constable Mark Field entered the lobby of a Sydney CBD skyscraper, EIG's world headquarters, with his partner. He stepped up to the security receptionist and displayed his badge. "Mr Harrison please." The lobby which was the showpiece of the insurance company's thirty-four floors looked spacious with a marble floor and brightly coloured walls. The walls to their backs were straw coloured with a few prints centred. One of side walls contained company emblems whilst the other two reflected paintings of rural Australia. The two detectives looked around whilst the fortyish female receptionist made a phone call.

"Level 30, officers," she said, flicking a switch which opened the glass doors. The elevator to the director's floor was inside, not available to the riff raff.

Moments later, another middle aged female met the officers and took them through to Fred Harrison's office. She closed the door once they were inside.

Mark Field shook Harrison's outstretched hand and then introduced his partner, Maury Riley. They were offered a seat and they didn't hesitate to settle into two comfortable armchairs. They weren't offered a drink.

Field surveyed the office. Large, darkly decorated, traditional conservative senior executive's look. There was no computer on the director's desk but a massive telephone which looked like some kind of internal switchboard. The desk contained some papers, loose and spread out. No files, no clutter.

"How can I help?" volunteered Harrison.

"We have examined CCTV footage from the RTA and noticed a

large hire truck exiting the garage of this building on the morning of the kidnapping" said Field.

Harrison suddenly became alert. "I see."

Field studied the man's face. "Are there records of deliveries somewhere?"

"I'm sure there are. Let me make a call. You realise I'm not usually involved with the day to day running of the company. Just now in the absence of the management team, I'm here every day."

Field nodded. He waited while Harrison, seemingly flustered, completed the call.

Harrison looked up at Field when he replaced the receiver in its creamy white cradle. "We keep records of deliveries but there were none on the day in question."

Field glanced at Riley who raised an eyebrow. Field said, "How does one get access to the garage?"

"By prior arrangement or if you are staff, then via the staff ID card."

Riley, a short wiry man with a well maintained moustache, said, "So either a staff member perpetrated the crime or a staff ID was stolen to carry out the job."

"It would appear so," said Harrison who was looking even more unpleased.

The three men were silent while Harrison's PA entered the room and asked whether coffee or tea was required. The detectives shook their heads.

A mobile phone rang, the Roxy Music tone making Field pull out a Nokia handset from his pocket. He listened for a moment then returned the mobile to his trouser pocket.

Field stood and said, "We'll have to go as we're due at another crime scene. Mr Harrison, would you be able to have your people check whether any employee ID cards have gone missing?"

"Absolutely. I'll organise HR immediately."

The detectives marched out of the office and didn't speak until they were back on the street. "It's looking more and more like an inside job," Field said.

"Who's checking with Orana Truck Hire?" ventured Riley.

"That's been checked. I went to Artarmon myself and discovered the truck hadn't been returned."

"That figures. And who hired it?"

Field used his key to electronically release the doors of the unmarked police car and waited until they were both inside, then said, "Probably a false name. But we're running it through the data banks."

At the same time, at a waterfront mansion in Watsons Bay, Detective Sergeant Jane Morris and Detective Constable Max Braxton were sitting on Rose Franks' white sofa. Braxton was content leaning back and enjoying the water views and yachts gliding by. Morris admired the internal decorations, paintings and fine furniture which, no doubt, represented the woman of the house's taste and design.

As wife of a Chief Executive of a major corporation, Rose Franks would have considerable spending power and it showed.

Rose Franks walked into the sitting room with a tray laden with coffee and sweets- Macadamia and white Belgian chocolate biscuits and Sticky date and pecan biscuits as well as some chocolate truffles. She had insisted the detectives be seated and relax while she arranged matters. Rose was a woman in her early sixties but she was well presented with fine long fair hair, beautifully manicured red nails and casual clothes which seemed to be especially made for her. They made her look almost slim although it was obvious she had issues with weight.

Once all had coffee cups and a small plate of goodies in front of them, Rose said, "You know I've already spoken to one of your colleagues."

"Yes," said Morris, "we're sorry to bother you again with perhaps some questions already posed but we need to explore all avenues as nothing much has come to light."

"Of course. I understand." Rose suddenly looked vulnerable as though their visit reminded her of the tragedy which had just occurred.

"Did Mr Franks ever mention enemies?"

"He had business rivals but he didn't consider them enemies in the sense that they were violent or wished to harm him personally."

Braxton who had been happily enjoying the biscuits observed, "What about troublesome staff or managers from the company?"

Rose put her cup down and looked at Braxton for a moment.

"Certainly there were a few but he rarely mentioned anyone's name who wasn't one of the top tier of executives. And he only had minor issues with them."

"And there was nobody who caused him to curse and show emotion?" Braxton persisted.

"There was a man from the Investment division who he said tried to blackmail the company.

But he never mentioned his name."

Braxton scribbled something on a pad.

The two detectives stayed a little longer waiting for Mrs Franks to remember something else which might prove useful but nothing emerged. They left and as they settled into the police owned Ford, Braxton who occupied the driver's seat said, "I hope we need to come back. I just love those biscuits."

Morris pinched his side playfully. "And it starting to show."

"What do you mean?" Braxton replied, hurt.

Morris smiled. She knew he worked out and was self-conscious. She was also aware that he fancied her and she wanted to prick his ego a little.

They were in a windowless conference room and they were both standing face to face. Chris Wolinski looked more closely at his assistant who had been very co-operative in her short tenure at the company. He said, "So you think it could be done by the end of the week?"

"Not a problem. I'll probably have it done by Thursday night. I'm working back most nights."

Wolinski admired her enthusiasm almost as much as he admired her smooth long hair and pert breasts. She was Indian with flawless light coffee coloured skin and dressed in a tight skirt and black heels. "I like your attitude but you mustn't neglect your social life because of work."

She smiled. "That's alright. I have no commitments outside of work."

Wolinski couldn't quite believe his good fortune. A beautiful young thing with no connections, no troublesome husband or parents. He knew she had arrived in Australia recently and was probably grateful for a job, any job. And he wasn't going to let an opportunity pass. He placed his hand on her bottom and pulled her to him. She struggled but not too much and he kissed her on the lips.

At that moment the door opened and the department's personal assistant came up short. "I'm sorry," she said, "but the police are here for Mr Wolinski."

Wolinski freed his assistant from his grasp so quickly it seemed like he was pushing her aside. He couldn't believe they were onto him so quickly. Then he regathered his thoughts and realised they weren't here for sexual harassment but on another matter.

"Right," he said, "we've just finished. Show them into the main conference room and tell them I'll be there in a moment."

Detective Sergeant Jane Morris brushed aside her dark hair whilst looking at the large screens on two walls of the main conference room. They were hooked up to equipment which she couldn't fathom. Meanwhile Detective Constable Braxton was fiddling with his mobile phone, checking for messages and accessing other applications. He was impressed by the Bloomberg feed in the department's main office on the wall immediately outside the conference room and wondered how people concentrated on their work with charts and numbers constantly changing. As a gadget man he was fascinated by all the technology lying around the place. He was particularly taken by the dealers and support staff having double flat screen computers side by side. How did they focus? There was simply too much data. It would drive him crazy but he would be prepared to take it on board.

Five minutes passed before Chris Wolinski entered the room. He introduced himself and took a chair facing the two detectives. He had composed himself since the sudden surprise from his PA and made a mental note to talk to her. He couldn't afford his assistant to complain, particularly as there was now a witness. But that was a problem to be sorted later. He breathed deeply, finally asked how he could be of assistance.

"You're the Treasurer, aren't you?" began Morris. "That I am, madam," said Wolinski.

"You can call me Detective or Jane if you like," she said.

Wolinski, a fair haired man with large spectacles and an accent many took to be American, nodded. He was in fact Canadian and found it annoying that nobody could detect that without being told. He was used to unsettling auditors so he expected that using similar tactics might disorient the cops. Wolinski who thought of himself as charming gazed at Detective Sergeant Morris and grinned.

After a moment, Morris explained their visit to Rose Franks and what she had mentioned regarding the person in the Investment Department who may have blackmailed the Group CEO. "Are you familiar with this?"

"Yes, he was the Deputy Treasurer, Brett Hasluck." Morris was getting impatient. "What happened?"

Wolinski stared at the female detective and wondered what she knew. However, in light of being caught out ten minutes ago, he thought it might be best to co-operate pleasantly. He smiled. "He was unhappy on missing out on a promotion and he became difficult, coming late, insisting on all procedures being followed to the letter and so forth."

Braxton couldn't restrain smirking and said, "Not following procedures was okay, was it?"

"Well we follow procedures but sometimes judgements need to be made and if we followed every last procedural requirement, things would slow considerably and money would be lost. We're in a fast paced business, the markets stop for no one and we need to be flexible if an opportunity arises," Wolinski spluttered. He drank from a water bottle he had brought into the meeting and wiped his brow.

The detectives waited.

Wolinski continued. "So the boss, on my recommendation, decided this was intolerable and sacked him."

"That was Mark Hovein?"

"Yes. Our policy doesn't allow the immediate superior to sack an individual. It has to come from the next level up. Anyway once he'd been gone for a month or so, he insisted on a meeting with the Group CEO and said he would contact the Insurance Regulator, APRA, if he was denied access."

"What do you mean, the regulator?" asked Morris, totally out of her depth with corporate matters.

"Insurance companies are regulated and reports need to be submitted annually. If an insurance company doesn't comply then the company could lose its licence. That would mean not being able to trade."

Morris nodded to indicate she understood but she was mystified as to how this threat would work.

Wolinski took another mouthful of water and realising he was the only one with water, asked whether the detectives would like some. Both shook their head. He said, "Brett saw the CEO and said he had made notes of certain transactions which should have been performed differently and which would have realised more profit."

"Was this true?" asked Braxton.

"Speculation. A deal could be carried out in different ways so it could have been possible, theoretically." Wolinski drank more water.

"What did Franks do?"

"He told him exactly what I told you. That his notes were of no benefit without proof and that he would not achieve either reinstatement or additional severance pay."

Braxton said, "How did you find out what had transpired?"

Wolinski adjusted his spectacles. "Franks consulted Mark after the meeting. He'd told Hasluck he would check out his claim before committing to any course of action. But I think this was merely a ploy to get rid of him. Mark then asked me to review the documentation Hasluck had left with Franks."

"Did you?" said Morris.

"I explained that there were a number of viable ways to do a deal. I showed Mark the results of achieving an outcome using Hasluck's proposed method verses an alternative way which is sometimes the way we do it in the Department. The net difference between him and us on a number of transactions Hasluck used for the shake down attempt was not significant. This was passed onto Franks who presumably then got back to Hasluck to tell him to get lost."

"Was this the kind of man who might hold a grudge and hit back?" said Morris.

"It's possible. I never liked the little upstart. Thought because he had a Masters degree he was smarter than everyone else."

The two detectives stood, shook hands with the Head Office Treasurer and left.

Outside they agreed that they should report this to Donaldson and that a team should be employed to visit Mr Brett Hasluck.

CHAPTER 27

Day 5

Stephen Burton was a tall elegant Englishman. But today he felt anything but elegant. He was being led along a corridor and down steps with a hood over his head. It was a far cry from being admired by women in his London office where he was the boss and treated accordingly. He recalled the good times when he would be invited to dinner parties by well meaning friends to meet young or not so young women when he had still been single. Because he had always worked long hours he had found little time to go to clubs like many of his friends. What the hell was he doing in this Aussie hell hole with people he could barely stomach?

Over the past three or four days he had been isolated in a room, apart from one brief interrogation session. He hadn't been mistreated, that was true, but he still felt indignant at the treatment. He'd had time to think as the reading matter was of no interest to him. Business magazines and Newsweek from past months were useless. Old news. The world had moved on. He'd rather a good novel or current newspapers.

He'd been able to determine that he was not interested in taking over from Franks, should he be asked to lead the company. He knew there were only three realistic contenders – Vincent, Tennyson and himself. He had no intention of moving to Australia and he was frankly a little tired of the games some of the senior managers played.

Finally Burton was shown into a room and led to a chair. He was asked to sit down which he did. His hands were tied but otherwise he was unshackled. The hood was removed and then a bright light shone into his face. The last time he was here he couldn't recall how he had arrived in the chair.

A voice said, "Hello Mr Burton, I hope you've had some good rest."

"That I have," Burton replied looking away from the light.

"I'm going to ask you some questions and depending on your responses, it may only be a short time before you are returned to your room."

Burton realised that there was no point in objecting or protesting. "Okay," he said. "Have you heard of James Johnston?"

"Yes. I knew James. He had been to the UK once and I often met with him when I visited the head office in Sydney."

"Are you also aware of Johnston's investigation of EIG operations in the US?"

Burton frowned. "I knew he went over to carry out a job but I never received any news of the results of his work over there. Certainly no report was circulated."

"Had you been to New York around that time, between three years and four years ago?"

"Probably. I haven't been there much as it is outside the region I'm responsible for, the UK and Europe, but occasionally senior managers would visit other centres to get a better understanding of conditions for reinsurance purposes. My last visit was in December, last year."

"And what was your impression of the operation?"

Burton smiled. He did not know how far he should go with this. These people had done their homework. This was not a random kidnapping for riches. It was well orchestrated. "It was different but I'm in no position to judge as I've only ever been there briefly."

There was silence. The light went off.

The voice said, "We can continue later if you like. When your memory improves."

Burton said, "Look I know there were some matters they wanted to keep quiet but I heard some rumours which I could not substantiate."

The light was switched on again and Burton shut his eyes. "What sort of rumours?" the voice said.

"Look, I would tell you if I felt they had any basis in fact but the department head who told me is no longer with the company and he was considered to be unreliable."

"That doesn't answer the question."

Burton debated with himself for a moment but, given the

circumstances, he decided he had nothing to gain by keeping silent. It wasn't as though he possessed a secret of such importance that it would endanger someone's life.

"Some of the business practices were less than good practice; in fact in some cases you could say they were nothing less than tawdry. The manager I referred to was called Ray Wilson. He popped over to London when he'd left the American offices and looked me up and we lunched. He told me that there were dealings in the South, Carolina or some such place, inherited by EIG as part of an acquisition that carried out dodgy business practices which should have been stamped out when Easy Insurance took over. It was confined to one particular insurance agency."

"So why wasn't it stopped by Tennyson?"

"You'd have to ask him that."

"What was your relationship with Tennyson," the voice persisted. Burton said, "It's awfully hot in here. May I have some water?"

After Burton had been supplied with mineral water, he continued, "Tim and I are not friends if that's what you mean but as business associates we tried to stay out of each other's operations."

"So you never mentioned what Wilson said to him or anybody else at EIG?"

"I may have queried it with him in Sydney once but I don't recall what he said. He usually had a plausible answer for everything. Even Franks found him difficult to get to the truth sometimes. He was a slippery character."

"Did he have any view about Johnston?"

Burton wondered why the change of direction. He answered after considering. "Tim didn't like him I know because I overheard him mutter something derogatory about him to Mittlehouse but it was Vincent who couldn't abide him."

"Expand please," the voice said in no uncertain terms.

Burton moved his head slightly to avoid the full brunt of the spotlight but all he could see was an empty room and when the light cut out it was incredibly dark, like a dungeon. He wondered whether tortures had been carried out in this room in a past life. For the moment he had to concentrate or he might end up as a current torture victim. "Vincent had little respect for Johnston from what I could gather. He once told me he asked the 'bean counter' as he was referred to by Vincent at any opportunity that he wouldn't help him raise an entry which would give the Division enough profit for all the executives in Asia Pacific to achieve a higher bonus for the period."

"So Vincent was a cheat?"

"According to Vincent it was simply a year end adjustment which would be reversed and nobody would be the wiser and nobody would actually suffer."

"And Johnston was despised for it?"

"Yes."

"And Tennyson? Did he have a similar grievance?"

"I honestly don't know."

After Burton was escorted back to his holiday flat, he wondered why all the questions about Johnston. He was a former financial executive who had since passed away. Confused, he stretched and did some exercises. He hated being cooped up and wondered how his wife and two daughters were coping. He hated travelling to Australia, simply because the flight was so long, and wished he'd heeded his wife's suggestion to send his CFO in his stead.

An hour later Mark Hovein was in the same chair which Burton had occupied. He was not a happy man. Used to getting what he wanted at the office due to his special relationship with the Group CEO, he wasn't able to accept being ordered about and denied any of his requests. He had asked to be released because his wife had an illness and he needed to supervise her medication. He said one less hostage should not make a difference. He also reacted when he was marched down the hall with a black hood over his head, saying it was unnecessary and undignified for a person of his station. His minders simply pushed him along and threatened to thump his head if he caused any more trouble.

Hovein was tied at his feet as well as hands and he felt extremely uncomfortable. He said, "You can't do this. It's inhuman."

Then the light was switched on and he moaned. "What is this? Are you Nazis?"

The voice said, "If you try my patience any more you will be taken back to your room and left without food or water for two days. Am I clear?"

Hovein was tempted to bark back that they could do what they wanted but decided he could not afford to antagonise them any further. He nodded his head.

"I didn't hear anything," the voice continued.

"Yes," he said.

"Good. Now answer my questions if you want to be treated better."

"Are you in charge?" Hovein felt if he appealed to an authority his needs would be handled in a more sensible fashion.

"I'm asking the questions, not you. Tell me about your US operations."

"I'm an Australian Head Office executive and don't know anything about America."

The voice waited a moment. "I see this is going to be futile. You will be returned to your room and handcuffed in the bathroom. While you're there consider this: you travelled to the States twice this year and a number of times each year before that. If you know nothing of their operations you are either the most stupid executive alive or a complete liar."

Hovein began to sob. "I'm not a strong man. You can't do this to me."

The light was switched off. Two men approached, untied him, pulled him to his feet, covered his head and forcefully pushed and pulled him along. When they reached his flat, they dragged him to the bathroom and handcuffed him to a pipe near the toilet. Then they pulled his hood off. They were wearing balaclavas themselves and Hovein saw from their body language that they would not reconsider their treatment of him.

They left, saying nothing.

JJ walked out the door of the interrogation room and into the control room and checked that the recording and videoing mechanism was functioning correctly. It was set up so that when the light was switched on, the recording process was activated. Turning the spotlight off deactivated the filming but another button stopped the audio recording.

After a few tests he noted that everything was working as designed. Satisfied he found Angela and suggested they stroll down the road to the cafe they adopted for coffee breaks. He needed time to think. He had expected that someone would test the boundaries but the meek-looking Hovein was a surprise. But then appearances were often deceptive.

On the walk down Arden Street with Angela, JJ explained what had transpired earlier. Angela said, "How long are you going to have him tied to the toilet?"

"A few hours should be enough to make him see reason."

"He might yell and scream."

"It won't do him much good. Nobody outside will be able to hear. He's also at the back."

Hovein was sitting on the tiles of the bathroom and it felt hard and uncomfortable. He pushed and pulled and all he managed to achieve was a sore wrist. He struggled to his feet and he stood crouched. Then he reconsidered. Even if he jerked free of the pipe, probably pulling it away from the toilet, the situation would still be dire. He would still be inside the flat and unable to escape. The thugs might be close by in any event.

Another thought occurred to him. The busted pipe might produce flooding, not that he knew anything about plumbing but he imagined that pipes and water went hand in hand. He might also be punished further when it was discovered. It was an impossible situation. He slumped down again and closed his eyes. The torment would continue.

He hated life. He wanted to go home.

CHAPTER 28

Day 6

Detective Inspector Donaldson was in his office eating a roast beef and salad sandwich when Braxton waltzed in. "Hey," said Braxton, "the hire truck has been found."

"Okay, surprise me," said Donaldson, "it's parked outside and there are fingerprints all over it tying it to known criminals. Better yet the culprits are handcuffed and inside."

"Very funny," said Braxton, "It was found in Wollongong in a paddock. Burnt to a crisp. However on a more positive note we've been able to enter Hasluck's unit in Randwick and insert some listening devices in a few strategic places. We also expect to interview him later today."

"Has he been sighted?"

"Yes," said Braxton. "He's currently employed in the trading department of the Commonwealth Bank. He usually gets home around seven pm."

Donaldson finished the remnants of his sandwich. "Ok. Talk to him. Doesn't sound like he's our guy if he's working late. But then again he may have hired goons or he might have connections with criminals. There've still been no demands made of anyone after five full days. Strange, very strange."

Brett Hasluck took one last look in the mirror. He brushed his hair and flashed his teeth. He was a good looking young man so why did he have so much difficulty convincing the pretty girls he was a catch. He left the men's facilities and strolled to his desk, shut down his computer and tidied the area. He buttoned his suit coat, said goodnight to Betty and Sam and exited the floor, passing Deborah with the big tits who didn't even glance at him.

Hasluck walked outside into the drizzly night and ignored other office workers as he made his way to his bus stop. He did not realise that a plain clothes policeman was walking behind him. They both caught the same bus.

He arrived inside his one bedroom unit at seven twenty two, after gathering mail from the block's bank of mail boxes on the right hand side of the hallway just inside the brick entrance. He always noted the time when he arrived home, a ritual he could not shake. Just as he could not help checking the time when he arrived in the office or when he walked onto the bus.

At seven forty six there was a knock on the door. He checked the peephole and was surprised to see a man and woman standing outside. The woman was holding a badge up. He opened the door, showed genuine alarm and said, "How can I help you?"

"May we come in, Mr Hasluck? I'm Detective Sergeant Morris and this is Detective Constable Braxton. We won't take up much of your time. We only have a few routine questions for you."

"This is very unusual. What's happened?"

"Would you rather come down to the station?" said Morris. Hasluck stepped aside, "No, no, come in."

Hasluck was a mild mannered man of medium height with no remarkable features. He wore round wire rimmed glasses and he had changed into a long sleeved shirt and corduroy trousers. He ushered them into his living area and showed them a couch which had seen better days and was set parallel to the large windows. He sat opposite them in a hard backed chair he dragged in from the kitchen.

Morris looked about. The young man had taste. Although the unit was small, it was clean and well set out with a cabinet against the wall, a large plasma screen above it and cords running to a DVD player as well as a gaming box. She compared this unit with ones of other men living by themselves and wondered whether he was gay. However there was a photo of a pretty girl on the cabinet. She was a brunette and she was beaming into the camera.

"Girlfriend?" asked Morris, nodding to the picture.

"She's actually my ex-girlfriend. Melissa. Is she in trouble?" Hasluck almost felt elated. Had she had an accident and had they found his name as the person to be contacted? Not that he wanted anything bad to have happened. He simply wanted her to take him back. She was such a sweet thing. And why had they parted? He couldn't recall.

"No, no, we've come to talk to you about your time with EIG."

"Right. I left or rather was made redundant about eighteen months ago." Braxton said, "Made redundant. We were told you resigned."

"I was the assistant Treasurer and I was told when first joining the Head Office treasury team that when a position opened up as a regional Treasurer I would be high on the list to get it. Well I did my job and the Treasurer in Singapore left and I was expecting the promotion, mainly because I'd received favourable reviews throughout my tenure in Head Office – for three years, each six months when performance review forms had to be filled out." He paused, took a deep breath, continued, "But a relative newcomer got the gig. And only because that useless bastard Wolinski liked the new bloke, an American. Wolinski is an American too and he and Hovein probably wanted to keep the goings on in the US kept quiet."

Morris, leaning forward, with hands clasped together said, "What things?"

"I found evidence of securities bought in that region which were in direct conflict with what the manual stated was permissible."

Morris said, "We were told that you tried to blackmail John Franks."

Hasluck smirked, "Yeah that scumbag Wolinski would say that. I did have a meeting with Franks some months after I left to inform him about some of the unsavoury practices I suspected were taking place around the traps but particularly in the United States."

Braxton prompted, "What was his response?"

Hasluck stood up, went to the table to the right of the couch, took a bottle of mineral water and poured himself a drink. He said, 'He said he knew but thanked me and suggested I be paid an additional bonus for my good work."

"That was it. You let it alone."

"Never thought much about it since. The additional money was welcome so I imagined Franks was on top of it and would have it sorted."

Morris said, "So you had no reason to want to harm Franks or the other senior managers?"

"Why would I? I got another job, I was rid of that prick Wolinski and I had just been paid $20,000."

Braxton whistled. "Wow, with that kind of send off, I guess you wouldn't harbour a grudge." Morris said, "Wolinski said you blackmailed Franks with knowledge you had regarding how Treasury personnel placed some deals."

"I knew Wolinski and some others were taking short cuts with some transactions which led to poor end results and I did mention this but it wasn't a key point. I just wanted to inform Franks so he understood what that Department was doing."

Morris persisted. "How did he receive that news?"

Hasluck frowned, then looked at Braxton, then Morris, and remarked, "It was something he suspected and he said he'd have it looked at but was basically at ease, saying he held Hovein responsible for annual targets."

"In other words he didn't care how they transacted business so long as profit targets were reached," said Braxton, displaying his scant knowledge of business from his days at high school.

"That's right. At no stage did either Franks or I raise our voices or argue."

Morris stood as did Braxton. "Thank you for your time. I will get somebody to obtain a statement from you soon but otherwise we're done."

Hasluck followed the detectives out and closed the door firmly behind them. In the car, Braxton said, "Do you believe him?"

"We can easily check with EIG's payroll people whether he was paid a bonus of twenty thousand. If they didn't, then we'll have to return."

Braxton started the vehicle and drove off without another word. He was beginning to feel frustrated with the case.

CHAPTER 29

Day 7

David Mittlehouse considered himself suave, well read and charming to the opposite sex. He was twice divorced and currently entered his status on forms as single. He had little respect for terrorists and vowed he would not give this group of thugs anything. Hence when he was quizzed by a voice behind a large spotlight, he decided to stay quiet.

Now back in his room, he wondered why they hadn't tried threats. He also wondered why they wanted to ask questions. Didn't kidnappers demand ransom then provide proof of life to the authorities or family members conducting the negotiations. He wanted to ask these questions but he had been determined to say nothing. He was prepared to resist even if tortured. He waited and waited when the voice had asked the questions and expected standover tactics. He had seen lots of American television.

He wandered around the room. He wanted to keep as fit as was possible under the circumstances. He was forty-six and the youngest of the group, apart from George Waites who was technically younger by a couple of years but looked and acted much older.

Eventually he gave in to boredom and went to lie on his bed. The reading material was of no value to him so he ignored it. He wanted books which informed him, not stupid novels. At least he could have been provided with some classics. The stuff in the room was beneath him.

Later the door opened and a tray was left on the floor. The woman delivered the tray and a man with a pistol watched. Both wore hoods and non-descript clothing. It seemed likely that the hostages would be released at some point otherwise the careful hiding of identity would be unnecessary.

Mittlehouse examined the contents. A bottle of orange juice, one sandwich with ham and cheese, a packet of potato crisps and an apple were neatly arranged on the tray. No one was going to get fat on this diet. Still the food held no appeal and he would wait until he was hungry enough not to care what stuff was served. He was used to dining in good restaurants most days as he travelled Australia and the Asia and Pacific operations. He loved Hong Kong and French Polynesia and Melbourne for fine cuisine. He was very well looked after by all the branch managers he visited. He missed the lifestyle. He wanted to get back to it.

Angela wandered back to the control room and noted that JJ was amused by something he was reading. She'd just placed a tray in Mittlehouse's flat and had removed the black hood once she left, carrying it in her right hand. She didn't like wearing the hood because it ruined her hair so she tossed it on a vacant chair. "Why are you so relaxed?" she said.

JJ looked up and smiled, "What's up? Bad morning?"

Arms akimbo, Angela stared at JJ. "You're treating this as a joke. We're in serious bother if we get sprung."

"Calm down. You look beautiful when you're angry. Your face reminds me of Emily Blunt. Back to the topic...it's under control. Mittlehouse who you've just served with light refreshments will not be given anything substantial until he talks. He's acting stubborn at the moment. He's always been an overblown self-righteous prick. I've met him a few times and he thinks he's some sort of super stud."

"What if he doesn't give in?"

"I have structured my schedule to deal with contingencies. We also have some flexibility with time, although I have an end time in mind. Why don't you sit down and relax. This guy is a great pretender. First we'll take the softly, softly approach. Without food and then water, this fuckwit will crack. "

Angela walked into the kitchen and grabbed a sandwich.

JJ said, "Whoever set up this flat, our control centre, did a marvellous job. Do you know who it was?"

"No idea," said Angela. She was annoyed but didn't quite know why.

It was 2 o'clock and Jack and Tony escorted a hooded man into the basement and guided him to the chair. It was the second interview of the day. The overhead light was on and stayed that way until the guys had their interviewee in the chair.

"Hey, not so rough," said Tennyson.

"Keep still or you'll know about it," said the voice.

The overhead light was switched off once the men had secured the American Chief.

Tennyson's hood was removed in the dark and then Jack and Tony who knew where the door was exited quietly. After the men had left the room, the spotlight was switched on. Tennyson closed his eyes. This was torture, plain and simple and he hoped these guys would pay dearly.

"Now that you've had time to think, you may be prepared to cut to the chase," said the voice. "What are you talking about?"

A button was pressed and an electric current went through Tennyson's body. It was brief but had the effect of giving him enough shock to cause more than mere discomfort. Tennyson now realised that they were prepared to enter the next stage of the program.

The voice continued, "No more games. If you thought you were going to be asked politely forever, think again."

After recovering from the charge, Tennyson said, "What do you want?"

The voice remained calm. "James Johnston visited the US and prepared a report which never saw the light of day. Why?"

Tennyson began to sweat. How did they know about this and how did they know James Johnston? He was dead. He couldn't be behind this. Tennyson knew what to say because he had already been asked to explain by more senior EIG executives and a couple of the directors at functions once they heard Johnston had visited the US on an assignment. Tennyson answered calmly, "The draft report had so many errors that it would have been irresponsible to have it sent to the audit committee."

"But Johnston wasn't an auditor."

"True, but he carried out an audit when he visited. I'm not sure under whose authority but he did it anyway."

The voice waited a moment. "The report had errors, you say. That's not what I understood. Do you wish to rethink your answer?"

Tennyson wondered who he was talking to. He seemed to have knowledge nobody else except John Franks and perhaps Mark Hovein had. But they were here in the same boat and he couldn't imagine either of them betraying him. He began to fear for his life. This was not a kidnapping for ransom. This was a whole different ball game. "Look," he said, "Johnston discovered we had investments outside what the company specified – some CDOs and other toxic debt. And he discovered that these derivatives were not disclosed properly. They were shown as investments fully recoverable. No provision for impairment was shown but we felt, that is Hovein and myself, that it would only be a matter of time before value would return."

"And the Group CEO knew about this?"

"Johnston did draft a report which I received for comment. I took the draft report to Franks and explained that if the company changed the figures at the last moment that the share price would plummet, particularly as it was such a hot issue."

"And how did you persuade Franks to get rid of Johnston?"

Tennyson said nothing for what seemed a long time. The man behind the spotlight waited patiently. Tennyson would rather get an electric shock than talk about this. He remained silent. He expected a quick burst of electricity and braced himself.

The spotlight diminished into darkness and it seemed that air had been sucked out of the room as well. A moment later he felt a syringe prick his upper left arm. That was all he recalled when he found himself back in the flat, lying on his bed. He promptly fell asleep.

Tennyson awoke later and wondered what would happen next. This ordeal was starting to make him go crazy. If only he had a pill to swallow, one which would end it all.

He reflected on the time Johnston had walked into his office in New York two years prior. He disliked the man on sight. He wore a typical accountant's outfit – pin striped suit, white shirt, red tie, polished black brogues – and his hair was neat and recently cut. Although he had met Johnston previously he had never taken any notice of him. But now he studied his appearance and false smile.

Tennyson was behind his desk and was not inclined to get up but Johnston stretched out his hand and wouldn't take a hint. Tennyson stood, shook hands, and then sat down again. "What are you doing here?" he said.

Johnston explained his brief which took Tennyson by surprise. If anything he thought Johnston, like many before him, was passing through and took the opportunity of visiting the office to announce himself and say hello to the US Chief.

Tennyson slid out of bed and went to the bathroom to wash his face. He still felt drowsy. He cursed aloud, furious with the world. Why the hell had Johnston been sent and why the hell couldn't the self-righteous bean counter work on the numbers and not poke around in areas which were of no real concern to him. He walked into the kitchenette, grabbed a glass and hurled it across the room. It hit the wall and was smashed into numerous pieces.

Accountants. He hated them. They caused more problems than they were worth. He had often thought of hiring non questioning book keepers to avoid getting into any discussions with financially trained individuals who thought it their right to question how things should be presented in reports and statements. And more to the point they often assumed if they understood the business then it was their sole role to show figures in their muddled way. He couldn't understand why they simply didn't show the cash position. What was wrong with that? An improvement in the bank meant that things were getting better.

He swore that when he was in charge he would reduce the number of people in the finance departments throughout the globe. That would cut costs as well, another benefit.

Tennyson had dropped out of school at the age of sixteen and began his insurance career at a small firm in Ireland. He worked his way up, getting to know all aspects of insurance, and reached the position of senior insurance manager in the underwriting department of Green Insurance Company when it was acquired by EIG. He was transferred to the US a few years later and because of his intimate knowledge of several insurance products became the Head of Insurance in the American division. When Randy Milton, CEO of the operation, retired Tennyson was installed as CEO on the recommendation of Milton with whom he had a good working relationship.

The only aspects of insurance operations Tennyson wasn't interested in nor familiar with were accounting and finance. He figured it was just a matter of adding stuff up and couldn't comprehend what they were jabbing about when they talked about amortisation, deferred insurance costs, deferred tax assets, swaps, derivative financial instruments, intangibles and so on. It sounded like drivel and he thought that some idiot had made it up to confuse investors and customers.

Now, thinking of this, Tennyson became indignant. Was this an accountant's revenge? He checked out the flat, looking at each wall, to find the weakest spot for a possible breach. Boarded up windows seemed too difficult to dislodge but he also didn't expect a simple one flight jump to the outside should he be successful. He decided the door might be the best bet to escape. He kicked it. No effect. He kicked again and again.

Suddenly the door opened and two hooded men, larger and taller than he was, grabbed his arms and forced him back. They subdued him with another syringe attack. When he woke, he discovered his shoes had been taken.

A note on his bed also informed him that he would have no food for a day.

CHAPTER 30

Day 7

Marion Vincent was a woman most would pass in the street without a second glance. She had a dirty blonde rinse through her hair which was not quite shoulder length. She was quietly spoken and wore neat but uninspiring clothes. She looked older than her forty-two years.

Marion was polite when Detective Inspector Donaldson and Detective Sergeant Morris met her at the front door of her Turramurra home. When they said they were police she did not bat an eyelid and welcomed them in. They walked to the kitchen through the living room which seemed to be in a shambles.

"Please excuse the mess," Marion said, "we're in the middle of renovations. Please take a seat.

May I offer you tea or something to drink?"

"No thanks," said Donaldson, "I understand you've already been contacted by our team and that you weren't able to shed any light on why anyone would wish to kidnap your husband."

"Yes, a few days ago I did answer some questions."

"And Mrs Vincent, have you had time to reflect?"

Marion looked up and Donaldson allowed her to speak. She said, "Yes, I've thought long and hard. The only concern Doug expressed related to an internal struggle to succeed the current CEO but both Tim Tennyson and Stephen Burton, the other contenders, have also been kidnapped. So I can't think of anyone else who would profit from this situation."

"Any nobody's contacted you regarding a ransom?" Morris said.

Marion looked like she was going to break down and weep but she stifled the impulse, wiped her eyes with the back of her hand

and shook her head. "I've not received one call from either Doug or somebody asking for money to release him. I just don't know what they want. Who would do such a thing? The renovation can't continue either whilst there this drama is in progress."

Morris was taken aback. Is this what North Shore matrons were most concerned about – their house!

Donaldson wasn't finished. He straightened his posture. "Your husband was a powerful man, a man who could make or break careers. Are you sure, apart from two of his peers, that nobody else had a grudge against him?"

"I can't think of anyone. The only problem he had was a few years back when he visited New York briefly."

"Can you tell us about that?"

Marion wrung her hands, pushed a cup in front of her to the side, looked at Donaldson for a fleeting moment before staring outside. She said, "Doug is normally a friendly guy and conducts himself as such although he can make tough decisions. I've seen him operate at social functions and he can be charming. He's well liked by John Franks too so he is regarded as a man who has the capability to lead a team or an organisation. I mention this because it is very unusual for Doug to come back from a trip so quiet and non-communicative. He's usually a chatterbox when he returns from London or any other overseas destination, keen to tell me all the gossip and how certain individuals are progressing. But on this particular trip, about two years ago, he was so different that I thought he was sick. But he wouldn't talk about it, not then, not since."

Donaldson nodded. "Oh," he said, "have you asked him about it?"

"I raised it once when we were on holiday on Hamilton Island in the Whitsundays but he said there was nothing wrong, simply that he had been tired from the pressure at work and an awful flight. But that's rubbish. I know him. He's had trips with delays or drama before and it hasn't stopped him being chirpy on his return."

Morris added, "So Mr Vincent never travelled back to New York."

Marion said, "Yes, he has but the other visits didn't seem to affect him. So it's a mystery."

Donaldson stood, shook Marion's hand and thanked her. As

they were leaving, he turned back at the door and asked, "How's his relationship with this Tennyson guy?"

"Much cooler ever since that trip. He's never invited him home since. Before that he would always invite either Stephen or Tim to join us for a meal, a home cooked meal for sad travellers, as he called it."

"Has Stephen Burton been invited back?" asked Morris. "Yes," said Marion standing at the door, watching.

Outside Donaldson said to Morris, "We need to follow up the US end of things. I'll get my contact in the NYPD to check on Tennyson's colleagues and family."

They drove off in silence, each pondering the latest piece of news.

Once they reached City Central and the car was parked, Donaldson suggested that he and Morris have a snack. They wandered through Chinatown until they found a place which served Yum Cha. Donaldson said he liked the custard tarts and said that Morris should have whatever she liked. They ordered some tea and after both had taken some items from one tray, Donaldson said, "I wonder if there's more to this than a simple kidnapping for ransom."

"What do you mean?" said Morris who observed that there were few customers in the restaurant at this time of day. She guessed that at 11 o'clock and after, one would see an influx.

When another tray of food arrived, Donaldson waved it away. "We've considered disgruntled employees, business rivals, personal enemies of people on the management team and professional kidnappers with nothing jumping out at us."

Morris sipped some tea. She was not fond of Chinese tea but knew it washed down some of the fatty food offered. "There's nothing obvious yet but we're still following up on all possibilities."

"True," said Donaldson, "But I have a hunch I'd like to explore."

Later that day Donaldson and Morris were with Zolinski in EIG's head office investment department. They were accompanied by a forensic accountant from the Darling Harbour division, a middle aged man who rarely smiled.

Zolinski showed surprise when the police again wanted to see him. He invited them to a meeting room and brushed his thin fair hair back with the palm of his hand as he awaited their questions.

He wore a blue shirt and dark trousers which were slightly crumpled.

Donaldson noted that he wore no tie. The same as last time. He wondered whether he was a genuine executive because all the previous executives he'd met wore ties, generally the latest to indicate they were up with the fashion.

"Mr Zolinski, I'd like you to meet Harry Dowling. He will be talking to your accounting people and he will need access to reports from your US division from three years ago until now."

Zolinski adjusted his posture and said, "Of course but I'm curious. Why are you reviewing information going back so far?"

Donaldson was getting irritated. "That is not your concern. However you can help us by telling what you know of situations in the US around two years ago."

Zolinski shifted in his chair and said, "Mark Hovein and Tim Tennyson kept certain information to themselves and I was not involved in the investment side of things. My role was restricted to Treasury issues and I can tell you that it was all above board. But I can't imagine that Mark would agree to covering anything up. After all we've been audited every year."

"Who are the auditors?" Dowling said. He was a quietly spoken man of around forty-five and he had seen many individuals like Zolinski who believed implicitly in the honesty of others.

"PriceWaterhouse Coopers. David Grant is the partner in charge."

"Can you arrange a meeting, today?" said Donaldson.

Donaldson had no skills in this area but wanted Dowling to pursue it immediately. He knew that fraud and other financial investigations took an inordinate amount of time and he wanted to eliminate the possibility that this was part of the case as soon as possible. He also knew that if he didn't follow up on this area he may be considered negligent. This usually occurred when things went wrong. He could just imagine a defrauded party getting back at the company. Then someone would accuse his team of not following up a possible motive. Of course then, with hindsight, another police officer would suggest it had all been very clear from the beginning.

Zolinski grabbed the phone and dialled an internal number. Once he had finished talking, he turned to the three detectives opposite him and said, "Mark's PA has it under control."

Donaldson and Morris had a word to Dowling in private, then thanked him for coming along and left him with Zolinski who was hovering in a far corner. Donaldson and Morris departed.

"This case is starting to freak me out," said Donaldson in the elevator on the way down. "Why? This isn't like you, the Mr Cool of the force."

"Jane, you are a sweetheart and it's just as well I'm married and that I'm too old for you. But it's not the difficulty of the case that's getting to me but...what can I say. I'll be honest. I don't like insurance types who are smooth talking and insincere."

Detective Sergeant Morris did not reply. She wondered whether her boss would ever make a pass at her. It was an intriguing prospect. She expected Braxton to do so and wondered what kept the keen young buck at a distance.

CHAPTER 31

Day 7

JJ and Angela were sitting across from each other at the Gelato Bar in Bondi, each with a section of the Saturday Sydney Morning Herald. They had ordered breakfast and their cappuccinos had just arrived.

JJ put the paper down. He stirred the coffee and tasted it. Good. He said, "The kidnapping drama is no longer getting much attention."

"That's good, isn't it?" Angela examined JJ's expression to determine what he meant.

JJ eyed Angela who looked so sweet, so innocent and with a face like an angel. "Yes, it is. But I'm surprised that the story didn't continue a little longer because the papers love this kind of stuff."

Angela smiled. She put one packet of sugar in her coffee and stirred. "Are you sure nobody can escape? I'm afraid some of the hostages are starting to get edgy and they might try something weird."

JJ waited while the waitress placed plates of Eggs Benedict in front of them. Once the young waitress in pigtails had departed, he said "Jack and Tony know what to do. I've been through the drill with them – to maintain the process of keeping everyone in their room, isolated and afraid. Random checks, no one in a room adjacent to someone else's room so that communication is prevented. It's all been thoroughly planned. Besides we have weapons, they don't."

Angela smiled but didn't say anything. Then she cut into a portion of her eggs and muffin, helped it onto the fork and tasted it.

"What? Do you still have doubts?"

"I'm not convinced that something won't go wrong. You can't plan for every contingency."

JJ placed his coffee cup down. "You're right but we're doing the best we can and we'll just have to deal with problems as they arise. I never said it was going to be easy."

After breakfast JJ and Angela wandered down to the beach. JJ took Angela's hand and they walked over the sand in silence. They had left their footwear in a pile near the steps. Although the weather was slightly breezy and still cold enough to deter many from the water, some die-hard surfer types were in rubbers paddling out a fair distance to catch a wave. JJ was amazed at their passion for this activity which seemed highly repetitive. He was keen to go body surfing in summer to cool off but he wasn't interested in going into water all that much and could never figure why some people were so drawn to it. It was shark territory after all. Did sharks come on shore – no way.

At the Northern end of the beach, JJ put his arms around Angela and hugged her. "You know I'm really starting to get used to having you around. If nothing else, this job has made me realise how lucky I am."

JJ bent slightly and stared into Angela's eyes which sucked him in. They kissed.

As they walked back to a car Nick Koutslakis had loaned his daughter, a Black Audi A6, JJ reflected on his last night with Maddie. They were in her unit and Maddie was cooking dinner. JJ was looking at her collection of CDs. He put on the Killers' Day & Age in her small CD player and thought that, apart from this album, his taste in music differed significantly from hers. She possessed Frank Sinatra, Sarah McLachlan, Johnny Farnham, Barry Manilow, Mandy Moore and others which would be classified in the 'Easy Listening' category.

"Oh, Jordan, please turn that off, it's terrible," yelled Maddie. "Sorry. It was in your CD holder."

"A gift from my brother. I hate it."

JJ ignored her and said, "Maybe if you listen to it a few times, you might grow to like it." Maddie came into the living room. "You're not into all that pop stuff, are you?"

JJ said, "I don't arrange things into neat categories. I like some of every music category and I dislike some of everything too. It's based purely on how I think it sounds."

When they were seated at the table, Maddie looked at JJ who was toying with the meal. "What's the matter, don't you like it?"

"I'm not too fond of stew."

"Well that's for dinner and if you don't like it, tough."

"Take it easy. Why are you so touchy tonight?" JJ said, wondering what was going on. "Did you have a bad day at work?"

"No, I'm annoyed that you scoff at my music and my food. I can visualise our future with your demands being paramount."

"Wow, you're looking that far ahead, are you?"

"And you live from day to day with no concept of making progress."

"Hold on Maddie. I had no idea you were seeing us in a permanent relationship. We've only just started going out."

"And we're getting to know each other gradually which is important," Maddie stated with force, "a necessary prelude to the next stage."

"Wow," said JJ, "I didn't realise anything about these stages. I thought we were having fun.

Isn't that enough?"

"You're so shallow, immature..."

"And you're so sensitive. I can't be with someone who's so reactive to such small things." Maddie stood. "Well, I've had enough. Maybe you should leave."

"Ok, if you want but aren't you over reacting? I mean..." Maddie pointed to the door. "Just leave."

JJ walked out and never looked back. He had no time for this nonsense.

Now as he climbed into the car beside Angela, he was happy the way events had unfolded. Angela was not moody like Maddie could be. She was confident and unassuming, qualities which he liked in a woman. As well as Angela's obvious physical attractions, she was affectionate and loving and JJ felt comfortable in her presence. To date she hadn't offered any criticism either but he knew that everyone who was together for any length of time would attract some critical comments, a human trait nobody lacked.

Maddie had displayed signs of being critical and even bitchy, a factor which would have resulted in future tension. And the one issue which had prevented JJ from trying to make up with Maddie was her thinking about a future for them when they hadn't really known each other long enough.

But when all matters were analysed, it really came down to one key ingredient – chemistry.

With Angela this intangible quality was present.

Angela stepped on the accelerator and the Audi glided smoothly down Campbell Parade, round a roundabout and back up a hill towards Bondi Road. JJ observed the locals and tourists wandering along the streets and then turned to watch Angela's face in deep concentration, her milky complexion in startling contrast to her dark hair.

EIG Ltd had circulated a memo via email asking for assistance in the kidnapping case. It had been drafted by the company's chief corporate lawyer, a pedantic but thorough individual, and was something that Maddie was currently assessing. It said:

"Good morning all,

As you know EIG's management team were taken hostage last week and the police have conducted initial enquiries which have not resulted in any conclusive leads. However they are of the view that the information the perpetrators were in possession of must have come, either knowingly or unwittingly, from inside the company.

Please consider whether you had aided anyone or been aware of any unusual actions by fellow employees. You may reach me with any information on my internal number and this information will be kept strictly confidential."

Maddie lifted her personalised cup which was three quarters filled with Earl Grey tea to her mouth and wondered whether she should respond and mention that she had given Jordan some details of Board meetings but then she thought better of it. He surely wasn't capable of doing something which would harm people they all knew and admired.

Later in the morning, Maddie reflected on the way Jordan had not tried to win her back and decided he needed to be taught a lesson. She picked up the phone and called the Legal Department.

Once the news of the tip-off reached police headquarters Donaldson and Morris visited EIG and arranged to meet with Madeline Manors in a closed conference room on a floor where she did not normally frequent so that the interview could be kept confidential and not be subject to speculation.

"Hello Madeline, I'm Detective Inspector Donaldson and this is Detective Sergeant Morris. First let me say thank you for volunteering information and that everything you say will be kept between us and will not be shared with any other EIG employee." Donaldson smiled at Maddie after shaking her hand.

Maddie liked Donaldson. He was a powerful man, a fatherly type to whom one could confide. They all sat around the table, a large round wooden piece of relatively new vintage.

"Ok Madeline," said Donaldson, "what would you like to share with us?"

The woman who accompanied the big detective, Sergeant Morris, put a recorder in the centre of the table and asked Maddie whether this was acceptable to her. Maddie nodded.

Maddie suddenly realised that this was serious and that she could alienate Jordan forever but she had come this far and there was no backing out. "I remembered something when I got the email but it's probably nothing," she said in a small voice.

Morris placed a hand over Maddie's. "That's ok, you're just trying to help and if we find there's nothing to what you say, that's fine. At least we can eliminate another potential lead. Does that sound reasonable?"

Maddie nodded. She sat up straighter and removed her hand from the table. "A fellow from a department downstairs – accounting or audit, I think – asked me about stuff relating to managers and schedules and at the time I thought it was routine but now I wonder..."

"His name," Donaldson said. "Jordan Johnson, level 2."

"Was the information he requested part of his usual duties?"

"Possibly but I'm not sure."

"When did this happen?" Donaldson asked in a pleasant manner. He needed to ensure she was not spooked otherwise she might pull the 'can't recall trick'.

Maddie provided the date but didn't mention that she had also provided JJ with succession details at her home.

"Thanks, we'll check it out anyway." Donaldson stood, smiled at the young woman and shook her hand. He exited the office.

Morris was left to follow up on his address and whereabouts. She returned to Headquarters around eleven and interrupted Donaldson who was enjoying a coffee and a cinnamon donut.

"Well," he said when he put his espresso down, "how'd it go?"

"Got his address and mobile number ok. But apparently he's on annual leave and nobody seems to know where he went. And his mobile is switched off." Morris sat opposite Donaldson.

"What about friends at EIG? And what does he like to do – golf, tennis, fishing, women?"

Morris smiled, "Sorry, I'll get Braxton to attend to that. I've got a ton of paperwork to get through."

Donaldson nodded. "Ok," he said.

Morris yawned. She was tired. Although nothing much had come to light, she had been working late and other cases had been banking up. "What next?" she said.

"I'm waiting for information from a guy I met on a seminar about a year ago. He works at the NYPD and I've asked him to track Tennyson's connections at EIG and also any family so we can check on the rumours surrounding the US insurance business. Don't imagine we'll find much but you never know."

Morris said, "What do you think happened to this management group? Do you think they've been killed?"

Donaldson wiped his mouth with the back of his hand. "I don't know but that would be quite unusual. No demands have been made. Murdering nine people for no discernible reason is bizarre, to say the least. I expect demands to be made at some point. Perhaps the kidnap gang is lying low until all the fuss in the newspapers dies down."

Morris watched as Donaldson stood up and twisted his torso. She said, "As far as I can see, there's little reporting apart from speculation. Nobody seems to know anything."

"Particularly as the Strike Force has shaken the trees in the underworld over the past few days. Nobody knows a thing. This would have to be the most brazen yet secret crime of this scale I've come across."

At that moment alarms raged. It was a fire drill. Both detectives followed others out of the building.

Outside in Day Street, Donaldson and Morris grouped with a few others from the Strike Force to chat and ask about progress in other areas of the investigation. Donaldson found that informal talks sometimes uncovered unexpected gems not always present in formal reports.

But today nothing emerged from these discussions which focussed mainly on the waste of time fire drills were.

Later that day Morris caught up with Braxton and she got the distinct impression he was going to invite her out if his gaze which almost penetrated her blouse was any indication. But he listened patiently while she informed him of Donaldson's suggestion that he should follow up on EIG employees friendly with Johnson. He agreed to look into it but said little else.

Was he really so cool or simply playing the part, she wondered, when he'd gone. Time would tell.

CHAPTER 32

Day 8

Tim Tennyson was pacing. He had been incarcerated too long. He was not going to submit to another interrogation. He was going to make a run for it and plans needed to be made. He realised now that someone had informed the interrogator of what had happened in New York and there was no possibility that he would concede anything. It seemed strange that the voice sounded distorted whenever the spotlight was switched on. It was linked to other equipment which created this sound and he wondered whether recordings were also being made. There was no doubt something odd was going on. Why else had there been no communication regarding money? Of course a ransom demand could have been made without his or anybody else's knowledge but nobody in the gang acted like this was important. No discussion of money had even taken place. Kidnappers usually only ever wanted to hold their quarry until cash was delivered.

Tennyson looked around for anything which he could use. Then he saw something. Yes it was small enough to conceal and he could use it as a surprise weapon. The hood he had to wear on the way to the interrogation room was a problem but that issue could be worked out. After all he was a CEO and he had not reached that position by being clueless.

They had taken his shoes and starved him but he would show them he was a fighter. He recalled one time when he was still married and his wife had invited her sister over for dinner. Conversation flowed easily and then the subject of help around the house came up. The women joked about his lack of support and that he was rarely home. Then whilst his wife went upstairs for a moment, the sister, Sara, berated him for his poor husbandly skills and said he should pull his socks up.

Tennyson, astounded that he should be taken to task in his own home by a stranger, was lost for words. Before he could respond his wife joined them again. He became so incensed that he brooded for the remainder of the meal. He visualised grabbing a large kitchen knife and striking Sara through the heart in front of his wife but decided he would address the matter in another fashion.

The next day he stopped at Sara's house on his way home from the office. When she opened the door, she showed surprise at seeing him. He'd rarely accompanied his wife to her place but when he did he usually made it obvious he regarded the visit as a chore. He smiled and said he needed to talk to her. She hesitated, but after a number of seconds staring at him, she waved him in. He walked down the long hallway and at the end there was a living area. Tiny but neat. Sara had divorced recently and probably resented men so he decided not to be too hard on her. He turned around and regarded her with curiosity. He couldn't figure her. She was attractive and could have had a happy life but her mouth probably wouldn't allow that.

"What do you want?" she said as she folded her arms across her chest. "Why are you so aggressive?"

She stared at him demanding an answer.

He began gently. "Look," he said, "about last night..."

"You've come to apologise for your boorish behaviour?"

His blood was now near boiling point. "I've got nothing to apologise for, you slut. I know why Bob left you. You're an ungrateful bitch."

"Get out," she said, pointing back towards the front door, "I don't need this."

Now totally out of control, he walked towards her and pulled her down by the ponytail she sported. When Sara was close to the ground, he put his nose near hers and said, "If you ever criticise me in my home again, I'll ban you forever. Got it bitch?"

Sara spat and a big glob of it settled on his chin. He dropped her to the ground then kicked her in the side, then again and finally he stomped on her head which she'd covered with her arms. She lay still and he waited.

A few minutes passed. "Tell your sister or anyone else and she will get a hiding she'll never forget." He walked out and since then he had never heard from her again.

These creeps would get the same treatment, he vowed.

In a room one level above him, Jennie Jones was starting to fear for her sanity. How long were they going to coop them up? What had they done? And why had there been interrogations? She didn't understand anything. She wanted to scream. Was that the plan? To break them down psychologically. She closed her eyes again. She was mentally and emotionally exhausted. She thought she'd kept track of the days but wasn't now sure whether they had been captive six or seven or more days.

She was a people person and this isolation was driving her to despair. She could understand how lonely people or people who felt unloved would harm themselves just to seek attention. And eventually that same despair might lead to carrying out outrageous acts or committing suicide.

Was that it? Did an ex-employee feel neglected and was this an expression of that situation? That, at least, made some sense. But the company had all sorts of help mechanisms. The intranet, the company's internal website, advertised that counsellors were available for people with problems, be they financial, substance abuse or grief. Each department also arranged functions, conducted its own social outings, as far as she knew, and did things to make employees have a sense of belonging. Nobody need feel alone or deprived.

Jennie stood up and banged her closed hands on the wall. But nothing happened.

Two doors down Don Nielson was sitting on his bed doing some stretching exercises. The captivity had made him realise how fragile life was. He came to the conclusion that if he survived this ordeal he would retire and enjoy life. He was wealthy enough and he did not respect the majority of the management team. He'd worked long and hard and was not really appreciated by the insurance types who thought all he did was count money. If only they knew the talents he possessed in doing deals, arranging finance, using his large network of contacts to get the job done. And if they thought promoting one of the in-house finance men to replace him would work smoothly they had a shock or two coming. To replace him EIG would need to search externally.

Don's wife, his second, had been very understanding and he knew he owed her time. He was going to take time and be with her and enjoy the sun. Of course this situation might end badly but he was philosophical and accepted that his fate may be determined by other factors, much as a meteor from outer space would change a thing or two, and be entirely beyond human direction.

John Franks was lying in bed, staring at the ceiling. He was not happy. He missed the day to day activity at the company. He felt insignificant when he was not doing something which related to the business. He had been with the group for thirty five years and couldn't imagine a life without being involved in some way with EIG. His wife had mocked him from time to time because EIG came first but she had no idea how important it was to him. EIG was his baby. He had moulded it and the discussions about succession had clearly unnerved him. Both Vincent and Tennyson had been at him and finally he had agreed to resolve it, at least decide who would take the reins when he retired. Not that retirement was something he contemplated in the near future. But he had to string them along, keep them with the company as they were integral to its success and if this meant having discussions regarding succession, so be it. He also began to share the accolades which he received. He loved being told how well he had managed the place. He loved the external acceptance of his greatness as a Chief Executive. He loved it all and now these hoodlums were upsetting everything.

He needed to brain storm with his team. For some reason, here by himself, he had no ideas whatsoever. It was as if somebody had taken away his oxygen.

He closed his eyes. If only it was a dream and he would awake with a bright new day of office wrangling. Oh, it had been so much fun. Particularly as he had called the shots for over a decade. And it was that level of control he was reluctant to forego.

CHAPTER 33

Day 8

Igor Radimovich was looking around the room as he waited for a cop to come into the room. He was a tall, blonde haired man of twenty five and the closest to a friend Jordan Johnson had at EIG. He was an IT specialist in the audit department and had travelled with JJ on a number of occasions. Detective Sergeant Morris had investigated individuals' profiles in the department Johnson worked in and then, after speaking to a few of them, she had ferreted out this information relatively quickly. Braxton had carried out further enquiries by phone to ascertain who else might have been close to Johnson but nothing useful emerged. He got on with most people Braxton discovered but, apart from Igor, Johnson wasn't particularly friendly with anyone.

Radimovich did not like the police. He'd only been in Australia for five years and had no cause to distrust them in this country but it was a different story in Russia where he had had a number of run ins and none of them he remembered with fondness. He toyed with his iPhone 4 and looked up when a female entered the room, followed by a male who seemed to be smirking at something she had said.

When Detective Sergeant Morris stood opposite Radimovich who stayed seated she introduced herself and Detective Constable Braxton formally. Braxton offered his hand and when Radomovich finally responded the detective shook his hand firmly. Braxton placed recording equipment on a solid table whilst Morris settled herself in a chair directly opposite Radimovich. Braxton finished the set up process and chose a chair side on to both Radimovich and Morris.

"Hey, what's this about?" said Radimovich who tried to recall what he had done which warranted a police visit at his place of work. He had simply been asked by the Internal Audit Manager to wait in the small conference room at the back because the police had some questions. He thought it may have related to his not paying his speeding fines but couldn't imagine that a recorder was necessary.

"Just routine," Morris remarked, continuing to press buttons to start the recorder without even looking at Radimovich.

When Morris had succeeded in getting the equipment to run, she, noting the hostile glare from the man across from her who was a friend of the only suspect to date, asked him to state his name. The Strike Force had been sweating on a break-through for over a week and Donaldson knew that the investigation would cool fairly quickly if nothing turned up soon.

Detective Inspector Donaldson entered the room and closed the door behind him. He introduced himself, then sat next to Morris and nodded to Braxton. Morris ignored him and informed the machine of the date and, checking her watch, said the time was ten fifteen.

"Mr Radimovich," said Donaldson, "May I call you Igor?"

"Sure, that's my name," said Radimovich who didn't like the man. Donaldson reminded him of beefy middle-aged Russian cops who initially appeared friendly but then reverted to issuing threats when the answers did not suit them.

"You're a friend of Jordan Johnson we understand, is that correct?"

"Is that a crime? Yes I work with Jordan and we are mates, kind of. We have a drink after a day away in one of the forgettable places we manage to work in."

"How long have you known him?"

"Around nine months," he almost snarled.

"Is that how long he's been with the company?" Morris asked, peering at a piece of paper.

"I don't know. He hasn't been with EIG long although he worked in another section before joining the audit team. His specialty is finance."

Donaldson scrutinized Radimovich closely. He rubbed his face and continued, "Do you know where he went on his break from work, for around three weeks I think?"

Radimovich screwed up his face. "I have no fucking idea. Didn't talk about it. He was cut up when his girlfriend Madeline from HR broke up with him. So he may have gone on a drinking holiday for all I know."

Morris looked at Donaldson. "So he and Madeline were in a relationship?"

"Sure were. He keeps it quiet but I caught him speaking with her a couple of times and when I said something about it he said 'yes' he was seeing her."

"We've spoken with Madeline who said he asked about schedules of meetings and so forth," said Morris, "would he need that information in his work?"

"Could do. Might have been part of an audit he was conducting. That sort of thing is fairly standard."

Braxton who had been sitting quietly sensed that his colleagues had run out of questions. He said, "Why?"

"Why what?" said Radimovich.

"Why would he need to look at meeting schedules?"

Radimovich looked at Braxton as though he was an irritant. "As auditors we review departmental requirements as part of our risk assessment and this includes an understanding of what they need to produce for board and executive management meetings."

Donaldson was getting tired of this. "You have travelled to cities with Johnson and probably had dinner with him drinks and you tell us you don't even know when he started with the company and where he was going on leave. Sounds highly unlikely."

Radimovich looked at Donaldson for ten seconds and shrugged. "What can I say? We talked about women and sport and sometimes how to get rich."

After a few further questions, Donaldson dismissed Radimovich and thanked him. He turned to Morris, "It seems to me that Madeline has it in for Johnson and wanted to make his life difficult. Typical woman."

"Hang on there," said Morris, "You're assuming a lot about women but I must admit it does look like we've been used in this instance."

"Oh well, let's have lunch and we'll talk about our next plan of attack."

"Great, are you springing for this?" Braxton said.

Donaldson gave him a look which suggested he was dreaming.

Radimovich returned to his desk, muttering under his breath. He was pleased he had lied about a number of things. He wasn't sure what the cops thought JJ had done but there was no way he was helping them. Board minutes were items auditors inspected, not their internal correspondence. If JJ obtained schedules of executive meetings for whatever reason, that was his business. As far as he was concerned, live and let live.

CHAPTER 34

Day 9

Lieutenant Stephan McPherson had a distinctive face with a hard edged jaw, sharp nose and bushy moustache. He was forty four years old, a career cop who had seen most of the evil that police officers encounter. He had seen death too many times to be unnerved by it and he had even been responsible for the demise of two individuals, both times in self defence. Although many of his colleagues had witnessed similar instances of watching a perpetrator die, they had suffered afterwards and needed psychological help to overcome the situation. McPherson needed no such assistance. He regarded the occasional violent episode as a necessary part of the job. He was an unflinching pragmatist.

So when his Aussie mate Detective Inspector Donaldson whom he'd met at a seminar in Honolulu asked him to quietly look into a potential case, he was only too glad to oblige. It was now three thirty in the afternoon and he had a few hours before things would hot up again. He'd looked up Tim Tennyson's details from the EIG site as well as vehicle records and decided to travel to Long Island to visit his ex-wife, Rita.

Rita had not remarried it transpired but she probably didn't need a husband to take care of her judging by the palatial mansion she lived in. McPherson was impressed. He'd never seen a garden so carefully tended before. It included trees, bushes, flowers of various kinds and lawn. He lived in an apartment in the Bronx and he was used to brick and concrete. When he knocked on the huge white door he had to wait a full two minutes before someone responded.

"Hello, I'm Lieutenant McPherson with the NYPD," he said, flashing his badge, "I was wondering whether I could speak to Mrs

Tennyson?"

The woman who was in jeans and a loose blouse smiled and said, "I'm Rita Tennyson but my husband and I have been divorced for years."

McPherson grinned. She looked more like a young girl than a woman who had been married. Rita continued to stare at McPherson, waiting.

"Did you know that your ex had been kidnapped?" asked McPherson.

"I can't help you there and I wouldn't give the kidnappers a dime for him. As far as I'm concerned they can keep him."

"Could I ask you some questions nevertheless," said McPherson.

"Ok, follow me. Forgive the way I'm dressed, I've just come in from the back garden, my passion." Rita led the way through doors to the left of the entrance and they walked into a large sitting room which adjoined a suitably impressive foyer from which a spiral staircase to the second level was visible. She pointed to a sofa and said she'd be a moment. When she re-entered she seemed to have been transformed into another, much more beautiful creature. She sat on a leather chair facing him.

McPherson now noticed how petite Rita Tennyson was. She was barely five feet tall, he guessed, and was very trim. Her figure was not the result of gym work but rather from keeping active in the garden, McPherson speculated. She had blue green eyes and fair hair. She was attractive in an innocent kind of way.

"A drink, coffee or something cold," she offered.

"A glass of cold water would be nice. It's a long drive from Manhattan."

She smiled which then reminded him of a smaller version of Kylie Minogue, if that was at all possible. McPherson noted that she was perhaps a little older than the Kylie he admired in a music video he'd acquired some years ago but he still found the resemblance uncanny. Rita bounced up and was back shortly afterwards. Her legs were amazing and he wondered why Tennyson would let her go or, more to the point, what he had done for her to send him packing. A maid followed with a tray containing a pitcher of cold water and another of cold lemonade as well as two large glasses. Once the maid had disappeared, Rita said, "How can I help you?"

"I take it you and your husband parted on less than amicable terms?"

"You could say that. He was a bastard of the first degree. The more I got to know him, the more I despised him."

"How so?"

Rita repositioned herself on the chair, like a cat rearranging itself during sleep. "We were married young and I thought he loved me for myself but as time went on I discovered differently."

"He cheated on you?"

"Yes but that wasn't the issue for me. If it had been an affair I guess one could get over it but it wasn't that. You see he liked me well enough when I was young because I resembled a woman in a child's body. I found out by using a private dick that he had many affairs after I sensed something was wrong. And all of the flings were with very small women and even girls. He had a thing for young girls and I mean as young as ten. He had the sexual bent of a paedophile and he tried hard to cover it up by marrying me. He would have stayed married to me and continued to be seen as respectable except when I eventually had had enough I confronted him. He denied his philandering and after that discussion, an almighty brawl, we fought all the time. Eventually the atmosphere got so toxic I asked him to leave."

"And you got the house in the divorce settlement?"

Rita pulled hair off her face. "No, I managed a decent enough settlement because he was a CEO of the US division of a multi-national insurance company, but I inherited this house from my family. Tim was such an arsehole he wouldn't part with anything he didn't have to."

"What's the name of the insurance company?"

"EIG. Stands for Easy Insurance Group. Can you believe it? The last thing they were was easy. I met some of the international executives when they visited New York on their annual junkets. They were tight and hard work. The only connection to the description of easy was in relation to their sleeping habits. They were easy lays as far as I understood it and Tim was the pimp."

McPherson was pleased. He was getting a picture of an executive team like many others he had encountered. Ruthless in business and party animals whenever they could indulge themselves with prospective clients, all on the business accounts they set up for themselves. These types made enemies as a matter of course. He could imagine that customers denied a large claim might resort to kidnapping or some other form of revenge. He scribbled some notes then looked at Rita. "Any idea who might want to harm your husband or extract money from him?"

"There'd be too many. Just look up the phone directory."

"Mrs...I mean Rita, seriously. A criminal investigation is in play. We need to obtain information because it's not only your husband who's a victim."

Rita poured herself more lemonade and took a sip. "I honestly don't know of any specific individual."

McPherson stood and tendered a card. "Should you think of anything I'd appreciate it if you gave me a call." He began to walk to the door. Then he turned and said, "Did your husband keep porn on his computer?"

"I never looked while we were together. But it wouldn't surprise me."

McPherson was almost tempted to ask her out but thought better of it. She was out of his class and he wasn't in the mood for rejection.

Lieutenant Stephan McPherson was in downtown Manhattan the very next morning on a routine job. He decided he would call into EIG's US Headquarters which happened to be near Wall Street. At the ground level lobby of the multi-level pale building, he flashed his badge at the male attendant and said he wanted to speak with Mr Tennyson's personal assistant. He was asked to wait. Two minutes later an attractive woman in her thirties arrived and escorted him up to level fourteen using her identification card. On the elevator ride up the woman who introduced herself as Lucy said that Mr Tennyson's personal assistant was currently in a meeting but that she would be finished shortly. Lucy showed him into Mr Tennyson's office and closed the door.

The personal assistant was true to her word and strode in a few minutes later, stretching out her hand and informing him that she was Miriam Muny. The confident Miriam settled into a comfortable visitor's chair facing McPherson who was in the other visitor's chair. "Mr Tennyson is out of town," she said, "how can I help?"

McPherson noted that Miriam Muny was dark haired and average in height and build and nothing like what Tennyson apparently fancied in women if his ex-wife's comments were to be believed. "Did you know that he's been kidnapped in Australia?"

"Yes, I heard something. Isn't it awful?"

McPherson appraised her. "Did Mr Tennyson have any enemies who might carry out such an act?"

Miriam Muny stared at McPherson. "I wouldn't know. You might be better off speaking with one of the managers."

"You may not know about his business associates but what's the gossip about him. You would be aware of that, right?"

She smiled and looked around the office as if to assure herself that nobody else was about. "I guess."

"Come on, anything might be helpful."

It seemed to the detective that she was weighing up what was appropriate and what wasn't, perhaps assessing how much might get back to Tennyson should he return. "He was not popular, I can tell you that. Some, not me though, thought he was a bit of a tyrant."

"In what way?"

"He was a bully and he made life hard for people he didn't like. He also kept employees who weren't in his immediate circle of advisors at a distance. That's why there are additional security measures for this floor, the executive floor, and only the usual security access to the other floors. And he also had a special security door to his office. Some would say, but you didn't hear it from me, so that he could engage in sexual activities with the ladies."

McPherson made sure his expression didn't alter. "With whom in particular?"

"Not with me if that's what you're thinking." Miriam's expression was one of unguarded indignation.

"No no," said McPherson quickly, "I'm not insinuating anything nor making any judgements. I'm just following up on what you were saying and assumed it had to be other staff?" He wanted to gain this woman's confidence and changed his approach from his usual tough style.

"Yes, it involved someone on staff," she said, crossing her trousered legs "Were there a number of women?" McPherson watched her closely.

"There probably were but I'm aware of only one." McPherson prompted gently, "Do you have a name?"

"Well there's Dolly. She's an actuary. Lives on the floor below."

After some more questions, McPherson established that the rumours were about a number of women but only Dolly was identifiable. He requested that Miriam ask her to come up. In the meantime McPherson wandered around Tennyson's office. The view was spectacular with a glimpse of water to the left. He looked at the picture on the desk which appeared to be of himself with some celebrity he didn't recognise.

A knock on the door, then a timid young woman with wide eyes entered. "Hello, I'm Dolly," she said. Dolly was only a little taller than Rita but she possessed lovely alabaster skin and a cute figure.

"Hi, I'm Lieutenant McPherson, please take a seat."

McPherson sat in Tennyson's huge leather chair which was set higher than the visitors' chairs so that the occupant could look down on his guests. He had always wondered about business leaders and their egos. He said, "You can't be more than eighteen surely."

Dolly blushed. "I'm twenty-three."

"What sort of a name is Dolly?' McPherson couldn't help himself. She looked like a lovely doll but he wondered what kind of parents would name a daughter Dolly.

"My dad was a big fan of Dolly Parton."

McPherson realised he was wasting time. He reverted back to the topic at hand. "How long have you worked here?"

"Around eighteen months."

"Do you like it here?"

"Yes. I'm an actuary and the team I work with is great."

McPherson placed his elbows on the almost clear desk, pushed himself forward a little and looked into Dolly's eyes. "And what about Mr Tennyson?"

Dolly swallowed and said, "He's ok, I guess."

"I see. I heard that you and he had something going."

It was a moment before it happened but when it erupted, it seemed the tears Dolly produced would not end.

McPherson waited a couple of minutes and then he tried to soothe her. "It's ok. He's not around anymore."

She sniffed and eventually rubbed her eyes. "What do you mean?"

"He's been kidnapped in Sydney, Australia."

"Oh," she said, "That's not good, is it?"

"So what happened Dolly, why did you break down when I asked about Mr Tennyson?"

She pulled herself together, then looked at McPherson and said, "He and I did have sex but he threatened me with being fired if I didn't respond to his advances."

"Did he rape you?"

"No, not exactly. At first he asked me into his office on the pretext of having me explain certain actuarial tables and I thought it was strange because it was usually the Chief Actuary who had regular meetings with him. In any event he got around to feeling my legs and bottom. I didn't say anything for a while wondering what to do, then finally I told him it was not proper for him to touch me."

McPherson watched her struggling with a story which she appeared to have been bottled up."Go on," he said.

"His reaction when I told him that was to laugh. He then asked me whether I enjoyed working at the company and when I said I did he said that as a team member I should go with the flow. He said others had suffered unusual career moves when they refused to co-operate."

"So you just did what was expected?" McPherson said. "I wanted the job badly. I needed it."

"You could have got a job with another insurance company, couldn't you?"

"Not after only three months in this job."

"So you've been having sex with Tennyson for over a year."

"Yes, and sometimes on weekends too. I hate him. I hope the kidnappers don't let him go. He is despicable but I didn't know what to do once I agreed. I couldn't really complain. I didn't know what to do." She wiped tears from her eyes.

McPherson said, "Thanks for your time. If he returns, I will have him arrested. In the meantime I will get one of my staff to get your statement." McPherson stood up and looked at Dolly and considered giving her a fatherly hug but decided against doing so in case she felt another male was seeking her affections.

McPherson despised people like Tennyson, powerful people who corrupted and soiled weaker members of society.

Although he said he would have Tennyson arrested, he knew this wasn't possible without evidence. But he planned to pursue this matter.

CHAPTER 35

Day 9

Katie was dancing with her friend Peggy who, eyes closed, seemed oblivious to all around her. Katie was blonde and dressed in a strapless white dress with green dots and circles giving an impression of swirling vegetation. The black haired Peggy however had a fresh modern look, black slinky skirt and heels. They danced to Beyonce on the Nightclub dance floor which now, at two in the morning, was packed solid with heaving bodies.

As the strobe lights flashed, the patrons, most of whom were either drunk or drugged, swayed, rocked or moved with guiltless abandon, all in their own imaginary world. So when Peggy accidentally stepped on another woman's foot, it did not register. However the woman who felt the stiletto turned and pulled Peggy's long black locks. When Peggy became aware of what was happening she retaliated with a fist to the other woman's nose. The woman tripped and soon others became involved in the skirmish. Men used fists or heads; women either cowered or joined in by pushing others or grabbing loose hair.

The bouncers soon joined in and whacked the most obvious with long black truncheons. The music which was deafly loud raged on. The floor was soon cleared and a few who wouldn't calm were taken outside and handled the way the bouncers had been instructed – hit first, ask questions later.

Upstairs in the club's central office, Nick Koutslakis was watching via a large screen. He was enjoying a drink with JJ who had popped in with Angela after having partaken in the activities downstairs.

"Got up here just in time," said Angela.

"Looks like it honey," said Koutslakis. "But don't worry, the boys would've looked after you."

"Does this happen often?" asked JJ who was impressed by the efficiency of the entire episode.

Now after ten minutes, dancing had resumed and the troublemakers had been despatched.

"Once or twice every month. It's fairly routine. Someone gets aggressive and then the drink kicks in and a fight starts. Usual human nature. They're nothing but animals dressed up, most of them."

The two men sipped their scotch, Johnny Walker Black label, and watched the dance floor which now appeared as if nothing had happened. JJ realised that the majority of dancers were so intoxicated or drugged that they probably wouldn't remember a thing the next day.

Koutslakis said, turning his attention to JJ, "How's the plan working out?"

"Patience is a wonderful thing," said JJ, "information is leaking out, a little at a time. Being patient is important. The long waiting period and increased suspense is beginning to affect them, it's quite obvious."

"How's the surveillance of their rooms working out?"

"It's been masterfully done, thank whoever designed it. So far none of the occupants seems to have spotted anything. It's been revealing. Seeing how they've reacted to their situation – a real character study if I wanted to write a book. But only one temper tantrum so far. And it was noted by Jack that Tennyson has a weapon which he fashioned from a piece of wood, so the boys are ready for him."

Angela who had dressed herself in black, tight trousers, blouse and stilettos stood up and wandered over to the sofa JJ was occupying and decided to move close to him. JJ took her hand.

"Good to see the both of you," Koutslakis croaked, "Now get the hell out of here and get some sleep. You can't afford to be tired in the middle of an operation."

JJ smiled and pulled Angela up when he rose. "Nice talking to you too Nick. Thanks for all the high tech stuff. It's really been useful and expertly set up."

"That's ok. Just make sure Tony checks it from time to time."

On the drive back to JJ's place, Angela remained quiet. It was raining but there was little traffic and JJ guided the car with care.

He liked driving the Audi and Angela was too tired to concentrate.

"What's the matter?" JJ eventually said.

"Oh just wondering how long this job will take. I'd like us to be able to live like a normal couple."

JJ placed his hand over Angela's. "I do too. The whole operation will be over in a few weeks so I hope you can hold on." He turned to her. "Look, if it's causing you any stress or anxiety you can opt out. The three of us are capable of managing the load. Jack and Tony insisted we have a break and they've let us spend tonight out. After all they're well trained. They are confident of dealing with any problems and they have the number of my mobile should they need to talk about anything, so everything's under control." JJ watched her face quickly before refocussing on the road.

"I'll be in this with you until the end," Angela said. "No need to worry. I was only expressing my feelings."

They arrived at Angela's flat at 2:50 am. The rain had become progressively harder and they ran from the street into the block of units as quickly as was possible with Angela's heels. Inside, they hugged each other, shed their clothes and waltzed into the shower.

Sleep finally welcomed them around 4am.

At 9:45am JJ opened his eyes and saw that he was alone. He ran his hand over his face and registered the roughness. He struggled up, walked into the bathroom and cleaned his teeth, using a fresh toothbrush that Angela kept in a drawer. Although she had some underwear lying around, JJ was not bothered by it. He took another shower to freshen up. Water flowing over his head made JJ gradually wake up and it got the brain into gear, his best thoughts usually originating in this environment. He decided not to shave. He could do it at the Coogee quarters if he felt he needed it, with the presence of his young lady the only possible reason for such action.

Fully dressed, he switched on the television and sought Sky News to see whether the kidnapping story was still playing. Angela entered almost immediately, laden with coffees and croissants.

"Good morning," she said.

'Breakfast. Wonderful," JJ responded, clearing the table of papers.
"You're a bad man," said Angela.

"What?"

"Don't you remember last night?"

"Sure, is my version different to yours?"

Angela sat down placing JJ's cappuccino and pastries at the place opposite her. "Don't know. You seemed hell bent on acting like a character from a porn site, wanting me to slide all over you with my bum while your tongue worked ..."

"I didn't want your generous proportions to go to waste."

They both smiled. The night had been a pleasant interlude, one not able to be repeated with the same freedom for a while. They realised the pressure of their current venture would return very soon. The risk of this illegal enterprise had begun to seep into Angela's consciousness and she hoped that JJ was aware too of the many dangers which lay ahead.

CHAPTER 36

Day 9

Doug Vincent sat on the bed, head in hands. How long had it been now? Eight days, fifteen days? All he knew was he was bored and worried about his safety and the future. He missed Marion. It was odd. Usually he didn't think about her. But now he wanted nothing more than to be with her and his son. It was such a cliché but he realised that family was the most important thing in life. He had fought and worked hard to get where he was, one of the heirs to the throne. Like Tennyson he could taste it – the power that came with being the chief.

He had discussed the succession plan with the other two front runners, Stephen Burton and Tim Tennyson many times. He and Stephen would have dinner in an expensive London Restaurant and talk about what they would do if they became the anointed one. He and Tennyson would do the same in one of the fancy bars in New York. Tennyson was the most fanatical of the three of them, he felt. He wanted the position more than the others, Vincent decided. It was as though he had to prove his worth to himself as well as to others.

Vincent rubbed his eyes. He would have liked a copy of the bible. He had not attended to his faith and needed to make amends. Here, confined alone between walls, he prayed every night. When he was free of this torment he would engage with the church again. He promised God that if he became free and allowed another chance, he would make sure he attended the local Catholic Church regularly. And when he was abroad, on Sundays he would seek out a service.

He asked to be forgiven for his irresponsibility in having Johnston made a scapegoat. At the time it was necessary for the company's reputation that expediency prevailed. And he couldn't now make it up to Johnston as he had died over six months ago. Johnston had been shunned and Vincent realised he didn't even know what sort of family he had, whether he was married or estranged or had children. They had never been civil, let alone close. He always quipped how much he hated bean counters and joked constantly about their boring disposition whenever in a meeting with him alone or when the meeting comprised many - always best for humiliation purposes. Of course he had no idea about the man but always felt, when they were both in the Asia Pacific Division, that Johnston was watching Vincent's extravagances and his personal expenses budget.

The door opened and the hooded female stepped in with a tray.

"Umm, look, do you have a bible around here?"

She shrugged and placed the tray on the floor near the door. Behind her, silent and as immovable as a stature, stood a powerfully built thug. Vincent wanted desperately to go for a walk. Not seeing any natural light was disorienting. He was on the verge of begging. But he held back. The woman left, closing the door with a thud.

Mark Hovein was sitting in the first class waiting lounge at Heathrow Airport. He had his legs crossed and he was reading the Daily Express and wondering why the Brits loved trash. All their papers seemed to be filled with gossip about celebrities and other bizarre happenings. There was almost no useful news. If politics were reported it was usually about the personalities involved rather than what was being planned for the country. And of course the bad news was headline stuff – an earthquake in Japan or a flood in Bangladesh but unless it was catastrophic, it didn't gain much space. Hovein tossed the paper aside. It struck a passenger next to him.

"I'm so sorry," he said, seeing the mystified expression on the woman's face, "there was nobody sitting there a moment ago."

"That's alright," she said, "I'll live."

"Can I make it up to you?" he said. "Would you like a drink?"

"It's free in the lounge. Are you proposing getting me a drink?"

Hovein blushed, "Excuse me. What I meant was having a drink out. Again I'm not making myself..."

"You're trying to pick me up, is that it?"

He smiled. "Precisely. I'm just no good at it." Although she was dark skinned, her accent was more British than most British people.

She returned his smile. "Sure, I'd love to have a drink with you. Do you live in Sydney?"

"I do. I suppose you're from Melbourne."

"I'm from Mosman in Sydney despite being Indian."

"Fantastic. I live at Cremorne. Not far away at all."

When Hovein opened his eyes to the door being opened, he blinked and tried to recollect where he was. The memory of how he met his wife dissipated and he wondered whether he would see her again.

Moments later he was back in the interrogation room, tied to the chair as before. He waited for the light, closing his eyes until it flooded the room.

With the light came the electronic voice. It said, "Explain the way the investment process works at EIG."

Hovein informed the voice and the video recording of which he was unaware that EIG had a strict policy on investments. This policy was documented in a manual and any breaches were noted in a register. Breaches also needed to be reported monthly in the Investment Report which was circulated to the Board. The register was available to both the internal and external auditors upon request.

After a drink of water supplied by a guard, Hovein continued. He said that as policy holders needed to be paid out on a regular basis, liquidity was important which meant that eighty-five to ninety percent of all investments were required to be held as cash or fixed interest instruments. Only around a maximum fifteen percent could be used for equity or non-liquid investment. He further explained that each region was expected to comply with these requirements and that the Head Office Investment Division was charged to monitor compliance.

"So why did the US region have CDOs which made up over fifty percent of their investment portfolio two years ago?"

"Where did you get that figure from?"

"Never mind. Just answer the question," the voice commanded.

Hovein swallowed. This was an inside job. Only a few people knew about the Collateralized Debt Obligations the company held. Who would have leaked this information? Perspiration trickled down his face and he wanted desperately to wipe it from his eyes. "Okay, I'll tell you but if I do will you release me?"

"I'm not making any deals at this point but honest answers may gain you some benefit." Hovein said, "Are you with the authorities? You can't do this. It's illegal."

"One last chance before we employ other tactics."

Hovein was in a bind. He was caught between two opposing threats. If he revealed what he knew then his life after the revelation would never be the same. If he didn't say anything then he might be tortured or killed. And it seemed that lying would not help. These people seemed to know a hell of a lot more than anyone could assume. "What occurred was nobody's fault. We acquired a US company which had invested in structured asset backed securities which you know as Collateralized Debt Obligations, information which didn't come to light until after the deal had been finalised. The manager of that operation New Hampshire Insurance Inc. also then absconded with many millions of American dollars and he's not been seen since."

"Was this reported to the police?"

"No, we took a decision that it wouldn't be favourable to our image if publicity of the theft got out. The sum of money was immaterial compared with the group's total cash assets so it wasn't going to affect the company's results."

"So twenty-two million dollars was simply ignored."

"Nobody knew that figure. How did..." Hovein stopped. Was this a rogue division of the FBI he was dealing with?

"And the CDOs which totalled hundreds of millions? How was this covered up?"

"You seem to know everything. Why don't you tell me?"

A painful sensation streamed through Hovein's body leaving his entire being shaking. He nearly expired from heart failure. After a few minutes he was able to accept that he had been stunned by a device and then he understood why the cords were wrapped securely and with a clasp holding his right forefinger. He may as well have been in an electric chair. "Please," he said, "there is no need for this. I have been co-operating."

"Cut out the stupid remarks and you will be fine. Continue."

"May I have some water please?"

Lights were extinguished and a man brought a plastic bottle and poured water into Hovein's mouth. When he had completed the job, footsteps retreated and Hovein wondered whether the voice had given him the bottle or whether it was the muscle. Not that it mattered and he thought better than to ask. As he peered into the black nothingness, he recalled newspaper articles of black holes.

Minutes later Hovein was ready. He had hated the US assignment when he had been requested by Tennyson to review the investment portfolios acquired with the new US corporation purchase. Hovein recalled his meeting with Tennyson who reacted strangely when confronted with the facts. The fact that the CDOs were worthless did not interest Tennyson. He simply wanted them to be classified something other than derivatives in the books. Hovein had baulked but Tennyson informed him that if Hovein wished to remain in his position after Tennyson's appointment to the Group Chief Executive Officer, he would remain quiet and do as asked. Tennyson had told him the promotion was a done deal and that he merely had to wait the appropriate period before he became the next Corporate Chief.

"Tim Tennyson and I agreed to place them in an account called US Bonds at six percent interest maturing in five years. They were simply consolidated as such and as they represented less than ten percent of our total bonds, nobody really noticed."

"What about the auditors?"

"They made enquiries and conducted certain tests but the topic never surfaced. I assumed they missed it or decided it wasn't a material issue."

"Who else knew?"

Hovein paused. "Only Tim and myself."

Another electric charge was emitted and at the end of the short sharp burst Hovein was exhausted. He was taken back to the flat where he flopped onto the bed face down. He lay there for what seemed like days but in fact it was merely two hours.

"Will he be alright?" Angela asked when JJ informed her that he had actually used the electric shock solution.

"Yes, we've only used a low current electrical discharge." JJ sipped his cappuccino which Tony had brought up to him. He had discarded his black clothes and changed into jeans and a T-shirt and was lounging on the sofa with Angela resting her legs on his.

The two lovers had just showered after a love-making session and were discussing the Hovein incident. JJ stroked her bare thighs.

"Sounds terrible," she said, wriggling her red painted toes.

"The belts we place around the hostages haven't been used on anyone previously and are perfectly safe. They administer a temporary high voltage but low current electric impulse. And I wouldn't have used it but Hovein lied and he needed to understand that there are penalties for that."

"Was he hurt?"

"He felt pain but that's the point. He may have been momentarily paralysed but he wasn't permanently damaged, if that's what you mean." JJ eyed Angela to see how she was reacting to his report. "Don't worry, I won't use the shock treatment unless absolutely necessary."

"You seem to be enjoying this." Angela examined JJ closely. JJ pulled her big toe.

"Ouch," she exclaimed, slapping his arm.

"I enjoyed that, your slap, but whether I enjoy playing with the hostages...maybe." JJ smirked. "Our next guest may require some of the tough treatment as well."

Angela did not ask any further questions.

David Mittlehouse sat where Hovein had sat three hours before. Mittlehouse had re-evaluated his position as he had been denied proper food. He'd been given fluid and just enough food to keep him going and now he was extremely hungry. He had been told that his refusal to speak was responsible for this treatment. He was beginning to dream only of having a meal. All other thoughts were short lived.

The voice interrupted Mittlehouse's train of thought. "Tell me about your visit to New York."

Mittlehouse said, "I can't remember. It was a while back. If you give me some decent food, I may be able to help." Mittlehouse thought that at least he was talking and sounding like he might help. Surely they would allow him something to eat.

The voice said, "Mr Mittlehouse you are being deliberately obtuse. If you persist with this charade your water will be reduced and you will get absolutely no further drinks. As for food, this will be denied to you entirely. This is your last chance."

After another moment Mittlehouse began. "All I recall is that Franks thought it might be instructive if I visited Tim's operation to help me with developing mine as I was relatively new to the position of Regional CEO. So I met with the US management team and was shown how they developed their business plans and so forth. All routine stuff."

"And how did you find Tennyson."

"He was very efficient and the senior guys respected him. Perhaps they were a little wary too."

"Why do you say that?"

Mittlehouse had no idea why this line of enquiry was taken. He did not care. He was starving and he would sell his mother to get food. He said, "Tim and I went out one evening and he was pumped. Apparently a finance guy, Johnston, who I didn't know well, had just got the axe and Tim was genuinely happy, saying that the bastard had it coming, that he had interfered in areas that weren't his concern. Anyway we had dinner, then Tim took me to a club and, well, it turned out to be a night to remember."

"How so?"

"At the club he introduced me to a woman who took us out back where there were some ladies.

And I thought they were underage but Tim assured me they weren't. They were so cute and..."

"So you each chose a girl?"

"It would have been rude to decline. I just thought this was the way business was done in New York – the entertaining I mean."

"What happened?"

Mittlehouse coughed, then cleared his throat. "I chose a young woman who was definitely eighteen or so and Tim chose his, a tiny dark haired girl."

The voice hesitated for a moment. "How old was she?"

"I don't know but she looked very young."

"You're lying," said the voice, with a firmness Mittlehouse hadn't heard before.

Mittlehouse imagined the worst. Food denied him for another long period. Water from the bathroom being the only sustenance to keep him alive until he was nothing but a shadow. He said with a quivering urgency, "I don't know, that's the truth. She could've been sixteen or even fourteen. I just don't know."

Silence, like a rock shattering a window, filled the room. It was another minute or so before the light became sheer brutal darkness. Mittlehouse nearly fainted from the tension he felt. He thought he was going to expire. His head was dizzy but whether it was from lack of food or fright, he hadn't a clue. Then footsteps advanced.

Mittlehouse was returned to his room and he was overjoyed to find that wrapped items had been brought on a tray. It ripped the packaging from the tray which rested on his bed. To his delight he discovered bread, chicken, salad and fruit juice.

As Mittlehouse was finishing off the meal, a luxury so glorious that he knew he would never take business lunches for granted again, he contemplated the interest the person behind the microphone displayed in Tennyson's activities and the focus on the prostitutes. Why was this of interest to these people? Kidnappers wanted money. The authorities sought justice. Nothing made any sense.

The empty tray was collected by a young woman wearing a hood however this time the usual hooded man entered the room and pointed a gun at Mittlehouse. He handed him a form which he gathered he had to complete. The form set out line items requiring details of his personal bank accounts.

Mittlehouse said he couldn't remember the details but the gunman left the room as though that was of no concern to him. Things began to make sense, he thought. The demand for money, directly and without resorting to third parties, was clever. Then again, that kind of transaction could be traced. At least that was his impression.

CHAPTER 37

Day 10

Detective Inspector Donaldson received a call from Lieutenant Stephen McPherson at 7am Friday morning. Donaldson was at home in Ryde reading the Sydney Morning Herald when his mobile phone rang.

He placed his knife and fork across his plate while his wife eyed him. He picked up the mobile and said, "Yep."

"How are you doin'?" McPherson said, "Hope I'm not interrupting your sleep or something else." He laughed.

Donaldson stood up and walked to the window turning his back on Jessie who disapproved of phone interruptions. "I've been up for an hour. You still funding the racing industry?"

McPherson roared with laughter this time. "At least I win every now and again, a little better than your dismal record."

"Yes, alright. No need to rub it in. I only bet on one race these days – the Melbourne Cup. So what have you got for me?" Donaldson admired his wife's roses outside. Jessie's passion of nurturing her small garden finally showed respectable returns.

McPherson assumed his professional voice and said, "After some digging I was able to convince my boss that we may have a guy, this Tennyson character, involved with child pornography. Hence we will be confiscating the computers at Tennyson's work premises as well as his home."

"Wow. I didn't realise that this would result from a few random enquiries. I was expecting to eliminate any connection to a motive."

"There you have it. I'll prepare a report and send you a copy."

Donaldson turned towards Jessie then turned away again. His thoughts were confused. "This complicates matters but I'm not sure how yet. Still, you've done a fine job."

McPherson grunted something which sounded like thanks. Finally he said, "Any other matters you'd like me to take a look at?"

"No, thanks for your time. You'll keep me informed about the outcome?"

"Of course my friend. Will you be coming over this way at all in the near future?"

"I don't know. It's difficult to get enough time off. But if I do, I will definitely let you know."

Donaldson finished his breakfast in silence. Jessie ignored him, sipping her coffee and finishing her crossword puzzle. She knew when he had a pained look on his face, as he now did, that he was deep in thought and about as much fun as a cat in a cage awaiting the vet.

At police headquarters, Donaldson called Morris and Braxton into his office and explained what had transpired.

"Interesting," said Braxton, "but how does this help us?"

"I just wonder whether there is a possible motive," said Donaldson. "I've been mulling it over in my mind but nothing makes sense."

Morris wriggled in her chair to get more comfortable. "It does seem strange. If Tennyson was the subject of the kidnapping then why take the entire top management group?"

"Exactly," Donaldson said, "maybe it's just one of those things and entirely co-incidental." He toyed with a pencil, then looked up again and said, "Or perhaps we're dealing with a foreign and very professional group who want to make the situation look like something other than what it is."

Morris screwed her face, "A little far-fetched, don't you think. There's no evidence to suggest that."

"You're right," said Donaldson who twirled the pencil around in his right hand.

Braxton was perplexed. He thought they were going way off track. He stroked his chin and said, tongue in cheek, "Perhaps they're all in on it."

Donaldson snorted. "If you're not going to take this seriously you can leave. We have virtually nothing to go on after more than an entire week. The Deputy Commissioner has been on my back and he wants to report something to the press who have been hounding him."

Braxton nodded. He was getting as frustrated as the rest of the members of the Strike Force. However he couldn't understand why some levity would go astray. He stood up and stretched his athletic frame. "Sorry Inspector. I'll get in touch with Interpol and run all their names through to see whether there are any connections to any sort of crime."

"Good idea," said Donaldson.

When Braxton had departed, Donaldson looked at Morris. "Any ideas?"

"No unfortunately. We'll interview Fiona again. We've spoken to all the tattoo parlours within ten miles of the city to see whether her description of the tattoo she saw was remembered but so far, no luck."

At that moment Constable Jackson entered. He waited after taking a few steps inside Donaldson's office until Donaldson looked at him.

"Sir, I believe we have a break through."

"Yes," said Donaldson quizzically, raising eyebrows.

Jackson straightened his shirt. "Mrs Hovein advised us that money has been electronically transferred from their joint bank account."

"How much?" said Donaldson.

"She said it was around two hundred grand."

Morris whistled. "No wonder they didn't want to make formal demands."

Donaldson stood up and waved his hands, "Get Peters from Forensic Accounting onto it straight away. Thanks Rob." He turned to Morris, "Can you check with other spouses to see whether any other funds have been stolen."

Morris said, "This could be the break we need. Hopefully it will lead to something concrete."

Donaldson nodded and watched Morris leave his office. If it could be traced to a specific individual, that would be wonderful and suddenly he felt elated. Now he had something to report. He decided he would pay a visit to Mrs Hovein himself.

Donaldson took an unmarked vehicle from the garage and headed out to Balmain where the Hovein family resided. Traffic in morning Sydney was woeful and he had to curb his enthusiasm. Sitting in the traffic on Victoria Road, drumming his fingers on the steering wheel, Donaldson knew it would be useless to become impatient. It would only achieve frustration and hence focus might be lost. He switched the radio to a classical music station and thought how he might conduct the interview.

Donaldson arrived at the terrace near ten o'clock. He had called ahead to ensure Mrs Hovein was in and that the detective waiting with her was aware of his visit. He showed his identification and was shown into a large well appointed lounge and asked to take a seat on a comfortable white leather sofa. At first he thought the dark skinned woman who led him inside was the help. But this short woman introduced herself once Donaldson was settled as the woman of the house.

The detective who had been sent to watch Mrs. Hovein and to assure her that she was secure walked outside. His job also included waiting for and listening to any possible calls from the kidnappers.

Mrs Hovein spoke with a British accent but was of Indian heritage. She wore traditional Indian garb and seemed polite and attentive. "May I offer you some tea, Inspector?"

"That would be lovely," Donaldson said, wanting to make her feel at ease before he delved into private financial matters. While she walked off to make the tea, Donaldson took the opportunity to look around. He got up and wandered over to the window where a view of the harbour could be glimpsed. The room was furnished with quality possessions and decorations. A large Sony television and top class stereo equipment tastefully located shouted designer inspired arrangements. To Donaldson it was plain that the Hoveins were wealthy. Perhaps the kidnapping was for money after all.

When Mrs Hovein returned with a tray, a pot of tea and chocolate biscuits, Donaldson said, "You shouldn't have gone to so much trouble Mrs Hovein."

She smiled. "Call me Daya please. Mrs Hovein sounds so formal." Donaldson sipped some tea. "You have a lovely home...Daya."

"Thank you. I try to look after it but I haven't been well lately and I can't do as much as I used to. Have you got any closer to finding my husband?"

Donaldson thought a moment so that he could choose the right words. He rubbed his forehead and looked at the woman sitting across from him, anxious yet expectant. “We’re doing all we can and we think we may have a lead. Which is why I’ve come to see you. I was told that you found money missing from one of your bank accounts.”

Mrs Hovein looked directly at Donaldson. “Yes. We have a number of accounts at the ANZ Bank and I noticed when checking to see whether the proceeds from the sale of EIG company shares had been credited to the correct account that a large withdrawal had been made. It wasn’t me and as Mark had been captured it couldn’t have been him.”

“And the amount?”

“Two hundred thousand dollars.”

Donaldson couldn’t help whistling. “Wow, quite a sum.”

“Oh it’s not much money and the money is not the issue but it might be a link to my husband.

I don’t know what I would do if he doesn’t survive.”

“You love him a lot.”

“Of course. We met at an airport lounge and found we both studied at Cambridge. We soon became friends. Finally after ten years we got married but we’ve remained friends despite the day to day domestic chores. So I would lose my best friend and my lover all at the same time. We don’t have close relatives or other people in our lives. Please do all you can to find him.”

Donaldson nodded sympathetically and waited until he felt he could get down to business again.

“What puzzles me,” said Donaldson, peering at Daya Hovein closely “is why the bank would allow that amount of money to be transferred. Aren’t there limits in place?”

“Mark arranged for a limit of two hundred thousand because he often deals in large investment transactions.”

“I see,” said Donaldson, “He’s the Investment Manager...I remember now. And he invests privately as well as on the company’s account?”

“Yes. It’s perfectly legitimate.”

“And insider trading? How does that work?”

Daya stood up and left the room. She returned a moment later with a file. “Here Inspector, this simply shows what he can and can’t do. He cannot trade EIG shares nor can he invest in fixed interest securities he transacts on behalf of the business. But he's at liberty to invest in other equities or commodities if he wants."

Donaldson accepted the file and looked at the contents briefly. He was mainly interested in whether the instructions were on company letterhead and signed. He handed the file back. "What about bank security checks – access numbers, passwords..."

"Mark knows the account details, password for transferring funds. He's got a good memory.

Does this mean he's still alive?"

"It's a positive sign," Donaldson said. "What I need you to do is to freeze the accounts so no further funds can be stolen."

"Sure. Do you have anything which might help track him or the perpetrators?"

Donaldson said, "We're getting our best forensic investigators to trace the funds. Thank you for the tea." He got out of the luxury chair and shook Daya Hovein's hand before marching out. As he strode out the front gate, Donaldson nodded to his colleague who was enjoying a cigarette. He drove off, down Darling Road, and was soon stuck in traffic again.

Later that day, Donaldson met the entire Strike Force contingent in the conference room and asked about progress, particularly in relation to funds withdrawn from other accounts.

Detective Constable Morris stood up and said she'd obtained a summary after talking to the detectives who made the enquiries. "As far as we can ascertain, apart from Hovein, the only other suspicious funds transfer came from the Waites family. Mrs Franks knew little of the family finances and said she was unsure."

"What seems to be the common denominator?" Donaldson was pacing the floor. "We haven't worked that out yet, sir."

A young constable from the back raised his hand. Donaldson nodded for him to talk.

"Does this mean that we won't be having any contact with the kidnappers?"

Donaldson said, "Maybe. But I wouldn't rule anything out at this stage. Every kidnapping is different although this one is extremely puzzling. All I can say is that we continue to carry out investigations into all areas. What I might suggest now is that we get in touch with EIG to ensure that no funds have been whisked away under our very noses."

Braxton said, "They'd have better security, wouldn't they?"

"Perhaps but you might talk to that Treasurer guy, what's his name Wolinski."

"I'm on it," said Braxton. He had been coming across dead ends and was anxious to do some serious detective work. He'd reviewed so much CCTV from around the city to try to fathom a direction the suspected truck had taken but found little of consequence. It was sighted going east on Castlereagh Street but where it had turned off was not seen. Braxton hated desk work and was pleased he would have to visit the company's premises and talk to people.

CHAPTER 38

Day 10

John Franks had always been rather stout and he had been bullied at high school for his nerdish behaviour and because he was chubby and wore glasses. He loved Rugby but never made the team. At school he felt like an outsider, never actually fitting into any group. So he focused on his studies and, although no genius, he worked hard and passed well enough to advance with reasonable grades. He chose accountancy, doing it by correspondence, and working in the day in a firm of accountants. However as he progressed in his chosen profession as a Chartered Accountant he began to gain respect. His professional career steered him to the audit division of PriceWaterhouseCoopers and he was assigned to Easy Insurance Group, an insurance company which was suffering financial stress.

Because of his audit work at EIG he built some key relationships. Then, in his early thirties, he was offered a job at EIG, as a finance manager. He accepted readily. There he rose through the ranks quickly and now as Group CEO he suffered no bullies. In fact, if anything, he became a bully himself, delighting in dishing out punishments. So when he was requested to complete his personal banking details he refused. Nobody was going to bully him now. The very idea of anyone questioning him was so alien to him as he had been a respected businessman for more than two decades.

These thoughts ran through his head as he faced the spotlight again. What was in store for him now? What tactics were going to be used? He knew he was mentally prepared for any assault. He waited. The voice had been silent. Did they think they could wear him down? Although he missed being back in his beloved office, he would remain patient. And despite it being contrary to his nature, this ability to wait for his opponents to show their hand had served him well during the years and he was not going to abandon it now.

An electric current suddenly pulsed through his body and he almost had a heart attack. Franks was rattled. He expected the voice to say something but there was simply eerie silence.

"What's going on?" asked Franks, his voice strident.

Silence continued for another minute and Franks feared he would be given more electric shock treatment. He held his breath and then began some deep breathing. He was not a patient man. He hated waiting.

JJ knew that John Franks was impatient and he wondered when the time was right to proceed. He decided to wait another five minutes to heighten the tension. He brought the special microphone which distorted his voice to his mouth. He was ready. The voice said, "Are you able to answer truthfully now?"

Franks said, "Yes, just get this business over with."

"Tell me about James Johnston and what really happened in New York prior to his departure from EIG."

Franks looked to the side of the spotlight and saw nothing but dispersed light. Eventually, considering all the facts, he decided he had nothing to lose. "Johnston had been asked to carry out a specific assignment in New York. His brief was to help a new finance head to understand how the numbers came together and to make him feel welcome and able to respond to our special requirements."

Silence.

Franks continued, "But he went beyond his brief and began to investigate all manner of accounts. This didn't please the US CEO who complained to me and I had to decide what was more important to the corporation – the findings from an overzealous employee or the support of an executive, integral to the business, one who was responsible for a sizeable amount of revenue and profit."

Another moment passed then the voice spoke. "Did the fact that you had substantial worthless assets in the US operation have no bearing on your decision?"

"How do you know about that? That's insider information. You must have known Johnston. So that's what this is all about."

The voice continued, "You didn't answer my question."

Franks considered his response. What did he want? An apology. And what good would that do now. Johnston was dead. "The business side of things was the province of my key executives, not Johnston. He prepared a report which made some quite impossible recommendations. He had to go. He was not authorised to carry out an investigation, especially as the executive committee had to rectify a situation which could have brought the group to its knees. You obviously have no understanding of these matters either."

A short sharp electric shock was discharged. Franks felt drained when it was over and he wanted this band of gangsters to be severely punished. After a while, the lights were extinguished. Footsteps approached and a glass of water was poured over his head and face.

A while later, time that Franks had no concept of, lights on again, the voice continued. "Last time I spoke with you, you said that Johnston had been dismissed because he wasn't ambitious enough."

"I said that because there was no other way to defend the decision to the broader employee body. It was expedient. I don't have to explain my decisions to you or anybody else. What I do is for the benefit of the company. Always has been and always will be."

"Okay Mr Righteous. For making that decision which was both immoral and commercially incorrect you are going to be fined a dollar amount. You will provide your bank details and access codes to us."

"I will not," Franks stammered. His face was red with rage. How dare this impertinent bastard make this suggestion.

The belt covering Franks midsection was activated and another electric shock was delivered. The cuffs securing his wrists to the chair and the leg irons cut into his skin. A moment later Franks was breathing heavily and clearly frightened.

The voice persisted. "Well then, are you going to continue to be stubborn?" Franks said, "I don't know those kind of details."

"So how do you carry out your electronic banking?"

"I log on to the site, use my password and review the accounts I have. But I don't know the account numbers from memory."

"That's not a problem. We have a laptop computer and one of my colleagues will watch you while you access the site. Then you can provide the information. Got it?"

Franks nodded. "And what happens to us?"

"Nothing for the time being. You will be advised in due course."

Franks, weakened by the ordeal, was escorted back to his room. Soon thereafter two hooded men arrived. The taller one had a laptop which he thrust into Franks' hands. The other man held a pistol. They watched while Franks accessed his Commonwealth Bank account and transferred the sum which the voice had nominated into an external account. They threatened the life of his wife if he didn't comply. They seemed to know all about his personal circumstances, where he lived, what the Franks' did in their spare time, probably even what brand of beer he drank. Someone had done some serious research. He clicked the appropriate lines and finally typed in his password.

The entire operation took three minutes. The men departed.

Franks went to the bathroom. He peered at an unshaven face and worry lines. He looked ten years older and he needed his blood pressure medication. Of course he had mentioned this to the girl days ago and she said she'd pass on the message. But nothing had happened.

He was emotionally exhausted and very angry. There had to be some way to deal with this situation. If only his team were with him. They could brain storm as they did on a regular basis, sessions which he delighted in, to arrive at a solution – that's what business was all about. But the isolation and infernal waiting was breaking down all resistance. He almost wept but he controlled himself.

CHAPTER 39

Day 11

His fingers traced a line along her right thigh and she closed her eyes. He began to explore the soft skin with his tongue and felt her stiffen a fraction in anticipation. Continuing on, he gripped the ample flesh around her buttocks and soon his tongue made her moan in delight as it searched and then discovered her sweet spot. Afterwards she rode him to fulfilment and they lay side by side, spent but feeling relaxed and happy.

Eventually she glanced at him and asked whether he was going to carry out his morning routine.

JJ found Angela's hand and squeezed. "That was better than my usual daily exercises and probably had the same value aerobically."

"I bet," she laughed. "You're just trying to make this your morning ritual, aren't you?"

JJ smiled and squeezed a little harder. "Sounds like a good idea to me. The exercises I don't mind but the running takes up too much time during the job."

They rolled together so that JJ was holding Angela loosely with his lips touching her forehead. For the next ten minutes they enjoyed the warmth of each other's bodies as the gentle breeze wafted in through the open window of the top floor of the apartment block. From this level, the eighth, Coogee beach was clearly visible.

"You seem pleased with something," Angela said after a while, shifting position slightly. "I guess," he said. "It's mainly you but also the job."

"It's going according to plan then?"

JJ kissed the top of her nose. "Yes, the funding has been sorted now and I don't owe your dad any money plus he's made a handsome profit."

"What do you mean?"

"As you know we asked all the hostages, under duress of course, to provide bank details. Only Franks couldn't recall his details precisely. This information was given to your father who employs or knows all sorts of useful individuals. He said he'd get one of his people to use the specifics to transfer funds out of their account to a foreign bank account. Yesterday we had Franks carry out a transfer to another Australian account from where they will be funnelled overseas. "

"Will that get Dad into trouble?"

JJ pulled her closer and hugged her. "Of course." He waited to gauge her reaction and when there wasn't any JJ said, "No, there's no danger as the funds can only be traced to a tax haven such as the Cayman Islands or Panama which won't disclose details of the account holder. Your father and I discussed this at length. Funds won't necessarily be transferred from all accounts and certainly not all at the same time."

"Why is that?"

"There are some in the team of hostages innocent of wrong doing and they will only be inconvenienced by being holed up for a time. Others who I believe are guilty will be subjected to a financial penalty."

"Wow. You're playing jury and judge, aren't you?"

"Maybe it can be construed that way. Let's wait to see whether I can prove my suspicions." Angela pulled away. "I don't like it. You're playing with fire."

"I admit there is some risk but what worthwhile proposition doesn't. You do see that?"

They dressed in silence. Angela walked to the window. "I'm going for a walk. It's a beautiful day."

As they took the elevator down, JJ asked, "When does your father refurbish this block?"

"I'm not sure but sometime in the next three months."

When they reached the ground level, Angela wandered out the door and half waved to JJ. He wondered what was amiss. She obviously perceived the funds transfer as either too risky or simply wrong. There wasn't much he could do at present as he watched her saunter off down the hill. But he needed to resolve it satisfactorily. He didn't want to lose her. He never fully trusted Maddie as someone with whom he could relate to or explain his ideas. She was pleasant enough company and would make some guy a fine companion because that's what she desired. She simply wasn't JJ's type, either physically or temperamentally. She was a woman who has too many personal issues to deal with and she displayed discouraging signs of random moodiness. And then there was the possessiveness, something which only raised its ugly head towards the end of their association. Angela, on the other hand, was an easy going individual without too many complications. She was honest and she had a great sense of humour. So why had she literally stormed off? Perhaps when he got to know her better, she too would reveal traits which were irrational. Women!!! He couldn't imagine living without them, yet to live with them might well be even more hazardous. He couldn't dwell on the Angela puzzle now because there was an objective he had to pursue and the distraction was unwelcome.

JJ, steeling himself to concentrate, turned away from the door and proceeded to the control room outfitted with surveillance screens. He asked Tony, "Any problems during the night?"

Tony yawned. He covered his mouth and spun his chair around. "Most of them slept all night.

A couple read and Jennie wept a little. I think the confinement is getting to her."

"Ok. Tony, you go and have some sleep. Jack and I will carry out the breakfast run."

"What about Angie?"

"She's getting some air. We'll give her a break."

Jack wandered in with a basket of pastries and bread. "Hi, want any of this before I organise the stuff into trays?"

Tony grabbed a Danish and JJ shook his head. JJ said, "Let's do the business before we enjoy our breakfast."

After all the deliveries were made, JJ called Angela. "Are you coming back for breakfast?"

"No, I'm going to have a coffee by myself and think."

JJ said, "Sure, take your time." Angela hung up.

Jack looked up from his coffee. "You got woman problems, boss?"

"She just needs some space." JJ studied Jack who was a young man who didn't often ask these kinds of questions. JJ wondered whether he too was having doubts about the assignment. The operation was more than a week old now and it was only natural for people to get jumpy. "How are things with you? Want to go back to Nick's?"

"I'm cool. Doesn't bother me much. I'd rather be doing this than some other menial job Nick would get me to do. It's actually quite exciting, this job."

"That's great. With any luck it should be coming to an end soon," said JJ who turned away and began to examine the flats using the internal CCTV. He had no idea how close to the end they were but he needed to sound confident in the company of his troops.

CHAPTER 40

Day 12

Detective Constable Braxton and Detective Sergeant Morris came into the interview room together. They both took a chair facing JJ across a table. Morris turned a tape recorder on and said, "Right. Please state for the record your full name."

JJ was unshaven and looked a little unkempt. He had been concerned when Angela had not returned to the apartment block and this concern was compounded when he had not been able to raise her when she didn't answer either her landline or mobile. At first he felt he just needed to give her some breathing space but then reconsidered. Something may have happened to her or perhaps she had gone to his apartment. JJ drove to his Bondi flat to which he had given her a key only a few days earlier when they were in the heat of the operation. He wanted to see whether she had taken up his invitation to visit any time. A call to her home suggested she hadn't gone there either.

Not long after he had checked out his mail and the fridge, JJ heard the loud thump on the front door. At first he considered not responding but his car was parked outside so that would have been foolish. Looking through the peephole he saw a police badge held up. Seeing the detectives when he opened the door almost gave JJ heart failure. How had they known? What had gone wrong? One of the plainclothes men then informed him he was requested at Police Headquarters. They allowed him to put on a fresh shirt before escorting him to City Central near Darling Harbour.

JJ was taken into a room with no windows, a table and some chairs. He was left alone for a few minutes before a male and female entered. They took chairs across the table from him. The woman asked his name after starting a recording device.

JJ looked at the female detective who was an attractive brunette and said, "Jordan Johnson."

"No middle name?" she enquired.

"No middle name," he said.

"Where have you been for the past week?"

"On holiday," JJ said, glancing at the silent male policeman who was a healthy specimen and someone who obviously worked out.

"And where did you go?"

"I took a car trip up north."

"Where precisely," Morris persisted.

JJ again glanced at Braxton who was observing his face closely. He knew that they wanted to assess whether he was nervous or agitated but he said, calmly, "I enjoy the beach so I decided to drive to a number of beaches up the coast and hang around for a day or so and then move on. I had no specific plans."

"So you just decided to take leave without any plans?" Braxton said, looking straight into JJ's eyes.

"Yes."

"It's a little cold to be going into the water," Braxton persisted. "Not for me. I've spent time in the UK recently."

Morris intervened, "It still seems strange for you to take a vacation without any plans. Is this normal for you?"

"Originally I planned a three week break so that I could do a few things around the place but..."

"Like what?"

"Painting the bedroom, cleaning up my book and music collections, that sort of thing."

"So what happened?" Morris prompted.

JJ shifted his position until he was comfortable on the hard chair. "I was going to tell you before you interrupted. I had a change of heart when it struck me that I wanted to have a complete break from Sydney. I needed to have some fun first. So I simply drove off, up north."

"Where did you stay nights?"

"Just any old motel that I saw when I'd travelled enough."

"Names?"

JJ had driven North enough times to know of cheap motels and he gave the detectives three names which they could check out. He mentioned spots in Port Macquarie, Coffs Harbour and Byron Bay.

Braxton said, "I'll check these out with your credit card details."

"The amounts weren't significant," said JJ, "so I paid in cash."

Morris pulled at her ear and studied JJ for a moment. "Mr Johnson, the company informed us that you took three week's vacation so why have you returned in less than two weeks?"

"I still plan to do the other things like I said. I also want to socialise and visit some nice restaurants in Sydney as well as frequent some night clubs, see movies, stuff like that."

"Why would you take three weeks off if you have no real holiday booked? Seems somewhat suspicious, don't you agree?" Morris seemed pleased with herself.

JJ peered at the sterile surroundings and figured it would be much worse in a prison cell. "I wanted some time to myself which is why I chose to go driving and surfing up the coast. Now that I've had that break which allowed me to get away from people and work, I'm ready to have some fun with some mates. I don't have specific plans but I intend to visit a mate in Wollongong and then hang out with some guys at clubs and pubs."

"Why did you want to see the schedule of management and Board meetings at EIG?" said Morris, changing the subject abruptly.

"That's a fairly routine request when carrying out a review of risk management governance."

"Can you explain further?" interjected Braxton.

"Communication of risk issues is an important part of the business. Establishing how often this communication occurs is useful. Routine agendas are also studied to ensure the appropriate topics are discussed."

After a few more questions, the detectives let JJ leave. On his way out Braxton said, "We may wish to speak with you again so don't leave the state."

JJ didn't respond. He now knew they had been watching his house and he suddenly knew that Maddie must have given them reason to talk to him. Luckily for him he had asked questions of her which were acceptable enough in his line of work. But he realised he had to be extra vigilant and ensure he wasn't followed back to the block. And the problem with the disappearing Angela was beginning to worry him.

After the interview was concluded, Braxton and Morris went into Donaldson's office.

Donaldson had his feet on his desk and he seemed steeped in thought.

"Are we interrupting boss?" said Braxton with a smirk he was unable to disguise. Donaldson removed his feet and sat up straight. He grumbled. "What have you got?" Morris summarised their interview with Johnson.

Braxton added, "We'll speak with his neighbours, talk to the motel staff and check out his mobile which we've retained."

Donaldson waited until his two detectives had completed their briefing. "Good. You might also examine available CCTV for evidence of his so called whereabouts. This may be difficult but I guess we need to check all avenues."

After taking a long and torturous way back to the block JJ told Tony and Jack to make sure they weren't followed when they left the block of apartments and that they should always monitor the people around them.

JJ had been asked to leave his mobile with the detectives but he had been careful not to use his regular mobile whilst the operation was in play. He'd kept his business mobile, a special one he'd purchased for this job, in the bedroom upstairs.

JJ took a couple of beers from the control room fridge and went upstairs to have a break and think through the next leg of his plan. When he stepped off the elevator he looked about and noticed the sound emanating from his room. He considered calling down for back up but decided against it. If there was a trap he doubted that they would be lying in wait playing old Beatles music. He entered the apartment and walked through to the lounge as quietly as he could. His spirits lifted when he saw Angela seated on the sofa, legs tucked under her cushy bottom. She was reading a magazine. He padded across the carpet and stood in front of her, waiting for her to look up.

Finally she did raise her head and smiled. "Sorry I've been hard to reach but I just went to my place and slept. I switched my mobile off and ignored the phone."

JJ went over to her and embraced her. "I thought you'd run off."

"No, I should have called you but I wanted to work out where we went from here. We've been going too fast and the situation, the pressure, may have been responsible. I needed to see things more clearly."

"Right," he said, "I understand. You thought once this was over we'd go our separate ways, that this was simply a crime fling, like a holiday romance."

"Something like that."

JJ informed Angela of his invitation to the police station and that for some reason they had found him from HR records which listed personnel who were currently on leave. He decided not to make mention of Maddie's possible tip-off. "They're probably checking on all individuals in this situation. Makes sense. They have precious few leads, I imagine, but we must be very careful."

"What does that mean?"

"The four of us must always come and go by different routes, just in case someone notices too much activity here."

Angela said, "There are not many people about when I go to buy supplies."

"That might be true but we have to work professionally and that requires us to do everything in such a fashion so as to minimise risk. It also means that as I'm a possible suspect I cannot be associated with you or Tony and Jack in public until this is over."

"Okay. How soon before we can finish this?"

"I think I'm getting close. Maybe another four or five days." JJ said, "I need a shave and a shower before anything else."

JJ felt refreshed after the shave and relished the hot water running down his back. He'd discovered over time that his most original thoughts and most inventive ideas were born when showering. He had no clue why this was but accepted it now without question. Hence he spent a good ten minutes thinking, letting the running water draw inspiration from him. Finally he stepped out onto a bath mat and used a large towel to dry. Next he dressed in newly laundered clothes. He was set for the day. He had his schedule of interviews, as he preferred to regard them, fixed. He also knew how he would arrange the questions.

He left Angela in the flat while he went down and got himself organised in the control room. Then he asked Tony and Jack to get Tim Tennyson. Knowing he could be trouble they were prepared. Jack opened the door and Tony entered only when Tennyson was visible. Then they got him to spread his legs with hands held above him. Tennyson was thoroughly searched.

With hood over his head and gun pointed at him, he was marched to the interview room.

JJ who had left to get some coffee returned to see that Tennyson was properly restrained. It never hurt for the interviewee to wait a while, letting doubt and intrigue play upon the mind. JJ had read books on interrogation techniques and applied his own approach to some trusted methods. Even without the spotlight, JJ was able to see his victim with the night vision goggles he kept in the desk drawer in front of him.

Tennyson sat there, looking ahead.

CHAPTER 41

Day 12

Tim Tennyson was nervous. He had been searched and man handled and he feared for his life. He knew that the person behind the voice had intimate knowledge of his business affairs and wondered how he had managed that. Only John Franks knew some of the details and he felt certain that Franks wouldn't disclose the truth. Unless Franks had been threatened or tortured.

The voice finally said after the spotlight was turned on, "Good morning Mr Tennyson."

"Good morning."

"Did you sleep soundly?"

"What is this? Since when have you taken an interest in my wellbeing?"

The voice waited a moment before continuing. "Ok then we'll get back to the business at hand. I would like you to tell me what James Johnston really discovered when he visited you. I don't believe for a moment that finding shonky investments would make you react the way you did."

Tennyson became alarmed. Perspiration was running down his back. "I don't know what you're talking about."

"We have elicited interesting information from Mr Franks and need to corroborate it."

Tennyson wondered for a moment whether a special police group was behind this. He knew his rights. He was an American citizen and entitled to legal protection. "I'd like my lawyer to be present."

The voice laughed. "Where do you think you are?"

"You can't do this," Tennyson whined.

A brief electric current ran through Tennyson's body. This left him limp. He was escorted back to his one bedroom flat. There he slumped onto the bed and wailed. He was going insane. What was happening? He couldn't take much more.

Was this the end of his life? He was fifty-one years old and he had almost reached the pinnacle, everything he had worked towards and dreamed about. What cruel God would do this? Not that he was religious but he had been brought up a Catholic in Ireland and his parents were God-fearing church- going folk. They had been dead for more than ten years now and he had not been a devoted or dutiful son. Was this punishment from above? He didn't really believe it but was it possible, he wondered.

CHAPTER 42

Day 12

Lieutenant Stephan McPherson had had one of those days which he would rather forget. Nothing had worked out for him and to top it off he couldn't recall making progress in any of his cases. And the weather had been wretched too, cold and windy and unpleasant. He just wanted to go to bed. It was ten after seven when he opened the front door of his apartment and announced to his wife he was home.

Ingrid shouted hello and said she was in the kitchen. After dropping his coat and boots in the entrance way, McPherson wandered in to find his wife taking out a dish from the oven.

"Smells great," said McPherson, "I'll grab some wine."

After placing the dish of lasagne on the straw coaster on the large round table, Ingrid walked over to him and kissed him on the cheek. "Hi, good day?"

"Don't want to talk about it. It was a nothing day except..." McPherson cursed silently.

"What?" she said looking concerned. She was a big boned woman with golden hair and fine Nordic skin, inherited from her ancestors who came to New York from Sweden a generation ago.

"I forgot all about it but I got the results on my Aussie mates' case. I have to give him a call."

"Can it wait until after dinner?"

McPherson hugged his wife. "Of course. I'm hungry as a bear."

They enjoyed the meal, the wine, a not so smooth Cabernet Sauvignon, and afterwards some coffee with a slice of cheese cake. He helped Ingrid clear the table, a task he enjoyed, as it allowed them to chat about the day. He discovered Ingrid had visited her sister in Brooklyn. Then, when the chore of washing up had been completed, McPherson worked out it was afternoon in Sydney and he called Donaldson. After dispensing with the small talk, McPherson said, "Our computer guys got some stuff on Tennyson's home computer. The office computer was clean but his personal computer contained hundreds of images of underage girls in various poses."

"Child porn?"

"Some, yes but it appears that he took many of the photos himself. In fact he actually took some of himself with girls in compromising positions."

"So he could be in trouble?"

"You bet. If he returns to the States, he will be arrested."

"Thanks, Steve."

McPherson ended the call and saw Ingrid tidying benches and organising breakfast dishes for the following day as he often left early for the office. He walked up to her and put his arms around her. "Why don't you leave that for now? I can think of better things to do."

She pushed herself into him. "I bet you can. But I thought you had a lousy day?"

"Suddenly I feel terrific and I have something in mind which will improve my day immeasurably. And you are the focus of my inspiration."

She turned to face him and they kissed passionately. She said, "You are in a better mood. Was it that phone call?"

"Partly. We got some evidence incriminating a high flying insurance executive. I hate those guys."

"Why?" She looked into his eyes.

"Because the Wall Street types always wriggle out of everything, no matter what mess they've made and who they've hurt."

"Was he on Wall Street? I thought they were kidnapped in Sydney?" McPherson smiled. "You're being pedantic."

She led him to the bedroom and they made love for an hour. Afterwards, McPherson fell into a deep sleep.

Day 13

Donaldson woke the next morning at 5:55am. Jessie was fast asleep, lying near the edge on the right side of the bed. Donaldson swung out of bed and relished the freshness of the morning. He thought about McPherson's call the previous late afternoon and, as he shaved and showered, he contemplated the situation. Was the fact that Tennyson had an interest in young girls a factor in this case?

He stepped out of the shower and took the left hand side towel from the heated rail and used it to dry himself, top to bottom. He enjoyed the morning ritual. He was a man of routine and he loved the quiet in the early mornings.

Dried, he selected a gray suit from the wardrobe, a blue shirt from a dresser drawer and a striped blue and red tie from his tie rack which held nearly twenty ties, most now thoroughly out of date. His son, married with children, often told him how old fashioned he was in the fashion stakes. He viewed himself in the mirror, scowled because he didn't measure up to his view of himself as tall, muscular and fit. Instead he saw a man with a disturbingly few salt and pepper hairs on top, a slight paunch and a face which was tired and decidedly older than the thirty five he felt inside. He moved away in disgust, through the bedroom and into the kitchen where he made himself coffee and a piece of toast. During this time he wondered whether any of the other kidnapped persons were involved in shady dealings. In his experience, few people measured up to their public persona. All had secrets which needed to stay hidden.

Then he wondered about himself. How was he perceived in the world at large, by his colleagues, by his wife, by his son and daughter? What secrets did he have which he needed to hide to represent the image of a decent man? None, he concluded. He was a boring bugger.

He drove through light traffic to his office.

Finally when he settled and viewed his emails and other incoming mail, he was ready to deal with people. Then, at his familiar Police Headquarters in Day Street, Sydney, Detective Inspector Donaldson set about organising a meeting in the large conference room. At 9am when all the required staff had arrived, he addressed the Strike Force, revealing what he had learned about Tennyson. "We need to consider whether this is a possible motive," he concluded, "although it may well be purely co- incidental."

A young man in the middle of the gathering, arms folded across his chest, offered, "Why would a kidnapping of nine people occur if only one guy had done something against the perps?"

Donaldson looked around the room to see whether this question had further support. "That's a good question, Barry. And the answer is I don't know. But what I do know is that we have another line of enquiry to follow up. Perhaps we should be checking each victim's history for any connection to a common individual. Perhaps others in the group have done something for which the kidnappers are striking back."

Braxton who was closer to the front stroked his chin in contemplation. Finally he looked at Donaldson and said, "I agree with that. We've been waiting for contact but none has come. We know that money has been extracted differently from the usual cash demand most kidnappers make. So looking closely at the people abducted makes sense. But how do we do this? We've already interviewed the families of each of these people."

Donaldson nodded. "You're right but let's check the databases to see whether any of these people has a record. Unlikely but it's necessary to ensure we know as much as possible. Then we need to re-interview the families from a different angle with the focus on the victim rather than who might have something against him or her."

The room stayed quiet but Donaldson could see from the body language that this approach was acceptable. "Right then, Jane, you co-ordinate the group and let's get on this."

"Yes sir," she said.

CHAPTER 43

The Past

The music was deafening and the place was jumping with mostly lean and fit bodies. It wasn't really a hangout for stodgy business types. Tennyson was in fine spirits though as he ordered drinks for his party of four. Mark Hovein was up gyrating on the dance floor with a woman of indeterminate age and appeared to be having a great time. John Franks was seated opposite Tennyson but seemed keen to engage James Johnston, sitting beside him, in conversation. Johnston who had also been invited out by Franks at the last minute seemed engrossed in the place, eyeing the dancers' bodies with an analytic passion, something Tennyson found irritating.

Tennyson downed his whiskey on the rocks and signalled to a passing waiter for another. He had consumed a few and he was feeling great. He saw that Franks had stopped trying to battle the noise to talk, had leaned back and appeared grumpy. He guessed that Johnston had only been asked along because he had mentioned something about irregularities and Franks didn't have the time to listen back at the office. Franks and Tennyson had been deep in planning another US acquisition, one which would give the group a very prestigious profile in the United States.

When the group of key executives had finished for the day it was already after ten o'clock. Luckily they'd been supplied with sandwiches for dinner or the effects of the alcohol would have reacted earlier. As it was some of them began to show signs of intoxication already. The disco was close to the American Headquarters and one Tennyson frequented from time to time with EIG guests near and far and certain clients. He felt Franks deserved some fun but wanted to give the boss some respite from work. Franks would work the night through if he were allowed; such was his passion for the business.

After more drinks and laughing at inane jokes, Tennyson paid the bill and had his three colleagues follow him. He hailed a cab and gave the cab driver an address while the others struggled to get into the vehicle. The yellow taxi sped through lower Manhattan and up Fifth Avenue and along west Central Park until coming to rest in a side street. The men waited for a moment surveying the dimly lit street while Tennyson checked that they had the right address. The building immediately outside looked like any other building in a street, a non-descript residential block.

The four men poured out of the vehicle and Tennyson, feeling light-hearted and extravagant, handed the driver cash, including an over generous tip. After ascending the stairway two levels, Tennyson knocked on a door. A moment later, after somebody apparently peered through the peephole, the door opened. A lady in her thirties led the men through to the back where a number of women were lounging about.

"Boys, take a seat," the lead lady said. She wore black see-through lingerie covering a taut body, towering heels and a flirting smirk.

When they were seated, Hovein whispered to Tennyson, "Is this a brothel?" Tennyson smiled, "No mate, this is a chocolate factory."

Women then began to parade before them. Tennyson urged his companions to choose a lady if they wanted. He simply sat back and took in the sights. After a while only Johnston remained seated next to Tennyson who got up and went into another room without choosing anyone.

Tennyson didn't like Johnston because he was a numbers guy and all these types ever did was nitpick, worry about expenses and sound superior when finance was discussed. Did they run a business? Did they motivate managers so that revenues increased? No, all they did was point out that profits were less than budget and that the company executives spent too much. Well, let him sit outside and wait while the three of them had some much needed recreation. Tennyson couldn't figure out whether Johnston was being moral or tight. But it didn't matter. He could watch as women were whisked away by other men. Tennyson didn't care what the prick did as long as he stayed away from him. This was an exclusive club known to only a few prominent businessmen who were only admitted by referral from another captain of industry. Each individual's particular tastes were noted and catered for. The establishment knew what Tennyson enjoyed and arranged a private room for his indulgence. Franks had chosen a fair skinned blonde whilst Hovein was lured by a slim Indian with soulful eyes.

Tim Tennyson felt good. He was king in this part of the world and he relished being able to demonstrate to the likes of Franks how well connected he was. He knew that Franks enjoyed female attention and it wasn't the first time he and Franks had been out on the town. But it was the first time he had brought anybody to this establishment from EIG. Once this deal, the acquisition of a prominent insurance brand, was cemented, Tennyson would be able to do anything he liked.

He could imagine being in charge of the entire EIG group soon and he knew he had leverage. He would remind Franks of what he had achieved for the group, of the businesses he had recommended, after suitable research, as fine acquisition prospects. Occasionally you bought a dud but that was part of business in this fast paced environment. At least he had the guts to make decisions. If it were left up to the Johnston types, after all the due diligence they would carry out, the opportunity would be missed.

Suddenly the front door opened and there stood Johnston, aghast. He stood there for what seemed a long time, several minutes, but it was only twenty seconds. He left without a word. Tennyson never had the chance to see Franks, Hovein or Johnston again as they flew out to Sydney the next morning. He took a cab home after the interruption, unable to continue his sport. He tried to think what he could do to mitigate the damage. He spent a restless night and eventually came up with a plan to discredit Johnston.

Tennyson's thoughts dissipated as he placed his toothbrush down.

Not only was the bathroom a dump but an insult to his status. He looked up at the mirror and saw his reflection. His face, normally always clean shaven, was now rough with bristle. He didn't bother shaving every day at weekends in New York but here he had no choice. Shaving gear wasn't part of the deal. His life had been disrupted from one of sheer joy at the prospect of being a major captain of industry to possible disgrace. There was no way he could reveal what really happened in that private chamber to the person behind the voice-distorted microphone.

On closer inspection of his face he noted it was beginning to show signs of strain. His usually perfectly set hair was also now a mess, strands hanging loose. He didn't care. He wanted this nightmare to end. He doubted, from the procedures to date, that he along with the other hostages were marked for death. Otherwise the gang would not continue to cover their identity with hoods and be so careful in their every move. No, they were after secrets and they could torture him and they wouldn't know how much of the truth he was telling.

Tennyson returned to the bedroom and sat down. He was bored. Breakfast had been the usual orange juice, coffee and pastry. He wanted bacon and eggs or a stack of pancakes with maple syrup. He lay back on the bed and tried to sleep but he'd had too much sleep and he felt incredibly lethargic. Then he had a thought. He jumped up and with a chair raced to the boarded up window and began to thump it. At first it felt as though he'd hit concrete, then he swung the chair in a wider arc and this time he could sense slight movement.

Within minutes two men entered and using a Taser gun rendered him helpless. The two men dragged him to his bed and bound him. They also placed tape over his mouth. They left without a word. The chair, the only one allowed to make eating breakfast at a table comfortable, was removed from the room.

Later one of the men returned to check the damage. He placed the hammer and box of nails down while he examined the boards with his fingers. He then ripped off the tape from Tennyson's mouth.

Tennyson said, "You can't keep me here, like this. Would you at least untie me?" The hooded, black outfitted man did not even glance at Tennyson.

"Please," said Tennyson, "I won't do it again."

After refitting the boards properly the visitor left and during the entire time didn't say a word.

After another few hours two hooded men, both dressed in black, returned. First, they both administered a solid blow to his midsection. They then untied him and left him doubled over. They left a note.

When he was able Tennyson crawled up the bed to where the note lay. It read, "A reminder.

You are a guest here. Any more protests, no matter how small, will attract unpleasantness."

CHAPTER 44

Day 14

The Audi pulled into the Shell service station driveway. JJ filled the car with petrol and bought Angela and himself a drink. When he got back into the driver's seat, JJ said, "Thanks for suggesting going to your flat."

Angela said, "It's too dangerous to go to yours. I'm sure it's still under surveillance. My dad knows all about that sort of thing. And the cops have probably installed some bugs to record your every utterance."

They drove to Angela's place in Watson's Bay. It was a large flat with panoramic views of the Harbour. The Sydney Harbour Bridge could be glimpsed in the distance.

"Lovely view," said JJ when they settled on the balcony. The pink and white cushions made the iron seats comfortable.

"Not bad. Dad was kind enough to buy this pad for me, particularly as I chose it. He usually likes to make the big decisions but he didn't have it all his own way in this instance." Angela smiled before disappearing.

JJ wriggled around in the solid chair and watched the activity on the harbour. Inside Angela made coffee and brought some excess pastries she'd bought earlier for the block in Coogee. She sat next to JJ and placed the tray on the little table in front of them.

After a few moments of peace enjoying the scenery, the apple turnovers and coffee, JJ said, "With any luck the final stages of my plan will be initiated later today and tomorrow."

"So what's it all about, Alfie?"

"Hey, I didn't know you'd seen the movie. Did you see the original with Michael Caine or the remake?"

"The classic with Michael Caine and Shelley Winters," said Angela.

"I've underestimated you, I have."

Angela smiled. "What, you thought I was some dumb broad with no culture." JJ laughed. "Not at all. I knew you had some culture..."

Angela slapped JJ on the arm. "So you figured I was a dummy?"

JJ laughed and pretended to edge away. "It hadn't occurred to me that you were any particular type of woman, just that you make me happy and it's nice to discover new things about you. You are marvellous, beautiful and bright as well." He moved closer and kissed her on the cheek.

"You're only saying that because I'm close to you."

"Of course. Once I'm outside I can alter my opinion." JJ stroked her arm. "We're getting off topic."

JJ finished his cup of coffee and poured some more. "This whole deal will seem corny when I tell you."

She waited, eyeing him curiously.

"It's about my father. His name was James Johnston. I changed mine to Johnson so that nobody at EIG would connect us."

Angela watched as JJ hesitated. "Go on," she said.

JJ stretched and rearranged himself to get more comfortable. He looked out to sea as he continued. "My father worked for EIG as a CFO of one of the company's divisions. Around three years ago, he was asked to visit the New York office as they had just lost their CFO and the division, much bigger than the Asian division, needed somebody to steer them through some recent large acquisitions. He set up their accounting procedures after examining the way they conducted their affairs but Dad being a perfectionist also delved into certain accounts when analysis suggested something was amiss. That's when he came across investments which had no substance. This led him to confront Tennyson who dismissed it as not significant and also informed him that Hovein said these toxic securities would come good in time and no write down was required." JJ paused and glanced at Angela who appeared totally absorbed.

"What happened next?" Angela picked up a Danish and bit into it.

"Not sure of the exact sequence but Dad then prepared a report for Head Office and the Directors. But it never saw the light of day as it was stopped by John Franks who listened to Tennyson on some pretext and my father was asked to resign."

"And he agreed?"

"He did because he was told if he didn't he'd miss out on a generous severance payout. But Dad withered at home. He felt guilty despite the extra cash he received. My mum left him because he was moping around and not much fun. And then he died prematurely from a heart attack."

"That's terrible. So that's why you want to get back at the company?" Angela pushed her hair from her face.

"There's more to it than that. Dad only revealed this to me when he was close to the end and distraught that my mother had left him. He said that EIG had a stake in a company which ran a prostitution business and which was also involved in illegally smuggled girls into the States."

"Did he have proof?"

"He was taken to a place in New York and he said it was odd that the madam seemed more than customer focused. It didn't really occur to him until he returned to Sydney. Being the sort of guy he was he couldn't let it go. He did his research and he finally discovered the link through an associate. By this time he had left the company but he was haunted by what he had seen and he couldn't let it go."

"Why did he tell you? Why involve his son?"

JJ grinned. "When mum left he and I grew closer. He wanted to warn me that not all things were as they appeared. He said he was proud of me, that to follow in his footsteps in finance was admirable, but then added that I should reconsider because sometimes there were forces in business which were ugly and that it might ruin my outlook on life."

"He said that?"

"Not in so many words but I caught his drift."

"Where do we go from here?"

"I need to find out who knew about the prostitution ring."

"Who's innocent and who's guilty?"

"Yes. The authorities would never catch them because we're dealing with well respected members of the community. And if somebody informs the authorities they will dismiss such claims as fiction but I want to know whether this information is restricted to one or two or a lot more within the company."

"Why do you think they'll talk?"

JJ raised himself and looked at the calm water. "I'm not sure anyone will but I have to try." He kissed Angela on the forehead and placed his hand on her head. "I'm going for a walk. Want to come?"

"No thanks, you go ahead."

He ruffled her hair and stepped through the living room to the front door.

A few minutes later, JJ was standing on the promenade and admiring the boats sailing out to sea. Joggers and walkers passed him. He wondered whether Angela's concerns weren't ones he should entertain. It was getting dangerous. Keeping so many people hostage and quiet for this length of time was bad enough but to imagine they would tell him what he wanted to know was potentially foolhardy. He needed to bring the whole sad business to an end.

He walked along the concrete path and reached Doyles on the Beach Restaurant, a place he would take Angela when this was all over, assuming the operation ended without him being caught or killed. The police were no doubt doing all in their power to find the hostages. Time was running out. His vacation period was ending soon and if he extended his absence, suspicion would grow.

JJ wandered back up the hill and just walked, letting the fresh air invigorate him. There was no point in worrying. What had been done was done. The next step would determine what course of action needed to be undertaken. There was no short cut. Pushing too much would elicit untruths. Better to continue applying pressure, much like a captain of a cricket team. Sooner or later something would give.

CHAPTER 45

Day 15

The sky was swollen with thick clouds and at any moment a downpour was likely. As Donaldson walked into City Central Police Station, he pondered how grimy the outside of the building was, matching the weather and his grim mood. After more than two weeks after the kidnapping had occurred, Strike Force Sigma, the daft code the computer generated for Task and Strike Force names, had come up with zip, diddlysquat, nothing.

Donaldson tossed his umbrella into the far corner of his office, removed his coat and wandered outside. In the kitchen he met Braxton who was rummaging in the cupboard for a cup.

"Good morning," said Braxton, finally able to put the blue cup under the coffee machine.

"What's good about it?" snapped Donaldson. He stood watching while Braxton dumped two sugars into his mixture.

"Like that, is it?" Braxton grabbed his coffee and said, "Are we pursuing the Tennyson link to child porn?"

"That's separate from this investigation. Unless you can find a link between that and a motive which links the perpetrators to the hostages, that line of enquiry will get us nowhere. I've told McPherson of our intention to find the kidnappers and left him to see what's to be done with Tennyson, should he survive his ordeal."

Braxton made a face like he understood then left the grumpy old man to do whatever he wanted.

Donaldson returned to his office with a cup of weak lacklustre coffee. His mood did not improve when he was reminded by the unit's secretary that he had back to back meetings from ten o'clock until lunch time.

Detective Sergeant Morris strode into Donaldson's office and he looked up from the report he was reading. "Yes?" he said.

"I may have some news. Fiona McDowell called to say she recalled something else."

"What?" said Donaldson, not tempted to change his mood setting to optimism.

"She wouldn't say. Simply said she'd be happy to provide a more accurate drawing of the tattoo she noted on one of the kidnappers."

"Good, well go and get it and then we'll sort out our strategy." He thrust the report aside, almost contemptuously.

Morris was taken aback and sensed that her superior was having one of those dark days which affects most people but police personnel more than most. "Sure. How did the forensic accounting pan out?"

Donaldson looked at her and pointed to the chair in front of his desk. "Sorry I'm snappy but part of the reason why is because I received news last night that our team could not track the funds. Whoever arranged the two known transfers to date knew what they were doing. We traced the funds to various places but they eventually disappeared in Panama." Donaldson studied his rather attractive subordinate's brown eyes which reflected disbelief. "We are dealing with a very slick team which seems to be ahead of us at every stage. However we will not give in. They must have made some mistakes. So let's hope your Miss McDowell can help."

Morris stood and smiled to indicate sympathy. Although the Strike Force had been unsuccessful with their plans to date, she realised that Donaldson, as the leader, would take the political fallout which would reflect on his career aspirations. "We'll get there sir."

Morris and Braxton took the latest data from Fiona McDowell and returned to the tattoo parlours around the inner city. Fiona had met the detectives at her home and had drawn what she now recalled. At first Morris wondered what the difference was but then saw that the snake had a distinctive cross towards the top end. When Braxton queried why she remembered this now, she said she'd had nightmares over the past few days with the attack of a fortnight ago including the image of the tattoo still haunting her. Eventually, from those dreams, she figured out that the image playing on her mind represented what she saw in reality.

Braxton wandered into the Bondi Beach parlour along Campbell Parade and noted that the shop was serving four customers. They were lounging on black leather chairs while the artists were doing their work. Nobody looked at Braxton and he waited until Morris who had stopped at a nearby shop to purchase some gum arrived before walking up to one of the chairs. “Where’s the boss?” he said.

A long haired, tattoo heavy, singlet wearing, stout man in his thirties looked up. “He’s in the back,” he said pointing to a door in the rear. “Be out in a moment. Who’s asking?”

“I’m Detective Constable Braxton.”

The man got back to his work without another word. He obviously had an aversion to the law and from his appearance, thought Braxton, had had prior invitations to the holding cells.

Morris walked over to the window and peered at the ocean. Gentle waves were visible and a few board riders could be discerned in the distance. Braxton moved beside her. “Lovely, isn’t it?” he said.

“Yes, places down here are out of our price range,” she said, “and I rarely come here but I can see the attraction. Do you surf?”

Braxton appraised his superior and wondered whether she was merely curious or whether there was some other meaning to her question. “I’ve tried it a couple of times but I don’t have the time...”

“Looking for me?”

The detectives turned and saw a big man with huge muscles confronting them. He wore a ponytail and tattoos on both arms. He looked like a bikie with attitude.

Morris said, “We’re from City Central.” She flashed her badge. “Some of our colleagues visited you a few days ago regarding a tattoo that one of your clients may have had done but the description has since been enhanced and we were wondering whether you’d take a look at the new design.”

“Ok. What is it?” the man said, not bothering to proffer his name.

Morris wasn’t interested in getting the man off side by requesting a name. No doubt he would never apply to become a diplomat. She pulled the drawing from the top pocket of her jacket. Fiona had given her a drawing scrawled on a thin piece of paper which Morris photocopied and it was the copy which Morris handed to ponytail who seemed less than impressed with this extra duty.

Ponytail regarded the image on the paper for some moments, screwed up his mouth then shook his head. "Nope," he uttered after a brief moment. But just as he was about to return the paper, he had a change of heart and walked over to his employees and asked them to take a look. The third guy eyed it curiously and said that it looked familiar. The detectives walked over and asked whether he could remember who may have requested it.

The tattoo artist, a short sandy haired man in his twenties, stood up and said, "I recall the guy who came in...oh, about three months back. Can't remember his name though."

Morris said, "Do you keep records?"

Braxton drove while Morris pondered the relevance of the information. "I just hope this guy didn't use a false name." Braxton stopped at the lights on Old South Head Road.

"Only one way to find out. I'm going to check our records for any motor or other violations and then I guess we'll let Donaldson decide whether the publication of the tattoo type in the media will elicit any responses." Morris watched a mother run after her young son and wondered what she, a career cop, was doing trying to run down lowlifes instead of running after little Johnny or Molly. She was getting to a stage in her existence where she craved a family. Time was passing.

They reached the city when the radio crackled and Morris was informed that Daniel Townsend had no record or motor violations.

"Damn," she said, "there's nothing going our way in this case."

Later, in Donaldson's office, they awaited his verdict. "Get the drawing copied and give them to the uniforms. Tell them to target the underworld informers. I think this guy is some crim who hasn't shown up on the radar yet."

Braxton took the drawing and strode out. Morris stayed behind. She stared at Donaldson who was in better spirits. "What do you think?"

Donaldson scratched his bald spot. "At least it's a start. We just need to keep working and hope something will break. I just pray it's not too late for the hostages."

"It seems odd, this case. No demands, no threats. Money extracted via electronic transfers. Will that be it? And what will they do with the people?" Morris tried not to let her sense of dejection show.

"Your guess is as good as mine. We may find bodies somewhere some day but I just can't fathom it. Why steal from only a few?"

"Could it be that the others couldn't supply details or that they didn't have a decent bank account," Morris offered.

"Let's get the fraud squad to check this out," Donaldson said. He leaned back and placed hands behind his head. "If necessary we'll get a full inventory of cash available just before the kidnapping and then have them track all transactions since."

"Will that be easy to do?"

"Don't know. I'm not a finance expert but these accounting types should be able to figure it out."

Morris left the office and Donaldson recalled another meeting he had to attend. He cursed, took a folder and walked down the corridor.

Braxton was sitting in Jane Morris' chair when she approached, her expression quizzical. Her desk was littered with junk, papers, pens, cups and files and she didn't like people looking at the mess. "What's up?" she said.

"Fancy joining me for a Chinese tonight?"

"You don't like Chinese."

"You do though," said Braxton standing to let Morris return to her seat. "So it's a date?"

"Call it what you like. What do you say?"

Morris sat down and looked up at the young man whom she liked more than she would let on. "Ok, we both need to eat, I guess."

"Great, catch you at seven, your place." Braxton walked off.

Jane Morris watched as he sauntered down the corridor. How did he know where she lived?

But he was a detective after all, wasn't he?

CHAPTER 46

Day 15

Jennie Jones had been in her one bedroom flat for more than a week, she felt, maybe even two. She had not been mistreated and she had had plenty of time to re-evaluate a number of things. Recently at work she had been so busy jetting here and there, to Hong Kong, to Singapore, to New York, to London, to Kuala Lumpur, to so many different countries delivering training seminars that she'd forgotten what it was like to be free from schedules and timetables. Each seminar consisted of a group of EIG international employees to whom the message of how things are done at EIG had to be inculcated.

The program had been devised by the Group CEO and herself with only a little input from her team of HR personnel. She prided herself on being professional and doing the best she could as she was the only female on the senior management team. Despite this, she found it difficult at times to swallow some of the crap the males handed out. Senior they might be but when it came to women they weren't much different from the young guns she met at night clubs and discos and around the traps. They all thought she was less intelligent because she was attractive, had a slim figure and wore fashionable clothes. They may not have said as much to her face but she could read between the lines in their mannerisms and gestures.

In a way, being here made her see things more clearly. However she had to admit she was curious to understand what the plan was. Why the entire executive team had been kidnapped and held here now seemed more puzzling than ever. Key banking information had been obtained on the basis that her family would be at risk if the information was withheld or false. So if they had obtained funds then what else was there, she wondered. After all, the identities of the kidnappers had been vigorously protected.

The door opened and it wasn't a meal delivery which had been regular and surprisingly good, under the circumstances. Sure the meals hadn't been five star hotel offerings but in the main they had been nourishing. The hooded men ushered her forward and she complied. Was this another interrogation and would she be any closer to knowing the point of the exercise?

Sitting down in the now infamous chair with its unusual belt binding, Jennie remained calm. The belt reminded her of a car safety belt except it was placed around her waist and not across her torso. Her hands and feet were also secured but the men did not apply undue pressure and she actually felt comfortable. It was only the fear which had prevented her from being relaxed before. She braced herself for the spotlight. She wasn't disappointed. Severe illumination blasted the room and she closed her eyes nonetheless.

The voice, a peculiar mutated sound, greeted her and she nodded hello. "How are you this morning?"

"I'd like to be out of here," Jennie said. She was exasperated. What was the purpose of the small talk?

"I can imagine. You have many important things to get back to, right?"

"Yes. My family would be at its wits end."

"You have a live-in lover and no children. What are you talking about?"

"Well, Adam will be worried."

"So if you cannot even tell the truth about the most basic matters, how can I believe you about anything else?"

"Adam is family. The bank information is correct. I don't have much in there but it is accurate data."

The voice waited a moment. Then it said, "Perhaps you can avoid a financial penalty and worse if you tell me the truth in some other areas."

Jennie became more alert. The hinted prospect of no harm coming to her made her accept that she had to pass the test. "I'll try."

"Ok. As the only female in the management team I'd imagine you would probably hear gossip about the men in the executive team from a number of employees as you travel around the company, both in Australia and abroad. Would that be correct?"

"Some, I guess."

"What I'm interested in is gossip from the US employees or about EIG's US management.

What have you heard?"

"Not much. Tim runs a tight ship. He can be rough with individuals who stuff up."

"Is that it? Do you expect me to accept that as your contribution for your release?"

"I don't know what you mean. What do you want to know?" Jennie was beginning to feel a sense of fear grip her. She thought she had mastered the captive situation but now understood that these people were after something very specific. And she had no idea what it was.

"What do you know of Tennyson's relationships? With women?"

The penny dropped. Jennie suddenly knew where this was going. "You mean his liking for the young ones?"

"Precisely."

"It was rumoured in the office that he liked not only young women but ones that looked like young girls. You know the kind, small and innocent looking."

"Did you have any actual knowledge of it?"

"No but I have noticed his selection of personal assistants and his attitude towards females at Christmas parties...that's all I've witnessed."

"Would you like a drink?"

"That would be nice."

Jennie waited while a man walked over and helped her with a bottle of water. She felt like an infant being bottle fed. When she had her fill, she was squinting into the light but could not get any real sense of anything to do with the individual who had assisted her. She had seen a couple of hooded men and one hooded female during her entire stay but, because of the dark clothing they all wore, she would not be able to identify any of them or reveal any distinguishing features. They'd obviously been very careful in their planning as well as in their execution of the operation. In a sense she wished some of the staff at EIG would be half as dedicated and conscious of performance.

The voice continued after a short break. “Who are Tennyson’s mates? I mean who normally hangs out with him?”

Jennie kept her eyes shut and let her memory take hold. She recalled a meeting only some months ago when Tennyson, Hovein and Waites stayed behind with Franks and wondered whether she would be invited to lunch. The others, led by Neilson, walked out of the boardroom.

The four men ignored her and she soon got the hint. There seemed to be a few factions, depending on the circumstances, but she didn’t fit into any of them. When she was travelling she occasionally met with Burton in London or Mittlehouse in Singapore but she rarely spoke with Tennyson. He had once grabbed her arse and she had looked daggers at him. Since then he avoided her and she only suffered him when in a group.

Mittlehouse and Vincent flitted from group to group. Neilson rarely mixed with Franks outside of the work environment and Waites seemed to court Franks at every opportunity.

Jennie said, “Tim and John are close and George usually tags with them. Tim does not get on with Don at all and I loathe him - Tim that is.”

“What about Hovein?”

“Mark and Tim are friendly but not great buddies from what I could see. Tim has a need for Mark’s expertise but he seems to spit people out once he’s got what he needs.”

Not long afterwards, Jennie was escorted back to her one bedroom apartment. She started to fathom that Tim Tennyson was a major concern of the kidnappers, their focus if she were not mistaken. Why the EIG Management team were all so unceremoniously spirited out from the office premises now seemed more confusing. She imagined that the risk of simply kidnapping Tennyson rather than a whole group would have been much lower. So many things could have gone wrong with the enterprise although it clearly hadn’t. And it seemed that the police had not been able to negotiate their safety. She had no idea whether contact with family members or authorities had even been made.

Jennie came out of the bathroom, having taken a shower, towelling herself. She was getting bored with being alone now. The novelty had worn off. She wandered over to the bookcase. She looked through the books and decided there was nothing she could do except amuse herself with escapist material.

Mark Hovein was the next person invited to the interrogation room to have a chat, as the hooded men put it to him when they arrived unceremoniously at his door. Hovein was not faring well and knew he had just about come to the end of his tether. He missed his wife who often consoled him with his worries. He was genuinely concerned for her and realised how much they needed each other. Together they were strong and apart he, at least, felt insecure.

The voice began. "Mr Hovein. We spoke last time of the junk assets or dud investments in the United States. What else is there in the books which is somewhat dodgy?"

"I don't know what you mean."

"If you want to see your wife again, you will be honest with me. I have spoken to the other members of the group and I know a lot more than you can imagine."

"So why do you need me to tell you?"

"Oh come now. I assume you verify information received from a source, whether trusted or not."

Hovein wasn't sure what this guy was after. He didn't believe him when he said they would see their families again but it was a glimmer of hope nonetheless. Besides even if they were murdered what good did it do anybody if he remained silent. Still he refused to cave in too easily, it was against his nature. "You sound like an auditor."

"Do you have a problem with auditors?"

"They are pests. They don't know your business and they only get in the way of a department functioning the way it should."

"We're getting off topic. Let's get back to the less than normal investments an insurance company would hold." The voice stopped.

"Are you meaning the whore houses?"

"Absolutely. I want to know everything about that aspect of the business."

Hovein's heart was beating too fast. He took a deep breath. This was dangerous territory but he may never see Tennyson again so what point would he prove if he kept quiet. "The investment constituted only a small percentage of the total...I mean the cost was small, yet the return was and continues to be significant."

"Go on."

"It was Tennyson's idea. He found that the company had acquired real estate with some of the large acquisitions and then came upon the idea that he could invest in brothels, list them as real estate in the books and show the income derived as sundry income. Again, compared to the billions of dollars the company generated, the income in absolute terms, rather than in percentage terms, from this aspect of the company's activity was immaterial."

"So the auditors wouldn't consider closer examination?"

"Correct. Only James Johnston asked me about it once."

The voice waited. Hovein thought that perhaps he had given the necessary information but was surprised when the voice said, "And what sort of women work in these establishments?"

"All sorts. I don't know exactly what you're referring to because I've only ever been to the one in New York."

'How many are there?"

"Four. New York, LA, San Francisco and Chicago."

"Thank you Mr Hovein. That will be all for today."

When Hovein was back in his one bedroom flat, he went to the bathroom and ran cold water over his hands and face. He was not feeling well. By keeping the hostages in separate units, there was no communication. This made it difficult to assess what the others had been saying. He was worried. Whatever happened, the outcome would be bad for him. He'd either be killed or, if the group survived, he would be seen as a traitor. He didn't know what to do. He had worked so hard to ensure his career was headed the right way. He had always been supportive of John Franks, had always been ready to go the extra distance if Franks required it and had hoped to be considered an invaluable and loyal employee. He sat in a chair and tried to think. What could he do to restore his position? Perhaps if the others had revealed information which he corroborated it would not be so bad. After all they had responded under duress. What was said under these circumstances didn't really count, did it?

He lay down and closed his eyes. He thought of happier times. He recalled the concerts he and his wife attended. He thought of the dinners they enjoyed in various parts of the world. His wife had accompanied him on a number of business trips and they went to many cultural places and events during those visits. He also missed his gym sessions. He attended the gym daily when in Sydney and sporadically when overseas. His employment contract included this very important perk which he had negotiated at the start, arguing it was necessary for men in his type of position to remain alert. He prided himself on his aerobic fitness. But what good did it do now? He felt thoroughly exhausted. Nothing was going right and his spirits were lower now than at any time in his life.

CHAPTER 47

Day 15

Daniel Townsend was tanning himself on the deck of his parents' house in Dee Why, one of Sydney's northern beach suburbs. His father was at work and his mother was inside making breakfast for her son who slept in until nine thirty. Daniel liked it here despite his father's questions about what he did for a living and why he hadn't a regular job to attend. His flat was a dinghy hole which he shared with some mates and he couldn't tell his parents he did odd jobs, and any odd jobs at that, for whatever cash he could hussle. The money from the kidnapping would see him right for many weeks yet.

Dan was day dreaming about being wealthy and scoring with the girls who paraded along the beach, only to be interrupted by a loud knock on the door. He ignored it. A moment later his mother appeared with a male and a female who promptly showed both of them police identification.

"Mr Townsend," said the female, "I'm Detective Sergeant Morris and this is Detective Constable Braxton."

"Yeah," said Dan, completely taken by surprise, "what do yuh want with me?"

"Interesting tattoo you have there," said Braxton, "a snake with a hammer across the head.

What's that meant to be?"

"I dunno. Saw it in a comic and liked it." Dan sat up. He was feeling a little uncomfortable. "Ok if we ask you a few questions?" said Morris.

"Not really," said Dan, gaining confidence from their gentle style. He settled back into a more comfortable position. It was a warm day but he felt a little exposed with two cops watching him. He wanted to cover up his bare chest but knew this could make him seem concerned about the tattoo he sported. He couldn't recall whether at the time of the job he had it all covered up. Of course he did – he wore a hood which reached down to the black shirt he donned. At the time of his entry into the boardroom he was completely covered. These cops were simply fishing.

Braxton took a step forward. "We can do this at the station if you'd rather."

"No, no I can talk to yuh here."

"Ok then," said Morris, "the questions are routine, ok?" 'What's this all about?"

"It relates to a kidnapping which took place in the CBD more than two weeks ago. Do you recall that?"

"What about it? I read about it."

"Please get dressed and we'll accompany you down to City Central. It's obvious you are not going to co-operate."

Mrs. Townsend came back onto the deck. "What's going on Dan?"

"Nothing mum. They want to ask questions about somethin' I know nothin' about."

"Mrs. Townsend," said Morris, "we'd like to ask your son some routine questions but it may be more appropriate to do that elsewhere. We trust you understand."

Dan's mother didn't look convinced but nodded and let Dan pass so he could get dressed. He finally appeared in scuffed jeans and a white T-shirt with the slogan 'Live today Die tomorrow' across it in large black letters.

The three drove to City Central in silence. Dan sat in the back of the Ford Falcon gazing out the window. He'd put on clothes and was annoyed that his lazy day had been interrupted. Although the weather had been mostly miserable until now, he felt cheated that he couldn't enjoy the glorious sunny day as he wanted.

Inside the police station Dan was led to a small interview room. A tape recorder was set up and he had to wait for fifteen minutes before the two detectives returned to talk to him. He was irritated by the delay but he wasn't frightened. He knew that, if he talked, Nick would not be pleased and that the Greek would get his boys to take care of him and that wasn't worth thinking about.

Finally everything was in place and Detective Sergeant Morris spoke into the recorder informing it of all their identities and the time and date of the interview. Then Dan was asked to verify his name and residential address. Dan learned that one of his share rental mates told the cops about his whereabouts.

Morris said, "Tell us where you were on 12th August?"

Dan screwed up his face. "How should I bloody well know – that was more than two weeks ago?"

"Don't you have regular employment?"

"I work jobs here and there but I've been on benefits for the past few months."

"That tattoo you wear was seen at the site of the kidnapping of EIG personnel. Do you deny you were involved?"

"You bet. I dunno what you're on about. I wouldn't do such a thing. I mind my own business and I'm a good person. Ask my flatmates."

Braxton said, "That tattoo of yours is not common and we have an eye witness who said she saw one of the kidnappers with that particular design. How do you explain that?"

"I can't. Maybe there's a mistake or there may be other dudes with the exact same one."

Morris continued, "You don't expect us to believe that, do you? We're going to have a coffee while you think about it."

The two detectives ended the recording and walked out.

Dan was starting to worry. He wished he could consult his mate who helped in the caper but there was no way he'd be allowed to make a call and it wouldn't be wise. He recalled the two of them tearing off after the job, both of them ecstatic with how easy it had turned out. The head guy sure had planned it well. Probably just as well he didn't know anything about him. In fact he'd be pushed to describe him now. And he only knew the Greek through a friend but he had heard about his reputation and he wasn't going to cross him. Apart from the name Nick, he couldn't finger him either. Dan mulled all this over and began to calm. He simply had too little information to do anyone any damage.

He settled back and wondered how long the cops were going to keep him waiting. He had no record so they couldn't blackmail him. Although he had been involved in some petty thieving, stealing from big department stores and a few minor bag snatching incidents he'd never been caught so he was clean as far as official records went.

An hour or so later, the two detectives entered the locked room. They set up the recorder again, repeated the time and who was in the room and waited.

Dan stared at them. Questions started again. They were the same ones asked differently and Dan continued to deny any wrong doing.

Morris finally ended the interview and informed him that he would be requested to come in again and that he was not to leave the city. He was also told that he may be made to take part in a line- up.

Dan left and smiled to himself. There was nothing they could do. He had to lay low though because he knew they would keep an eye on him. He also understood from some of the more experienced criminals he knocked around with that they might bug his flat and record his telephone conversations. He needed to stay out of trouble and keep his life simple. Perhaps he could stay with his folks for a while and they'd keep him on the straight and narrow.

Morris and Braxton sat together and replayed the recording. "What do you think?" said Morris.

"I think he was involved but it's possible he only took part in one part of the operation. He's not smart enough to be a key player."

Morris nodded. She said, "Let's keep an eye on him, who he associates with and who he talks to. This is the only positive lead we have."

"Nice bluff," said Braxton, "telling him not to leave the area."

"All we can do is apply a little pressure."

Braxton smiled. "Are you free tonight to pop over? I'd like to apply a little pressure myself." Morris said, "Maybe after this case is closed."

"Nice one – in another few years then." Morris grinned.

CHAPTER 48

Day 16

George Waites woke from a nightmare. He shook his head to confirm he was not in the cave he dreamt he was in. It was dark and he wondered what time it really was. Without his mobile phone and watch, he didn't have a clue what time or day it was. He was disoriented. He had a reputation for being late, not getting around to heaps of paperwork which he blamed on his heavy schedule but now he wished he had a personal assistant to advise him on his next action. He had misused the resources given to him. He often told Kay, the PA he shared with others, not to worry when she popped in to say his next appointment was in ten minutes or that somebody was asking about their report which he had thrust into his in-tray with no intention of reading it until circumstances or need suited him. If only Kay were here to tell him whether it was day or night. He lay back thinking of missed opportunities. Why had he listened to his wife who had worked at EIG before she was pregnant all those years ago to take the job offered at EIG due to a forced vacancy.

Time passed but George could not get back to sleep. Then the door opened and light entered. He expected breakfast as he was starving but instead two masked men arrived and in their possession was a dark hood. He knew what this meant and he wasn't keen to do the interrogation thing again. But he was escorted to the 'interview' room, as they insisted on calling it.

Bound with electric conducting material, George feared what was to come. The truth usually spared him and he realised that this gang knew more about issues at EIG than anyone could imagine. Surely an insider leaked information and he'd often speculated who the traitor might be but to date he'd drawn a blank. The hood was removed and the two hoods walked out the door.

The voice began as soon as the spotlight blinded him. He cursed silently. He should have learned by now what was going to happen.

"Good morning Mr Waites," said the voice.

"Morning." Waites was not going to sound pleasant. This treatment was nothing less than inhuman. These people would be convicted at the Hague if they represented a country.

"You're the Chief Risk Officer, are you not?"

"That's correct. It says so in the Annual Reports."

"But you replaced James Johnston originally, isn't that the case?"

Waites screwed up his face. "I'm a qualified accountant and quite capable."

"You worked for an insurance company which went bust, isn't that so?"

"It was a reinsurance company and the fact that it went into liquidation was not my doing."

The voice sounded a laugh. "As the Chief Financial Officer you saw things which very few people could see."

Waites felt ready to explode. He had never been interrogated in this way. To question his competence was going beyond the pale. If this character knew how much work and energy he put into his job, he would be more respectful. "It was not a finance problem although at the end we weren't able to continue our lines of credit. One deal went bad, an underwriting decision which soured. It was something nobody could have foreseen."

"That's not what I hear. But you retain the delusion if that helps you."

"You know nothing. I'm not deluded and I'm sure you don't know the first thing about reinsurance which is far more complicated than... most businesses. Johnston was considered not right for his position."

There was a pause and Waites wondered whether he had said something which made the person reconsider his attack. He had no idea why replacing Johnston was even raised.

The voice finally said, "So, as the Risk guy for EIG, you carried out your duties diligently or did you find that you were out of your depth?"

"I did my job and I was promoted on the strength of my dedication and ability. You can ask John Franks how well I performed."

"What puzzles me is how the US situation evaded you."

"What do you mean?"

"Are you saying you're still ignorant of the sham investments?"

Waites thought his head was going to pop. "There are no sham investments. We inherited some investments which you could argue should be written down but Franks discussed the position with Tennyson and Hovein and decided, after due consideration, that those investments may prove more resilient than many people believed."

"What was your role in this?"

"I was informed of their decision."

"You agreed with their analysis?"

"After the facts were presented I was happy, yes."

"I see."

"What's this all about? Are you a disgruntled shareholder? We cannot control the share price, you realise."

The voice ignored the question and said, "Investment in brothels... what's your position there?"

"Oh...well that's a decision Tennyson took without consulting the executive."

"So you were all aware after the event?"

"Johnston pre-empted Tennyson informing Franks because they had visited one of the sites. Hovein knew and I was informed by Franks at a later stage but I don't know whether anybody else was told."

"Why was that?"

"I don't know. Franks made that decision. I guess he felt I needed to know because of my visits to the States on a regular basis. Hovein needed to understand what was in the investment portfolio and Franks was the boss. "

"Thank you Mr Waites. Now you may have your breakfast."

After Waites was returned to his flat which he regarded as a not-so-friendly prison, he sat on the bed and tried to think of some way to negotiate his release. He had been successful in negotiations with employees, peers, superiors, friends, neighbours and even his wife. He was known as a talker, someone who could talk his way out of anything or someone who could persuade, in a mild, reasonable way a point of view which, in most instances, achieved the desired result.

But to date he had not been allowed to communicate properly. He was being interrogated as though he were the criminal, not the other way around. He had to turn the tables. Perhaps he could break the cycle by requesting an audience. He thought that at any moment his captors would be back with some food and drink. Was that the opportunity?

He waited. He tried to construct an opening gambit.

Then the door swung open and he saw that the female was accompanied by the usual large male with the ridiculous balaclava and black uniform. He wouldn't be able to challenge the pair physically. He waited until the tray had been set down.

The woman retreated.

Waites said, "May I ask you something?" The woman turned back but remained silent.

Seeing that she wasn't going to speak, perhaps to maintain additional security in the event that he were able to recognise her voice in some future time, he said, "Would you please ask the person who has been asking the questions whether I could have a time with him where I could express some of my thoughts?"

The woman departed without a word.

CHAPTER 49

Day 16

Detective Inspector Donaldson was roused from his sleep when the mobile phone buzzed. His wife shook him as well so he was well and truly brought abruptly back to the real world. He picked up the mobile from his bedside table after flicking on the lamp. He glanced at the clock which showed it was four thirty four. He almost cursed but restrained himself as Jessie didn't much care for foul language no matter what the provocation.

"Yes," he said as he placed the phone near his ear.

"There's been a break-through in the kidnapping case. Don Nielson was found drugged at Balgowlah."

"How is he?" Donaldson rubbed his face. Jesus! Balgowlah was on the Northern Beaches near Manly.

"He's been taken to Royal North Shore Hospital for tests. Do you want to talk to him once he's got the all clear?"

"I'm on my way."

Jessie glared at him. "What's so important it can't wait until morning?"

Donaldson shuffled out of bed, grabbed his dressing gown and said, "A hostage from the EIG kidnapping has been found. Not sure about the details but I'm going to see what I can find out."

"Can't one of your subordinates do that?"

"Jessie, I know I've been spared going to crime scenes for a while now but I instructed my people to alert me as soon as something significant occurred on this case, a very high profile case that the Commissioner and Deputy Commissioner have been bugging me about. So please be a little understanding."

Donaldson looked at his wife who simply appeared resigned. She lay back and pulled up the covers. "Give me a kiss before you leave."

Donaldson didn't bother showering and hastily flung on his clothes, got to the door, then hurried back and pecked Jessie on the cheek. He wanted her in a decent mood when he returned for whatever meal he could manage. He didn't know whether this was a real breakthrough but it seemed promising and he was going to see this through.

On the way to the hospital, Donaldson called Morris and told her the news. He also told her to bring a recorder. They met in the foyer of the emergency area of the Royal North Shore hospital and debated tactics. Morris made attendants aware of their status and were shown to a second level room where Neilson was in his own room. A policeman was posted outside.

Donaldson and Morris entered and were surprised to see that Neilson was looking relaxed and unharmed. Donaldson introduced himself and Morris. A nurse who had been taking blood pressure and other vital readings left the detectives with the patient.

"How do you feel?" said Donaldson, moving closer to the bed.

"Fine. What happened? Where am I?" Neilson was clearly disoriented and looked uncomfortable in the white gown he had been given.

"That's what we're here to find out."

"I see. Of course I'll help but I mean I cannot even remember getting here."

Donaldson said, "I was told that you were found lying on a bench by uniformed police as they were driving around. You were identified from a photo and brought here by an ambulance."

Neilson frowned. "On a bench. God. Was I drunk?"

"Can you tell us how you got to be on a bench?"

"I have no idea. The last thing I recall was having a meal – dinner. Perhaps there was something in the food which knocked me out because I can't remember the next part."

"It appears you were not mistreated," said Morris.

"By whom?" Neilson appeared puzzled by the question. "Why would anyone..."

"You do recall being kidnapped?" said Donaldson who was

beginning to feel a sense of unease.

Had his memory been wiped?

"Of course...it's coming back...oh yes."

Morris persisted, "You seem to have been well treated?"

Neilson pushed his hand through his thick wavy salt and pepper hair. "That's right. I was asked plenty of questions but I wasn't hurt in any way or physically abused." He explained how the interrogation process worked, how the men always donned masks and how he was kept in a one bedroom flat.

Donaldson listened and waited until all that was said was recorded by the machine which Morris had placed on a chair between the bed and the standing detectives. Finally he said, "So you only witnessed three people but you think there may have been a fourth person doing the interrogation?"

"If there were others I didn't see them. We were locked up and had no contact with each other and it's likely there were people behind the scenes."

A nurse entered and said, "We need to carry out more tests. Please be brief Inspector." Donaldson nodded and the buxom nurse moved out of the room again.

"Any idea of the whereabouts of this block of units?" Donaldson said.

Neilson shook his head. "No. All I know is we were placed in a large truck and drugged before landing in a room, then knocked out again to wake up in a one bedroom flat. From that point on I was given a hood to wear each time I was moved from the flat. I'd imagine the others were dealt with in a similar fashion"

Donaldson said, "Were any threats directed at you?"

Neilson said, "Look I'm happy to help but if at all possible I'd like to see my wife. I really can't think of anything which might lead you to these people."

Morris said, "Your wife has been notified and will be arriving soon. I sent a message to another colleague before we visited you."

Neilson sighed. "Thanks. I don't know what happened to the others but at least I can say I wasn't hit or threatened or anything. The whole thing seems bizarre."

Donaldson walked about and peered out the window which was useless since it was dark outside. “Were you asked for money?”

“No.”

“What about your possessions...rings, watch, wallet?”

Neilson pointed to a cupboard and asked whether someone could bring over his jacket. Morris opened the cupboard, found some clothes but not his jacket. She searched in other parts of the room and then noticed a jacket hanging behind the door. She handed it to Neilson who pulled out his wallet. He checked the contents. “Everything seems to be here, including my credit cards and the two hundred dollars of cash.” He then pulled out his watch from the pocket of his jacket. “They weren’t after our money it seems and I’ve got my expensive watch back too,” said Neilson with a note of incredulity in his voice. “Initially they took watches, mobiles, wallets etc but it seems they’ve replaced them.”

“Strange, very strange,” said Donaldson.

Morris said, “What were the questions they asked? Company secrets?”

Neilson looked away, deep in thought. “To tell you the truth they weren’t interested in client lists or internal workings of an insurance company so again I can’t see how they would benefit.”

Donaldson said. “We have discovered that funds had been electronically transferred from the accounts of two individuals.”

“I see. I don’t know why that would be. Selective stealing.” Neilson laughed. “The more I know about this operation, the weirder it gets.”

At that moment Mrs Neilson walked in. She strode over to her husband and hugged him.

Donaldson walked over to Morris who had turned away a little to allow the couple a moment of privacy. He whispered, “We need to scour all unit blocks within a five mile radius of where Neilson was found.”

Morris said, “He could have been driven to the bench from a lot further away.”

“You’re right but I’m hoping a mistake has been made.”

Donaldson went back to Neilson who was sitting on the bed with his wife beside him, holding his hand. Donaldson said, “Is there anything you can tell us which might lead us to the place you were held?”

Neilson looked thoughtful. He finally spoke. "The flat I was in was poorly maintained. It had boarded up windows. It had walls which were shabby – needed fixing and painting. I think I was held on a level up one from the room which was used as the interview room. I was hooded on the way to this room so I don't have any idea of the condition of the hallway. The interrogation room itself was large and bare save for a chair in the centre and a spotlight which was turned on when interrogations began. That's about all I can tell you."

Donaldson noticed tears escaping from Neilson's wife's eyes. She brushed them aside and hugged him a little tighter. Donaldson guessed she was pleased to see him. It took no genius to realise that these two were very close. Donaldson continued, "One last question and we'll leave you alone. Although you couldn't see the gang members who gave you food and escorted you around, can you describe their general appearance?"

Neilson turned to his wife, smiled, and turned back again. He closed his eyes. He said, after opening them again, "Let's see. One of the men was tall...say around six three. Don't ask me about centimetres. He was powerfully built but not as much as the other guy who was muscular but a few inches shorter. Both were formidable in their black outfits." Neilson paused. "The woman was much shorter, about five six I'd imagine and she had a curvy figure...big breasts but in proportion to the rest of her."

"Did you hear them talk?"

Neilson let go of his wife's hand and looked thoughtful. "The woman said a word or two and she sounded refined but definitely Aussie. The men didn't speak in my presence, just the occasional grunt. But there was a sound, I'm not absolutely certain but the sound of waves seemed to intrude sometimes..." Neilson didn't say any more.

Morris smiled. "I guess you can't recall how long you were being transported." Neilson stared at the ceiling. "Can't recall the drive to the bench at all."

"And immediately after you were kidnapped?" Donaldson asked.

Neilson frowned then said, "The initial drive in the van, yes I remember bits although we were frightened and talking kept us occupied. There were many turnings I recall and the time taken was around an hour I guess. Perhaps one of the others checked their watch but I didn't. No I recall we had our watches taken before the ride so I really couldn't say."

Donaldson squeezed his chin between thumb and forefinger. "Thank you for your time. I'll give you my card in case something else comes to mind."

"Do you think you'll catch them?" said Mrs Neilson, an attractive middle aged woman with a red tint through her hair.

"We'll get them, don't you worry," said Donaldson.

Neilson accepted the card then hugged his wife who was still teary.

The detectives walked down the hall of the ward in silence. Morris wondered why all hospital wards were white. Donaldson looked forward to his first cup of coffee. He wouldn't be able to think properly before then.

They drove to City Central with the radio on but there was no news of any of the kidnap victims when the news came on. Donaldson said, "Don't let the media get word of this for now."

"Sure."

"Jane, when we reach the station I'll drop you off and I'll take the car to get back home. I need a shower and a shave. I'll also have some breakfast as my stomach seems to have woken up."

'Okay. I'll leave some instructions for Max and then I'll cab back home myself. I can't believe there's so much traffic this early."

"It never stops," said Donaldson as he stopped the car. "Has Max made a pass at you yet?"

"No way, he's too young and I'd tell him where to go should he be so brazen." Morris said, keen to keep her affairs private.

"Of course," said Donaldson who couldn't help grinning.

CHAPTER 50

Day 16

JJ was sitting on a chair at the head of a table in his upstairs unit. He was facing his male colleagues and they waited for Angela who was getting her hair sorted in the bathroom. Eventually she appeared and the men whistled their approval.

"Oh shut up," she said playfully, taking her seat beside JJ. She didn't like being fussed over unless it was from JJ.

JJ smiled at her. "You're looking super, Angie." Angela blushed. She said, "So what's the big news?"

JJ took a sip of his coffee. "You've all done a fine job and I want to bring you up to date and inform you about our plans from this point on. The first thing I need to say is that the operation is nearly complete. That should please you all."

The two Koutslakis assistants looked at each other then returned their gaze to JJ.

Over the next fifteen minutes JJ outlined the next steps. He spoke in measured tones and made sure they all understood the plan. There were few questions and JJ felt confident his people understood how important it was to execute the plan without deviation. JJ explained the consequences should mistakes occur and evidence left for the authorities to discover. He urged them to appreciate that they would be treated without mercy should they be caught. Kidnapping was not a crime which would be viewed favourably no matter what the justification.

The time was 9:25am when they concluded the discussions. Angela waited until the two big men left before turning her attention to JJ getting him to join her on the sofa. She leaned into him and said, "I'm so glad it's nearly over. You seem a little nervous."

"I hope the others don't see it. It's important we remain confident."

"Maybe I'm just perceptive."

"Absoutely, my darling," he said before he turned serious. "The key is not to get overconfident. Angie, you make sure that any visit to the hostages from now doesn't leave you exposed. You appear to be happy that the end is in sight and this very feeling may make you vulnerable - to making a misjudgement, to displaying certain feelings. You wouldn't be the only one who, with the prospect of the finishing line, acts out of character. What this means, basically, is that you need to play the game as you have before - no perfume is to be worn that can be detected, no changes in dress or anything which might connect you to being here afterwards."

Angela said, "Ok, I won't reveal my feelings nor make any changes. Are you close to knowing what you need to know?"

"Pretty much. With luck, the last day will be tomorrow. But we have a lot of work to do before then."

"At least we have one less guest."

JJ smiled. "The transfer worked like a charm. If only other things would pan out as well. The drive to the Northern Beaches was about an hour in the early morning so hopefully no cops will poke their noses around here."

In another part of the Coogee complex, the day was beginning.

Tennyson left most of his breakfast. He was getting sick of the routine and the sameness of breakfast. In the States he always ate out and he frequented a different place most days depending on his mood. He was generally in his office by 8am but there were occasions when he arrived at 10:30am. He didn't like routine; he was an entrepreneur, a deal maker.

The door opened and the two hoodlums, his reference to the two big guys for now and it would be the same description he would apply to them later when he was back in charge, strode in. They sauntered either side of him and when he tried to resist he received a nasty chop to the kidneys. A hood was placed over his head and handcuffs applied, roughly. He was then marched to the interrogation room and forced down into the chair and shackled.

The hood was not removed, a deviation from the standard

procedure and Tennyson wondered why the change. He waited and waited. Was this another form of torture? Hadn't they got all the information they were after? Or was asking stupid questions what got them off? Sick bastards!

Some time later, perhaps ten minutes or more, Tennyson couldn't say, his hood was removed but it was too dark to see anything. The last glow of a torch faded. Tennyson expected the big spotlight to stun him so he prepared himself, keeping eyes closed.

Then a light was switched on but it wasn't the spotlight. It was a fairly bright overhead light and Tennyson, when he peeked, noticed he was not alone. Four chairs had been placed in a kind of circle and each chair was occupied by a hostage. Apart from himself there was John Franks, directly opposite, Mark Hovein to his right and George Waites to his left.

Each of the hostages looked at each other, almost afraid to speak. Finally Franks opened the exchange. "I don't know what this is all about but I suggest we remain quiet."

Tennyson saw that Hovein and Waites nodded assent. He wasn't going to conform though. "Why, what else can happen that hasn't happened?"

Franks regarded him with a look of disapproval. He realised that should anyone succeed him, it shouldn't be Tennyson whom he held responsible for this mess. To cap it off the man was arrogant.

How was it that he was suckered into acceding to many of his outrageous demands? Franks said, "You don't know what has been planned and being quiet is the best policy."

"Do what you like," Tennyson retorted, "I really don't care anymore. The bastards have our bank details and credit cards and once they've had fun with those, they'll let us go."

"What makes you think so?" said Waites.

"They're playing games, that's all. If we were to be killed, they would have done it by now.

And why all the questions? Not necessary if we were meant to die."

"There's some logic there," said Hovein.

Elsewhere in the building, JJ was monitoring the discussion whilst reviewing images on a large flat screen on his MacBook laptop. At the same time it was all being filmed and recorded by other equipment. His men had set up the room as instructed and the surveillance equipment had to be rearranged slightly so that nothing was visible to the men in the room. JJ felt the four key hostages may suspect they were being spied upon but he had no desire to confirm anything. Doubt was a powerful emotion and could play tricks on the mind.

JJ didn't know what would come of this plan but he was prepared to be patient and let it play out. By now Neilson would have been able to make his way to the authorities or home. Before letting the others go, he had to eliminate them from suspicion conclusively. It seemed that the four on view were the main culprits but he was prepared to wait a while longer to be certain the other executives had not been involved. The operation was running behind schedule and he had little time buffer but he had enough time still to work the latest strategy, he felt.

Angela entered the room and placed a cardboard cup of cappuccino on the table in front of him.

She peered at the laptop and shrugged. "Anything of interest?"

"Not yet. One has to be patient. Why don't you read your book?"

"I will." Angela walked over to the sofa and made herself comfortable.

Nothing of note happened for two and a half hours. Then Hovein said, "While we are here, tied down like animals, why not let us in on some decisions you've made Tim. Why did you buy the whore houses?" Hovein was beginning to become agitated and he thought Tennyson was the one who had brought this on all of them.

Tennyson shrugged.

Franks said, "Yes Tim, why? You still haven't explained why you carried out such a transaction without even consulting the executive." Franks had decided after some examination of the situation there was little to gain by being silent. Besides he was bored to distraction.

Tennyson looked at Franks. He snarled, "Because I was sick to death of safe and sure no return type of investments. We were being killed on our investment portfolios. We were the laughing stock of the industry."

Waites suddenly came alive, "That's not true. The CDOs earned us nothing and the fixed interest investments had low rates of return but we were in line with the US industry."

"Is that so? Well I wanted more."

Hovein said, "The amount we had in whore houses was small comparatively so a higher return did not alter the figures much. What you say is not logical.'

Now Tennyson's face changed to an almost red curtain and he shouted, "Stop it. You people make me sick. All you think about is making money for the corporation. There's more to life. I had needs which could not be expressed in a balance sheet or profit and loss statement."

Franks said, "Settle down. You're doing yourself no favours."

"I don't care anymore. You probably wouldn't have appointed me the next CEO anyway."

"I don't have the power to appoint my successor, that's the board's job. I can only recommend."

"So tell me, was I in the frame?"

Franks glared at him. He was ready to clock him. "After going against my suggestion to be quiet, what do you think?"

Tennyson continued, "What's going to happen? All our corporate mistakes have already been aired. I want to know what my chances were prior to this catastrophic mess."

Hovein and Waites eyed Franks. Was he going to reveal his choice? This had been the hot debate amongst the management team and other key personnel for months. They felt there was change in the air and all the hot money had been on Tennyson and Vincent.

"Alright," said Franks, "I will tell you on one condition."

"What's that," said Tennyson, grinning.

"Tell me whether you're into underage girls."

"Why, is that a job requirement?"

"As you said, we've been through much of the corporate dirty laundry and should we get out of this, I would no longer consider you suitable. So you can speak the truth." Franks had had enough too. This man was a criminal. How the hell had he passed muster with everyone of significance?

Tennyson waited and looked at each man in turn. He said, "I guess it really doesn't matter now. I have always admired petite women and young girls. That's what gets me excited. Everyone has their thing and that's mine. I don't consider age. I don't care if they're six or ten or fifty as long as they have a certain look."

"What look – tiny?" said Hovein.

"Yes," snapped Tennyson. "You like the Indians, so don't be critical."

"I don't discriminate. I'm attracted to intelligent and classy women. What's the age of the youngest girl you've actually been with?" asked Hovein.

"I suppose the youngest was around eight but what a beauty she was."

Hovein screwed up his face. "Disgusting."

"Have you done it with midgets?" said Waites, a large grin forming.

Tennyson looked at him with disdain. "Please, you don't know anything you fucking accountant."

Franks coughed. It was a device he used to get everyone's attention, a ploy he often used in meetings.

After a few moments, the room was again quiet. Finally Tennyson broke the silence. "I've told you what you wanted to know so tell me John, what was the deal before this kidnapping stunt?"

Waites and Hovein looked intently at Franks. They were intrigued by how this man who they had respected would handle this. Hovein no longer cared for his opinion. He realised that he wasn't so powerful after all. His bullying manner only worked in circumstances made possible by the artificial corporate settings. In the outside world he wasn't so terrifying.

Franks considered his response for a moment but then decided whatever he said would be under unusual circumstances. He would be able to deny everything later should the situation return to normal.

He said, "When I looked at the possible candidates, I had listed four individuals – you, Burton, Vincent and Neilson."

All eyes were on Franks. Waites was particularly interested in the reasoning Franks would give as he harboured major ambitions.

Franks continued. "Neilson was the first I delisted. He is older than the rest and would only be able to serve a few years. Vincent was a likely candidate because he is eager, young in outlook and prepared to do anything for the company. He's a real company man with only his inexperience in running a large business against him."

"Doesn't he have experience running the Australian Operations?" proffered Waites.

"Yes," said Franks, "but he asks my advice about many aspects of the business. He's still being minded and I worry that when I'm gone for a year he may struggle."

"So he's off the list," offered Tennyson.

"Not quite however if better all round candidates present themselves he would be overlooked."

"Which leaves Burton and myself," said Tennyson with an arrogance he was famous for.

'Which left Burton and yourself, correct. But now you've eliminated yourself."

Tennyson grinned. "Nice to know. At least I was a major contender and should something happen to Burton, well it doesn't bear thinking about, does it?"

Franks ignored him. He knew this man had an ego but he did not know the full extent of it. He was impossible. There was no way on earth he would recommend this vile creature. Having a paedophile in the executive was too much. He had to go, no matter what the consequences were. If only he had listened to Johnston. Johnston didn't know about his sexual exploits but he knew the man was unstable and dangerous, making key decisions without waiting for approval. Franks had always felt he had an eye for talent and recognised people of substance. The decision to promote this American egomaniac disappointed him. Why hadn't anyone picked up on it before the final recommendation was put forward?

Franks wondered how he was going to negotiate Tennyson's departure with the Board so that there was no taint of scandal. His first priority was to ensure that the company's reputation remains intact and any suggestion of impropriety or wrong doing by a senior executive was totally unacceptable. The Board needed to be convinced as Tennyson's stature was at the top management level. Johnson's departure required no Board approval so it had been relatively straight forward to dismiss him with little explanation required. He looked at Tennyson. Bile almost rose from him as he focused on the man.

What a disgusting human being, one who should never have been given authority over anything, let alone the reins of a wealthy division. Tennyson was the reason they were here, he felt certain. He had compromised the EIG brand and this was the worst sin imaginable to Franks. He would have given him up to the kidnappers except he considered them unpredictable.

Tennyson's oily grin sickened him. If only the kidnappers realised that nobody but Tennyson had poisoned the place with his stupidity - the ugly investment in brothels and perhaps even human trafficking. He would not lose sleep if Tennyson were eliminated. He shut his eyes. It was all too much.

Oddly, Franks believed that they would be released. There was no point to this exercise otherwise. The identities of the gang had been carefully hidden. There had been no ransom demand. It all added up to someone or a group finding out specific information. Perhaps these people were with some secret authority, like a black military operation or police outfit. That made a certain amount of sense.

The lights were suddenly extinguished.

The men were led back to their cells, each individually, albeit that the cells happened to be apartments in some abandoned facility.

When Franks re-entered his flat, he lay down and thought. He was not going to let Tennyson back into the frame. He needed to be sacked and it was up to Franks to construct a plan which would be acceptable to all, so that no scandal would attach to the company. Now at least he had something else to think about other than fretting about his personal safety.

CHAPTER 51

Day 17

A soft breeze wafted across the water and Braxton was enjoying the cool of the early morning as he walked across the Darling Harbour Bridge. At this time of day, before seven, some office workers were beginning to make the trek to their offices. But the peak period was yet to come and Braxton savoured the relative emptiness of the walkway. He thought about breakfast but wasn't really hungry. As he strode along, coffee cup in hand, he pondered what lay ahead for the day. More specifically he wondered when this case was going to finish so that he could enjoy continuing his chase of Jane Morris. She was looking more and more glamorous each time he saw her. Did she make an extra effort or was he becoming obsessed with her? He had no idea.

Strike Force Sigma had a lot on its hands. During the night, more of the CBD EIG kidnap victims had emerged from who knew where. They had been discovered in various parts of Sydney and seemed to have been dumped at bus stops or other places where members of the public would find them and report the bodies to the police. All were gathered up and transported to either the Royal North Shore hospital or St Vincent's hospital but were found unharmed except for the effects of knock out drugs.

Jennie Jones was found in Sydney's south at Cronulla, David Mittlehouse in the west at Parramatta, Doug Vincent in the far north at Hornsby and Stephen Burton in the city at Darling Harbour. All were being questioned but none could throw any more light on their captors or the location or region where they had been detained than Don Neilson had done.

Donaldson was reviewing the reports in his office when Morris and Braxton entered.

"Anything useful?" said Morris who had been forewarned. Braxton was surprised with developments as he had visited a mate the previous evening and had been out of touch as he hadn't returned home.

"No. Each one has been questioned. None could recall how they were drugged but Vincent suspected it was in their drinks at dinner. He said they were given a glass of wine which was not a usual occurrence."

"That's five of the nine kidnapped victims. What about the others?" Morris studied her boss to assess his mood. He didn't appear particularly happy with the outcome.

"So far they are still missing." Donaldson rubbed his eyes. "All of the current batch of dumped people reported that they had sessions like Neilson, sessions where they were questioned. It almost seems like the kidnappers were trying to find very specific information but it's not about anything which makes sense."

"Have their bank accounts been raided."

"That's odd too. They all report that details of their accounts were provided but funds have only been withdrawn from the missing four."

Braxton looked at Morris then Donaldson. He said after a moment, "Were the amounts the same?"

"No, they weren't."

"Do you think it's worthwhile analysing how much was taken from each account?" Donaldson said, "Do it but I can't see the relevance."

"Maybe a certain amount needed to be recovered. Perhaps they were customers of a drug lord and they owed money."

Morris smiled at his dimwit remark. "Somewhat farfetched, don't you think?"

Braxton nodded. "That would make some sense. Nothing else does."

Donaldson said, "At this point I'm prepared to believe almost anything. Get to work and see what you come up with."

A few hours later Braxton cornered Donaldson in the cafeteria. Donaldson ordered some coffee and a meat pie with tomato sauce. The two men found a table and sat down. Braxton watched while Donaldson poured the tomato sauce satchel over his pie.

"You shouldn't be eating that stuff," said Braxton, a surfing enthusiast and fitness freak.

"I know. My wife's been at me as well but I can't resist food, and bad food at that, when I'm under stress. So how did you go with the funds business? Any pattern?"

Braxton leaned a little closer. "I think so. Amounts transferred were different for each. Waites had $200,000 taken, Hovein $400,000 and Franks $1,000,000. We can't find out what, if any, funds have been taken from Tennyson's account because he lives by himself."

"Hovein had $200,000 transferred as far as I recall," said Donaldson.

"He had two lots of $200,000 taken. Perhaps Mrs. Hovein didn't think they would strike again after the first withdrawal."

Donaldson scooped up the last bit of pie and ran his tongue over his lips. "Umm. Interesting. And there were no funds taken from the others, all of whom are now safe and on the road to recovery."

"Physically if not mentally," added Braxton. "Precisely," said Donaldson.

"It seems that the four men still in captivity committed some crime against the kidnapper or kidnappers and that this is all about revenge or payment of dues translated into cash."

"Looks that way. Perhaps drugs are involved but it doesn't seem likely. I've had some of the boys shake the trees in the underworld and stir up their informants to discover whether any major debts from these people are outstanding but so far, nothing."

Braxton signalled to Morris who had just entered the cafeteria and she grabbed some food and a coffee and then came to join the two detectives.

"What's that?" said Braxton. "It's a muffin," said Morris.

Braxton said, "That's a breakfast thing, not lunch."

Donaldson laughed. "You really take the health gig all the way."

Morris poked her tongue at Braxton who brought her up to date with their conversation.

Donaldson said. "We need to go over the transcripts of the interviews with these guys and consider going back to the wives if we deem it necessary. Brax you look after Mrs. Hovein, Jane you review Mrs. Waites and I'll read Mrs. Franks' statements."

"And Tennyson?"

"I'll get in touch with my New York mate Stephen again."

While Donaldson and Morris wandered off, Braxton grabbed an apple and went back to his desk. He brought up the transcript on his computer and began to read.

Donaldson prepared an email for Lt. Stephen McPherson asking whether anymore had happened in New York on this case and informing him that all but four of the kidnapped individuals had been freed.

Morris looked at the data on Mrs Waites and realised that it was fairly sketchy. She decided to drive to Glebe herself and conduct a fresh interview.

Although it was a short drive to Glebe from Darling Harbour, the traffic made it seem a lot longer. The day was beautiful, blue skies and a pleasant temperature for this time of year, and Morris enjoyed getting out of the stuffy office. She also wondered whether it was wise to allow Braxton to pursue her. She probably should make it clear that she didn't want his attentions. But it was flattering and he was a handsome man.

Morris arrived in front of a two storey terrace which looked like it had been renovated recently.

Mrs Waites looked pale and anxious. She let Morris in once she identified herself. "Any news about George?" she said.

"No, I'm sorry. What I need to understand is how money could have been taken out of his account. The last time we asked you said that nothing had gone."

Amy Waites bit her lip and screwed up her face, thinking. "That's odd. We only have one joint account and I used it this morning and it hasn't changed since I checked it last time. Maybe he's got another account in his name. I don't worry about the finances because George takes care of the bills."

CHAPTER 52

Day 17

Lt Stephen McPherson had initiated investigations into the brothels owned by EIG without the case being requested by Donaldson or anyone else. He realised after talking to more individuals from EIG's New York office that their boss, Tim Tennyson, had used a location in West Manhattan to entertain clients. A raid was made and the NYPD discovered illegal immigrants, underage persons, women held against their will and a madam who boasted they had some cops as clients.

After reading Donaldson's email, McPherson called Tennyson's ex-wife to find which bank and branch Tennyson used. Later that day McPherson had a colleague from the fraud department accompany him to the premises on Court Square, Long Island City to seek information. At first the bank's personnel stonewalled them, saying their client's privacy was protected by law which the police should be well aware of. Finally the Bank Manager was called and he offered the officers a seat when they entered his office.

"What's this all about?" the Bank Manager said. He was a man in his fifties with short grey hair on the sides and in the few areas on top of his head where he wasn't completely bald.

The detectives informed him about Tennyson's situation and explained that funds may have been illegally transferred from his account.

Now the bank manager listened and agreed to review the account. After a moment on his computer he turned to the senior officer and informed him that one transaction of eight hundred thousand dollars had been transferred recently.

"Doesn't the bank insist on a daily limit for all withdrawals?"

said Mancini, the fraud specialist. "That's right detective unless the customer otherwise arranges," said the bank manager.

"And what did Tennyson use as his limit?"

"One million dollars."

The two detectives looked at each other. "Wow," said McPherson, "who needs that sort of cash?"

The bank manager shrugged.

McPherson thanked the bank manager for his help and wandered outside where he pulled out a packet of cigarettes and offered one to Mancini who shook his head and looked at McPherson who contemplated the revelation while enjoying a few puffs in the sunshine. "Well well, I wonder how that was done."

Mancini informed him of how easy it was these days with internet connections.

Later that night Lt Stephen McPherson called Donaldson during work hours and advised his Sydney counterpart of the visit and their findings. Donaldson whistled and explained that the transfer of such a sum fitted the trend, one whereby funds had been withdrawn from four hostages apparently for a purpose they were yet to discover.

McPherson did not know what he was talking about and didn't ask. He was more interested in closing down the brothels and laying charges where appropriate.

Tennyson needed to be arrested, that was for certain. McPherson came to the view that Tennyson would return to New York should he be released by the kidnappers who had already devised a way to obtain his money. From what he had learned, the identity of the kidnappers had been closely guarded which suggested that there was no need for the hostages to be eliminated.

He wasn't concerned with the kidnapping crime but he wanted Tennyson badly. He was someone who was guilty of a lot more than theft. He was a sleazy guy who should be punished to the max.

CHAPTER 53

Day 16

Time passed slowly and the room which kept the four men bound to their chairs arranged in a sort of circle had been relatively quiet for the past hour. Desultory conversation occurred but little more. Franks had finally got the group to remain calm. After his revelations about succession, it seemed that the men wanted to mull it over.

Waites wasn't surprised with Franks' admission and he knew that his attempts to win over Tennyson on a number of visits to the USA had been sound. He'd always prided himself on his judgement and felt good about this one as well. It was rumoured that Waites was a cold fish, outwardly sympathetic but unable to really connect with his staff whom he drove relentlessly into the night to obtain obscure pieces of information which would stand him in good stead with the powers in the organisation. He had no regrets except that some situations, like the current one, could not be controlled or contained.

On the other hand Hovein, who was not surprised that Tennyson had once been in the running for the CEO's job, was now suspicious of the move. Had Tennyson been the reason for their capture? Had he been out of line, not only in his contempt for authority within the organisation but also in his private life? Why else had all been kidnapped rather than Tennyson alone? He was no longer going to remain the meek geek. What had he to lose anyway? He doubted he would ever see his sick wife again.

Hovein glanced at Tennyson who had closed his eyes. "Tim, looks like you stuffed it good and proper."

Tennyson opened his eyes. "What do you mean?"

"Now you'll never be in charge, you despicable human being."

Tennyson smirked and glanced at the faces of Franks and Waites who awaited his response with looks of expectation. He was centre stage. He was the man of the moment and he had no more interest in being compliant. He'd always hated the rules imposed on him by this little Australian dictator and his mob of suck ups. Only Neilson showed spunk. Only Neilson challenged the order of things.

That's why Neilson hadn't stood a chance and the poor sod wasn't even aware of that fact. Or didn't he care? "There's one little secret that nobody knows," he muttered.

"Which is?" demanded Hovein.

"Did you know that Johnston had a daughter?"

"What of it?" said Hovein.

"She and I had a fling during one of my visits to Sydney years ago."

"How did you meet her?" asked Waites.

Tennyson was enjoying himself. He said, "Johnston was working late and she popped in by train to meet him at the office. I happened to be around and invited her to join me for a cup of coffee until her dad was finished as he was doing some claims analysis on the American division. I took her across the road to the Westin where I was staying. She joined me in my room and one thing led to another."

Franks suddenly became very alert. "Johnston's daughter was only fifteen when she suicided."

"Oh," said Tennyson, "I didn't know that."

When JJ heard this in the monitoring station his face paled. It took a moment for him to compose himself.

Angela saw that he was upset. "What's the matter?"

"Nothing," said JJ, "I need something to drink. Sitting down for too long is not good for you. I also need to go for a walk." He needed to be by himself, to think. Angela had not heard this confession by Tennyson and he was pleased because he needed to get his head around it.

"Do you want company?" asked Angela who was stretched out. She placed her book down. "No, I'll be back shortly."

He went down to his assistants and issued an order. The ordeal was finally over. Jack and Tony had been very efficient with delivering the drugged bodies of the released hostages to designated locations but this time there would be slightly different arrangements.

JJ's family had suffered at the hands of EIG and in particular Tennyson and Franks. To a lesser degree Hovein and Waites had been complicit.

JJ's younger sister, Emily Johnston, had committed suicide at age sixteen, not fifteen. Nobody in the family had any idea why this had happened. She had always been a pretty teenager, popular with her peers. She hadn't been bullied, had no weight issues and seemed to get along with her teachers and other people. It had been a complete mystery until now. Tennyson's revelation had shocked JJ. JJ had no notion that Emily had sex with this monster, let alone met him. Clearly James Johnston had not known either.

After Emily's death, Sonja Johnston, JJ's mother took to the bottle and she left. James Johnston was shattered by these events as it came soon after his sacking from EIG. He thought his inability to earn a living had caused his wife to leave him but possibly it had been Emily's death. No one knew for sure and Sonja was also now deceased, a victim of a car accident.

James Johnston survived a little longer but he grew more and more morose as time went on. He needed treatment for depression but refused to entertain visiting a psychologist or psychiatrist. And then he took to the bottle and died of a heart attack. But JJ felt he died of shame and held EIG responsible. He had done all in his power to learn about his father in his last days and he learned much of his efforts with the company, his discoveries in New York, his report which was never released, his sacking for inexplicable reasons and the personnel at EIG. James Johnston, during his drinking binges towards the end of his days, behaved with less discretion and told JJ things he would normally have kept to himself. He had always been loyal to the company and his colleagues and absolutely close mouthed. He rarely talked of anything to do with his work.

JJ then also embarked on his own research into the company and the structure of the board and the key people on the management team. He joined EIG determined to learn even more. The plans he devised had been formulated early but the details changed as time went on.

JJ's family had been destroyed not only by the paedophilic Tennyson but by an organisation which looked after top brass ahead of others. There was no point in getting upset, complaining or challenging key people in the company. Nothing would have been achieved except for JJ being made to feel stupid for pursuing something which others would deem an unintentional outcome of circumstances beyond anyone's control. JJ had formed another view.

He was prepared to die for his actions.

CHAPTER 54

Day 17

Nick Koutslakis sat back from the table, reading the Sydney Morning Herald. He smiled when he finished the article. He placed the paper beside him, took his cup of coffee and drained it. He waved to the waitress for another while he surveyed his daughter's face.

"Why so glum?" he asked.

They were seated outside a cafe in Balmoral and the view of the water and the people who walked along the promenade was peaceful. Koutslakis often came here for breakfast. Today he and Angela had arrived in his new Audi, a silver A8.

'I'm fine," she said, "Just a little concerned about what's going to happen now."

"Worried about Jordan?"

"Yes. He's back in his flat and doesn't want me to be seen with him until the police surveillance is over."

"He's a bit paranoid, isn't he?" said Koutslakis.

"He likes to do everything with little room for error."

"Good policy. I could use a man like that."

"He's going to quit EIG in a few months when all the fuss has died down."

"I see. Do you think he'll work for me?"

"I don't know. He said he'll think about his future in a while. First he has to make sure he's clear of the law."

A seagull flew by. Koutslakis recalled his childhood when he and some friends used air rifles to target small birds. They hadn't managed to hit many but it was fun. Now he did things to win and half hearted efforts were unacceptable. What Angela said about Jordan Johnston impressed him. Of course he realised that the young man was using the name Jordan Johnson and wondered whether he was going to revert back to his real name at some point in the future.

The two young men Koutslakis had lent JJ would soon be available for other work. Jack would be back with the nightclub where he kept the peace better than the most of the others in his employ. Tony was also a useful hand and would be employed profitably. Dan however would be left to go his own way. Given the police interest in him, Koutslakis thought it bad news to have him connected to his organisation at this time. Perhaps he would be hired in a few months when the kidnapping affair was of less interest.

Jack and Tony were both strong and wiry and could handle most trouble makers and problems.

JJ had been pleased with them, Angela had confided to her father. "Honey, why don't you have some breakfast?"

"Okay, I've had a coffee and my stomach has now woken up. What do you recommend?"

"The big breakfast is good. I like Eggs Benedict too. Have whatever you want."

Angela ordered French Toast with strawberries and watched the people stroll by until it arrived. She had her breakfast in near silence as her father continued reading the paper, a habit he had always had. Her mother tolerated it but rarely came out with them. Although her parents were divorced, they remained friends and occasionally enjoyed each other's company. Angela thought their relationship was quite civilised. They realised they were incompatible after the first flush of lust had passed and decided not to destroy their affection for each other by being married and becoming miserable over the years like so many people.

Angela also enjoyed a good relationship with both of them. She saw her mother more often than her father who loved her company but who managed to let her live her life as she saw fit. When she'd spoken to JJ about her family he said he admired them. He said his own family had been broken by events out of their control and he was saddened by their deaths. He said he was now alone and that he didn't see much point in going on at times. Angela was drawn to him even more when he showed his vulnerability. For someone who was generally very guarded and preferred to keep his feelings bottled up, JJ allowed her an occasional glimpse of what made him tick. She was flattered that he felt he could let himself be unguarded around her.

Angela peered at the water, noting some vessels farther out. She felt good. The last few days had been particularly tense and she was glad the whole criminal episode was behind them. She hoped she and JJ could stay together without the bond of enforced togetherness through a tough and dangerous situation.

It was interesting that her father didn't ask for details of her work with JJ. Was it because he trusted her? Or was it because the less he knew, the less exposed he would be should the police link him to JJ and begin to ask questions?

CHAPTER 55

Day 18

Headlines around the globe screamed out:

HOSTAGES FOUND ALIVE

KIDNAPPED EXECUTIVE TEAM UNHARMED
BIZARRE END TO KIDNAP DRAMA

ALIVE AFTER 17 DAYS – HOSTAGES RELEASED

POLICE BAFFLED BY EVENTS IN AUSTRALIAN KIDNAP ORDEAL

Donaldson who read the listings from a communication sent to him before breakfast was surprised, annoyed and relieved, all in equal proportion. The fact that the first five and now the other four of the kidnapped individuals were alive was cause for genuine relief and joy but he was plainly irritated that the Strike Force had been unable to break the case. He would get his team together and, like a good sporting captain, urge his men and women to continue the vigorous pursuit of the perpetrators.

He now needed to read the story in detail and wondered how the press had gained the information before his people. His wife had left the Sydney Morning Herald on the kitchen table as always and he grabbed it even before making coffee. Jessie was at the stove cooking bacon and eggs and he pecked her on the cheek and mumbled, "Good morning."

He sat down and began to read. The article was on the front page.

'This morning a message was received by this newspaper regarding the whereabouts of the remaining four kidnap victims from the daring broad daylight kidnapping of the entire senior management team of the prominent insurance conglomerate Easy Insurance Group, known to most as EIG. The message said that the latest senior executives released were part of a cover-up and criminal network and that tapes would soon be made public to provide evidence of this crime.

John Franks, Group CEO, Tim Tennyson, American CEO, Mark Hovein, Group Investment Chief and George Waites, Group Risk Chief were found in an abandoned building in Redfern, an inner suburb of Sydney. They had been drugged and left lying on the ground level of the building. They had been tied so that they were not able to move had they woken from the effects of the drug. Ambulance services had been contacted by this newspaper. The men have been transferred to hospital but appear to be unharmed.'

Donaldson tossed the paper aside. He needed to talk to the journalist who received the communication and he was not going to accept any nonsense about confidentiality. He finished his breakfast with his mind working rapidly.

He got to his desk in quick time and summoned Braxton and told him to get information regarding the contact made to the newspaper anyway he could. He also needed to understand whether they would receive copies of the tapes as well.

This case had turned into a publicity stunt. The kidnappers were hailed as good guys in some quarters from what he could gather as he started researching the internet. They had uncovered crimes and were being praised rather than being seen as the law breakers they were.

As expected his superiors wanted to meet with him. For the next few hours Donaldson attended a variety of meetings with senior police and politicians wanting to know how the media had obtained this latest information. By the time he got back to his office, he was in a dark mood.

Braxton and Morris came in and he pointed to the visitors' chairs. Braxton sat comfortably with a pad on his lap. Morris crossed her legs and waited for Braxton to inform them of the interview at the paper's headquarters.

Braxton said, "The journalist with the by-line said he received a text message and that this led him to where the captives were held. The text also mentioned the tapes."

"Can we track where the text emanated from?"

"The journalist tried and we examined the data but it led nowhere. A disposable phone seems to have been used."

"Damn," said Donaldson, clearly annoyed. "What do we do now?" said Morris.

Donaldson rubbed his chin, deep in thought. "Let's wait for these tapes. Get our experts onto it. They'll examine their origin and hopefully that'll provide a break."

CHAPTER 56

Dark clouds spread across the skies, JJ noted, as he exited the block of units he lived in. He considered taking an umbrella but retreated as far as his front door before turning back again to proceed forwards. Damn, he would take what came. Rain was not the worst thing that could happen. JJ walked to the wrought-iron gate to his block of flats, pulled the stiffened metal open, and set off to the Bondi Beach cafe which was fifteen minutes away. He was alone and he kept a keen lookout as he strode along the footpath, down the slope. The beach was relatively deserted at this hour of the morning with only some surfers braving the waves. The ocean looked magnificent in the distance. He wasn't being followed. Perhaps the police had given up on him. In any event he would continue to be vigilant. He called Angela on his new mobile phone once he was settled near the window of the cafe and asked her to join him. In the meantime he consumed two cups of cappuccinos and read the newspapers which were scattered around some vacant tables.

The discovery of Franks and company still generated interest and comment in the papers. One story suggested that this gang of crooks, not the kidnappers but the EIG executives, should be locked up and the company placed under administration. Of course that was absurd but JJ knew that the reputation of EIG had been damaged. He would ensure his stock holdings in the company, small though it was, would be liquidated over the next few days.

When Angela walked in he put the paper down. She looked breath taking in a new outfit. A raspberry peasant blouse and tight white trousers made her look stylish, the sleek lines of the pants showing off her obvious curvaceous figure. Her hair was cut and coloured a slight shade of dark red and she appeared relaxed.

"Hi gorgeous," he said, standing and kissing her on the lips, "I love your red hair."

"It's actually called badious," she said, smiling.

"I wouldn't call it bad."

"Chestnut is something you've heard of, I trust."

JJ nodded whilst still looking dumbfounded.

She sat in the comfortable chair across from him and smiled. She was pleased with the response her freshly acquired current fashioned clothes brought. After being cooped up for weeks, she felt good being able to dress nicely and apply the usual feminine extras to herself. Makeup had been a secondary thought at the concentration camp in Coogee.

A waiter arrived and she ordered coffee.

JJ added, "Get us two of your famous big breakfasts too." Alone, JJ kept his gaze on her. "You look spectacular."

Angela said, "I'm still me. You look like you haven't seen me before."

"I've missed you. I only realised after spending a few nights apart how much I missed you. I haven't been fair to you either. But now that the operation is over, I'll be much more attentive.'

Angela placed her elbows on the table and came closer. "What's going to happen now?"

"One of your father's computer geeks, Gerard, will send excerpts from our stay in Coogee to the internet, with written text and with some voice feeds."

"What will that achieve?"

"I don't know exactly but it will explain a number of things that the newspapers and perhaps some of the public have been curious about. The tapes we originally made available was a teaser, like a movie trailer."

"Have you left the selection up to Gerard? He might send stuff you don't want aired."

JJ smiled and squeezed Angela's arm. "You know me better than that. I'm a control freak. I've edited the segments and made three tapes which Gerald will upload at the times I specify. I haven't left anything to chance."

After they finished the breakfast of bacon and eggs and grilled tomato, Angela kissed JJ and left the establishment by herself. JJ insisted that they don't appear together for another few days so that any watchers wouldn't be able to connect Angela to him. Once all the tapes were released, JJ hoped the focus would shift.

However JJ had not planned on an undercover police officer being in the cafe when Angela seated herself next to JJ. The cop who had kept watch of JJ's flat had recognised the man as he wandered down the hill and had maintained a reasonable distance along the way. When the woman joined him, he was curious. He immediately sent a text to Donaldson so that a tail for the lovely young thing could be organised.

Hence, when Angela returned to her flat, she had been followed and photographed. This was emailed via mobile to the Strike Force's co-ordinator.

Braxton was soon able to discover that Angela was the daughter of Nick Koutslakis who had been a person of interest to the police for some time.

Donaldson was ecstatic. Could this be the break they were after? He arranged for a few of his police officers to work this angle.

That evening, Joseph McCrae, a Strike Force member visited the nightclub which Koutslakis owned and ran. He ordered a soft drink and bided his time. After six hours he knew that he couldn't expect Johnson to simply turn up. The stakeout was an idea but it might take days or weeks for the plan to work as easily as they imagined.

The next day he reported to Donaldson who agreed it had been a knee jerk reaction. He also told McCrae that Angela Koutslakis had stayed in all evening.

CHAPTER 57

Lt Stephen McPherson was in a great mood. He had been going about his business at the office when a junior cop popped by his desk and asked whether he had seen the item posted on the internet regarding the US CEO of EIG. McPherson was soon led to the site which had already caught the press' attention. The site was in two parts. The top section included an article which provided basic information about a Tim Tennyson, a 51 year old man, who managed to climb the corporate ladder of an international insurance conglomerate and then tragedy struck. First he was kidnapped but then he was exposed as a child molester but more significant was the revelation that he used insurance funds specifically set aside for the payment of claimants to acquire brothels.

In the second part of the website was an accompanying YouTube clip of a young woman, called Mona, who looked about fifteen years old but said she was nineteen and she spoke of being assaulted by her uncle when she had been thirteen. She told the story of how Tim Tennyson, her uncle, had raped her when he had visited his brother's house. Both brother and wife were away in Chicago to visit friends. At first Tennyson showed interest in her hobby of collecting sea shells. She went on to detail the change in him when she bent over to collect a shell which had fallen down. She described the horror as he grabbed her, ripped her clothes off and began to fondle her. She was so terrified she couldn't move. Later he threatened her, saying if she revealed what had happened, he would make sure his brother, her father, lost his job at EIG.

McPherson had initiated steps to have Tennyson arrested as soon as he returned to New York but this website was gold. It meant that the judicial process would be much smoother and less likely for lawyers to have this sick individual let off on bail or for them to engineer a defence to secure his acquittal. McPherson had experienced a host of slick lawyers representing wealthy defendants and using the most bizarre tactics to generate reasonable doubt. Of course they would search for Mona who would be a crucial witness.

In Sydney too, City Central was buzzing with the news.

Donaldson ordered the apprehension of Franks and Tennyson and wondered whether others were implicated.

Later that day the papers took the story. One release on a newspaper website read: 'Tim Tennyson, CEO of the US operations of EIG, a global insurer, was charged with various offences including having sex with an underage girl.'

Morris caught Donaldson in the corridor and asked, given these latest developments, what the status was on the kidnappers.

Donaldson said, "That's a separate matter. We continue our investigations."

"Nobody was hurt and it seems that the real criminals were insurance executives," said Morris, apparently quite agitated.

"They are separate crimes. It's our duty to uphold the law. It's not for private individuals to assume the mantle of law enforcement. You don't condone vigilantes, do you?"

"No sir." Morris walked off. She didn't believe in citizens taking the law into their own hands but, in this instance, she felt the corporate bigwigs would have got away scot free like they usually did without an incident such as the brazen kidnapping highlighting what was turning out to be a huge scandal. The media was seeing to that.

Polls indicated that people were disturbed that a blue chip corporation had indulged in activities both criminal and morally corrupt. Talk back radio was having a field day and insurance companies, like banks, the target of public loathing, were being denigrated. Enquiries were being called for and politicians, eager to appease the populace, began to make noises to suggest that investigations would be launched.

The web spread the news far and wide. In the USA the FBI was called in. They were tasked to find what else the company had shown as assets which were dubious in nature. This was aided by the release of the second tape indicating that it was well known amongst the top executives that assets in the USA were materially over-valued, that the company held CDOs at full value and that certain acquisitions brought disreputable personnel within the ranks of EIG. The global reputation of the company could no longer be sustained. In London, the company was not as badly mauled in the press as in the USA but it was probably only a temporary situation as regulators were beginning to place the corporation in its sights.

Having being named as accomplices, George Waites, Chief Risk Officer, and Mark Hovein, Chief Investment Officer, were also being investigated by the insurance regulators in Australia.

JJ watched the spectacle from his home. He had another day's leave prior to the weekend before his scheduled return to the office. He realised he needed to attend work to ensure that any broken routine would not be misconstrued. JJ knew that the police would still be seeking to check out whether he had any involvement in the kidnapping, mainly because he had been away and, because of Maddie's allegations, he was the only person the police could consider a potential perpetrator. Using a new mobile phone, he had advised Angela to lay low for a few weeks.

What JJ failed to understand was how the You Tube film of Mona had been uploaded. It had come out of thin air. It certainly helped the cause and he wondered how many people had been hurt by Tennyson whom he considered a vile human being.

Naturally JJ wanted to enjoy a week's break with Angela, somewhere well away from Sydney, but now was not the right time. He thought about the monies the gang had stolen from the four key executives at the centre of the saga. He had not benefitted. All the cash went to Koutslakis to fund the operation as well as provide a hefty business margin. Koutslakis felt the cash was more than adequate compensation for lending out labour and providing other resources and facilities.

Koutslakis knew the police were sniffing around to find out what the word on the street was. But he and only a select few knew what had occurred and they were tight lipped. These associates who were in the loop all understood the penalty should there be a leak. Koutslakis had not been involved in any major criminal activity for a while prior to the kidnapping so there was little leverage the police had to force any of his associates to talk.

Nick was impressed how the website leaks fed the mainstream media and how this created speculation about the integrity of the entire company. He noted how the share price had retreated by twenty-two percent in only a few days.

JJ was hurting this organisation in more ways than one. He was a smart boy, Koutslakis realised, and he was pleased his daughter had chosen him as a boyfriend. So when a detective asked to see him he was not at all surprised.

Detective Ryan Smith was shown to his office at 11pm one night. He was well known to Koutslakis as a man who knew the Cross and he was a down to earth man who appeared quite reasonable on the surface. But he could show a tough side if he felt someone was lying.

"Nice to see you again Ryan," Koutslakis said, not getting up to shake hands. "You're well Nick," Smith said, standing and looking a little uncomfortable. "Can't complain. How can I help? More fights around the Kings Cross area."

"I'm here on another matter. I was wondering whether your daughter knows a Jordan Johnson."

"I'm sure she knows lots of fellas but she doesn't always tell me who she's seeing. That's the new generation, as you probably know." Koutslakis upturned his hands in a gesture which said he was kept in the dark by his own flesh and blood.

Smith nodded. "Yeah, I guess that's right. Have you heard her mention a Jordan by any chance?"

Koutslakis looked at the ceiling as if pondering the question. "No mate I haven't. She rarely introduces her boyfriends. In fact she usually dumps them after a few occasions."

"So she's had no steady partners?"

"One I recall was a few years ago but, yeah she hasn't had anyone for long enough since then to have them introduced to the old man."

Smith seemed stumped. "What do you say to the fact that Angela was seen in the company of this Jordan Johnson a day ago?"

"Really. Well maybe you should ask Angela about that." Koutslakis eyed Smith keenly. He wasn't going to be cowed by some stupid comment. Did they think he was an amateur?

Detective Ryan Smith smiled and walked out of the office without another word. He reported his interview to Donaldson who then informed Morris to talk with Angela. "Shake her up a little. We have nothing to lose."

Morris had Braxton come along and in twenty minutes the car pulled up in front of Angela's new unit in Pyrmont. She lived in a security building and Morris had to identify herself to be let in. They took the stairs to the first level and knocked on flat number 12.

A moment later the door opened to reveal a beautiful woman and if Braxton didn't know better he would have taken her as being Italian. She possessed large eyes, a smooth olive complexion and a bosom which made his heart race. He was tongue tied for a brief disorienting moment.

She invited the two detectives in when Morris flashed her badge.

Morris appraised the unit and was favourably impressed. It was evident that it was a female's home. Everything matched and the colours on the walls were a creamy apricot with a darker shade on the cornices. They were asked to sit on a cream sofa with numerous cushions.

Braxton thought the entire lounge area was extremely feminine. There wasn't even a large screen television in sight. He wondered whether it was located in the bedroom for viewing with any lucky sod who came around. Everything looked clean and tidy and Braxton was almost afraid to lodge his big frame on the sofa.

Angela sat in a leather chair opposite the detectives and smiled. "How can I help?" Morris started softly. "Do you live here by yourself?"

"Yes," said Angela, "it's a one bedroom flat."

"What about boyfriends?"

"What about them?"

"Do they stay over?"

"What is this all about? Is it a crime to have a boyfriend now who sleeps over?"

"Is Jordan Johnson your boyfriend?"

Angela remained calm. She had been warned that this might occur and she and JJ had decided that it was of no value to lie about anything which could later be proven to be incorrect. "I've been out with him but it's too early to suggest he's my boyfriend."

"So you know him?" said Braxton.

"It's difficult to know anyone after a few dates, don't you think?"

"Johnson has been implicated in the kidnapping of EIG's management team," Morris said, staring straight at Angela.

"Oh, I had no idea."

"Don't act coy. You must know. Did he brag about it?"

"Not to me. I met him for a meal only the other day and he seemed no different than at other times."

"Where was he when the kidnapping saga played out?"

"He's been on holiday, that's all I know."

"By himself?" said Morris who began scribbling something in a note pad. "I don't know. We didn't discuss it."

Braxton said, "Don't give us the run around. Doesn't it seem coincidental that he's available to see you after the kidnapping incident has ended?"

"I can't answer that. I haven't been following the news," said Angela. She stood up. "If there's nothing else, I have an appointment to get to."

Morris looked at Braxton. "Just one more question Ms Koutslakis. How do you contact Johnson?"

"I don't. He calls me on my mobile."

Outside Morris said to Braxton, "We haven't been getting much activity on Johnson's mobile so I wonder whether he's bought other disposable mobiles."

"I wouldn't be surprised. But I don't think we should ask Angela for her mobile to collect his number, just yet."

"I agree. Let's wait until a little later when we have something more tangible to pursue."

On their drive back to headquarters, Braxton looking out the window mumbled, "Where do we go from here?"

Morris, who chose to drive for a change, slowed to a stop behind a Toyota waiting for the red light to suddenly show green, then turned to her colleague. "Donaldson said we will take Johnson into the station tomorrow to explain to us where he's been over his holidays and to provide proof. In the meantime transcripts of phone conversations are being prepared."

Morris reported to Donaldson who seemed out of sorts. "What's wrong?" she said.

"There is nothing on any telephone taps of any value whatsoever. Either he's very clever or innocent."

"And that's a problem? Being innocent, I mean." Morris possessed a strange quizzical look.

"I guess not," Donaldson admitted, "it's simply that we've made no progress and the powers up stairs are getting impatient."

"Aren't they happy that nobody was killed?"

Donaldson studied Morris for as moment. "Are you starting to get soft? A crime has been committed which is being played out across the world and we're looking like we can't organise a booze party."

Morris smiled then departed. He was right. It was far more important to look good than to have results turn out well by their own accord.

CHAPTER 58

The next day a further tape was released on the internet and this one was more devastating for the corporation than the previous two. The contents were reported word for word by major newspapers throughout the country and then picked up by the international media. It showed not only that Franks and Tennyson were the drivers of decisions which reflected poorly on the company but included an audit report to Franks which had never been distributed. In fact it had been suppressed from management and the Board of Directors. This report also revealed that Tennyson had hired a convicted criminal to head up one of the USA's key East Coast insurance businesses.

John Franks was reading the Sydney Morning Herald which included the story on the front page under the heading 'EIG Cover-up'. He was going red. He pushed his half-eaten breakfast of eggs and sausages away. How the hell did anyone know about this? He muttered to himself. He slammed the paper down.

Rose looked up from her breakfast. "Ooh, what's that for?"

"This report," he said pointing to the newspaper article and then thumping the table, "was shown to nobody except George Waites and George wouldn't have shared it or leaked it."

"What about Tim?"

"He knew about some of the contents but he didn't see it. This report is quoted verbatim and I had destroyed the original years ago."

"So how would anyone access it?"

"I have no idea. It's a complete mystery."

"What about the author?"

"He's dead," snapped Franks.

Rose said in a moderate tone, "Was it left on the system perhaps?"

Franks stared at his wife, deep in thought. "Johnston wrote it and I had the IT Department delete it from the system. The only way that

that report could survive would be Johnston himself, if he took a copy home. But who would he show it to?"

"Family members."

"A wife who left him and a daughter who committed suicide. I don't think so."

Franks stood up, ignoring Rose. He went to the bathroom to finalise his preparations to visit the office. Tie on, shoes polished, hair combed, Franks went to the garage but a police vehicle pulled up. The officers approached and almost apologetically invited him to go to the City Central police station.

Franks grudgingly complied. He wondered whether the police had more questions regarding his stay in the one bedroom establishment or were they interested in company matters which he had already mentioned was largely confidential. During his initial interview he was asked about the unusual investment portfolio which had been leaked but he remained resolute that regulators and auditors had already reviewed the company's books. The police accepted this area of enquiry was outside their brief, particularly as APRA was showing revived interest.

Franks was installed in an interview room and had to wait for ten minutes before Detective Inspector Donaldson walked in. He had been provided with coffee which was not up to the standard at the office. Donaldson apologised for keeping him waiting.

"What's this all about?" Franks said, feeling comfortable talking to a senior man.

"Mr Tennyson is being held in custody pending extradition to the United States. The Americans are now asserting that you too should be charged as you must have been aware that Roberto Mussolino, a well known criminal, was hired to head up one of your US operations."

"That's EIG's prerogative, surely. He hasn't broken the law since he's been with us."

"Well, according to my US sources, he has."

"What do you mean? I'm not aware of any crime he's committed."

"They are in the process of gathering the evidence to send."

"You can't keep me here."

"We're not going to hold you. I'm just giving you advance warning of what's in the air. You should get yourself a good criminal lawyer."

Franks assessed Donaldson. "Why are you doing this?"

"I like to see justice done. I don't think you intended to hurt anyone. Tennyson's a different story and he's going to be convicted in the USA on a number of counts. I also believe that any wrongdoing regarding the financial side of things will be dealt with by the Insurance regulator. That's not our brief."

"And what about the kidnappers and the money they stole?"

"That's still being investigated. We're confident we have a lead."

Franks stood up and shook Donaldson's hand. "Thank you. I'll keep in touch. You never know when I'll be able to return the favour."

When Donaldson met with Braxton and Morris, he informed them of his chat with Franks. They were in his office and Braxton scratched his head. "Why did you do that? It's not our job to warn people."

Morris waited for Donaldson to reply. She was as puzzled as Braxton.

Donaldson said, "Franks already knows about the report which has appeared in the newspapers. He'd be on alert so I wanted him to think he was clear of any criminal charges. In the meantime I had someone bug his office and telephone."

"To see whether he is involved?"

"You can never tell. Why would a guy who is a prominent captain of industry deliberately allow a big time crim to be hired unless he was unaware at the time of his appointment? I think Tennyson is the bad egg and he's dragged Franks into this mess."

When John Franks arrived at his office he was welcomed back by all the head office staff on his floor. He spent a few moments informing them he was unharmed and that he wanted to carry on business as usual. Once he was by himself, he checked the share price which had fallen again. The leaks had done untold damage to the value of the company and he was worried EIG might become a takeover target. He couldn't allow that to happen. He had to restore the company's reputation and hence its share price.

In another part of the building, JJ was also welcomed back after his three week holiday. He talked about how good the break had been and how good it was to be back at work. His colleagues seemed to believe him and at ten o'clock a few of them went across the road to a cafe where they enjoyed coffee.

JJ knew that everything had to look natural. He chose to return to work at EIG but planned for it to be short lived. He had carried out his plan and flushed out the truth. Tennyson would be convicted, it seemed but the others in the senior management team would simply have to deal with the directors, now that the report had been exposed. JJ had only heard of the report from his father and he had taken it upon himself to find it amongst his belongings after he had died. His father would never have shown it to anybody. Johnston was angry that he had been denied an opportunity to send it to stakeholders but he would never have gone over the CEO's head. He was that kind of man. JJ admired him for it but still felt it was wrong not to fight the corruption.

As the coffee members wandered back into the foyer, waiting for the elevator, JJ saw that Maddie was entering the building with a cup of coffee in her hand. She smiled at him but otherwise ignored the group. She had taken the break-up badly. JJ didn't expect anything else. He vowed not to get involved with anybody else from the work place in future should the opportunity arise and assuming he and Angela ever broke up. The romantic adventure with a colleague was foolish but of course he needed to find this out for himself. The fact that his father had cautioned him previously about this sort of danger counted for little when he made his choices.

Later that day, Morris called JJ at the office and requested his presence at City Central after work. She said a number of fresh questions needed to be addressed. JJ agreed, saying he was happy to help and said he appreciated that the police had not visited him or prevented him from coming to the office. Until they were satisfied he wasn't guilty of the kidnapping, JJ understood that he would be under surveillance.

At six fifteen that evening, JJ was in the interview room with Morris and Braxton opposite him. JJ was dressed in a pin striped suit, white shirt, yellow tie and polished black lace-up shoes, much different from when he was first interrogated and it seemed the police accorded him more respect in his business outfit.

"Mr Johnson," Morris began, "thanks for coming in. We need to clear up a few issues. So you know a colleague of yours, Madeline Manors, told us you had requested sensitive information..."

"A spurned lover, you mean?"

"What was the nature of your relationship?" asked Morris, fiddling with a pen.

"Maddie and I were seeing each other but I broke it off and ever since she has been awkward and unpleasant. So it wouldn't surprise me that she landed me in it...female revenge."

Morris couldn't help herself. "Why did you break it off and was that just before your annual leave?"

"I don't recall the exact date but I quickly realised we were completely different people with little in common and I felt it was better not to get too involved."

"But that's not the case with Angela Koutslakis?" added Braxton.

"Are you interested in my love life? I can provide you with a written summary of all my conquests, if you like."

Morris said, "There's no need to take that tone. What we would like you to provide is a summary of places you've been to during your time off and a list of people who can verify it."

JJ smiled and said, "I don't keep a diary but I'll do my best."

"Credit card details will suffice," said Braxton.

"I think I paid cash for everything but I can check. When do you want the details?"

"By tomorrow at six o'clock should do," said Morris who stood, dismissing JJ.

JJ left the building, made a call, and hailed a cab. He told the driver to take him to Paddington where he got him to stop near a pub. He paid the driver then hailed another cab. Checking that nobody was watching, he told the driver to take a particular long winded way to another pub in the Rocks. Alighting, he kept an eye out for anyone who might be following. He didn't spot anything suspicious.

Inside the Lord Nelson he found his man sitting at a back table on the ground level. He ordered a special beer and sat opposite Fred Trott, an associate of Nick Koutslakis. They enjoyed a few drinks and then JJ outlined what he needed. Trott nodded and said it would be no problem. He and a few others also in Koutslakis' employ would be able to provide the police with evidence of his whereabouts.

The men shook hands and JJ departed first. He checked the people as he walked out and walked a distance up Kent Street before finding a cab. Convinced nobody had tracked him, he told the driver his destination, a street a few blocks from his place. Then, to ensure there wasn't anybody who showed too much interest in his movements, he strode quickly to his unit block.

Arriving home, he made himself some bacon and eggs before sitting down and inventing his journey, using maps and the internet for details. Having completed his summary, he printed a copy and put it in his briefcase for the next day. He watched some television before getting a good night's rest.

The next day he again visited City Central after work hours and asked for Detective Sergeant Morris who happened to be out on a job. He gave an envelope marked for her attention to the receptionist and went home. He expected that the police, as much as they could from the information listed, would check the statement. He knew that the people who had been placed in the correct locations would do their job. After all they would be paid handsomely from proceeds of the funds transferred by Koutslakis' electronic experts.

CHAPTER 59

The three men waited outside the Group CEO's office. The inner sanctum where all the key executives lived was secured even more than any other floor which had keypads outside each entrance.

Not only did this area have a separate code, in addition to the code needed to enter the reception area, but it had reinforced bullet proof glass. The receptionist was a trim blonde woman in her fifties who took no nonsense from anyone. She sat in a separate glass office between the corridor to the elevators and the sectioned off executive offices which occupied half the floor space of level thirty-three, one down from the top level where Board meetings took place.

The three men whom the CEO's personal assistant, Ruth, had asked to wait were all from the Internal Audit Department. Alan Wilton was the Internal Audit Manager. He was a down to earth man with over twenty years experience as head of the company's internal audit services. Then there was the head of the Australian team, Tony Allson, who was a veteran auditor with significant specialist experience. Finally there was JJ who was brought in because of his specialist IT experience. They had been summoned for a 10 o'clock meeting. JJ checked his watch. It was ten fifteen.

JJ noticed that Ruth was hopping around doing whatever she'd been instructed to do. She was a large woman and she had a pleasant disposition but she seemed devoted to John Franks and she worked diligently, often working until the very late hours. Her reputation preceded her but JJ felt sorry for her as he regarded Franks as nothing but a corporate bully, if not a tyrant.

At ten twenty-five the auditors were ushered into Franks' large corner office. They were asked to take a chair opposite Franks who hid behind an enormous desk which was extremely tidy, almost bare, in fact. JJ wondered what this man did every day but assumed he spent his time in meetings or on the telephone. There was no computer in sight. Obviously he got others to do anything which required technical expertise.

Franks hardly waited for the three men to be seated when he began, "Thanks for joining me this morning. I know you're all busy but I have an urgent and important job for you."

For the next ten minutes Franks outlined what he wanted and how confidential this assignment was. He stressed that it was top secret and that they report to him directly and to him alone. This in itself was unusual. The Chief Executive rarely had other than a copy of the report going to him and although he espoused support of the audit team, actions suggested otherwise. He always took the opposite side of the audit issue and recommendation if any operational manager challenged it.

Essentially, although JJ knew the real purpose of the project, Franks went to great pains to suggest that security breaches in the computer systems were a serious threat to the company and its operational secrets. He wanted the teams in Sydney to co-ordinate an investigation into all potential weaknesses into breaches over the past two years with an emphasis on reports prepared by financial heads. James Johnston's name was not mentioned but JJ knew that this was the essence of the investigation.

When Franks had concluded his sermon about absolute confidentiality, he said, "Due to a number of issues related to the arrest of Tim Tennyson, the American Internal Audit Department has been officially disbanded. I sent a message this morning. I'm telling you so you do not engage in any communication with that department from now onwards. Is that clear?"

Wilton and Allson nodded. JJ simply stared ahead.

"Thank you gentlemen. Alan, please report progress at the end of each day."

"Yes John, no problem."

The three audit men stood.

"Oh, Jordan, could I have a moment?"said Franks as the group turned to go to the closed door. Once Wilton and Allson had left and had reclosed the door, Franks stood beside JJ and said, "The

Investment Division's reports need to be looked at carefully, on the system. You'll need to liaise with the Deputy Manager to achieve that."

"What about Mark Hovein?"

"He's going to be made redundant."

"You mean sacked?"

"Yes but that's between you and me, understood?"

JJ elicited a wicked smirk. He said, "Is that because he lacks ambition?"

Franks frowned, not certain what JJ meant. The irony seemed to be lost on him.

As JJ exited the fortress like inner sanctum, he passed Hovein who was on his way to a meeting inside. Hovein didn't even acknowledge JJ as he seemed lost in thought. But JJ didn't expect anything different. He was a cold fish and a most unlikeable man. During his visits to the Investment Division, JJ had not heard any of his subordinates or team say anything positive about him.

In another part of the city Nick Koutslakis peered at the rain smashing against the parked cars. He was enjoying a morning coffee with one of his associates in a street corner cafe in Kings Cross. The rain had started suddenly and Koutslakis thought that the kidnap operation had begun much the same way, in a flurry and then ended quietly with most observers and law enforcers taken by surprise at the outcome. Nobody hurt but plenty of damage done to reputations and lives. The rain would be the same. Nobody would die but there would be inconvenience and lasting collateral damage. Flooding, stalled cars, hung washing drenched, gutters clogged. And the investigation would continue on for a long time.

Meanwhile Donaldson was pacing. Morris had just delivered the news that the summary provided by Jordan Johnson had been checked out and there were witnesses who confirmed his presence.

"Damn," he said, "we're back to square one."

Morris said, "I know it's disappointing but better to have the information to eliminate someone than persist with a theory which is flawed."

Donaldson stopped pacing, "You're right. We have no real leads so I guess we'll have to review the case again and begin looking at other angles."

"What's going to happen with the Strike Force?"

"I think we'll select a few guys to stay and have the rest return to other duties. This operation has already cost too much for what we've delivered."

"Why not look on the bright side and accept that a paedophile ring has been uncovered?"

"Sure. But hardly our doing."

Morris walked out to her desk, activated the computer, to see what was on her email. Office work could be so boring.

CHAPTER 60

Mark Hovein rose late. He had a headache. He looked at the bedside clock which showed a digital eight-forty-two. He rubbed his head. His wife, Daya, was lying beside him and she looked worse than ever. The cancer was beginning to eat her up. The chemo treatment was useless, he felt. But he had to continue it for her sake. And it was expensive.

Now that his job had evaporated because Franks had decided to remove all those who might be seen to be responsible for the demise in the value of their investment portfolio, Hovein's source of funds had dried up. He needed the money. The severance pay was substantial but he would run through that quickly if he continued gambling. And he knew he would.

His chances of finding a new position soon would be difficult, particularly locally because he knew word would get around that he had been dismissed by Franks. Today he would consider dispensing with the live-in nurse who looked after Daya every day. That meant he had to become a nurse. God! It was all such a nightmare.

He walked into the bathroom and looked in the mirror. He was pale and he wished he could disappear. The shock of what had happened in Franks' office was still raw and it had not quite sunk in. In fact the experience was worse than the kidnapping which was totally outside his control. But with Franks he should have argued, negotiated, at least tried to deal with the situation rather than submitting passively, like a child being told he had to leave the class.

Hovein brushed his teeth, then shed his pyjamas and went into the shower cubicle. He turned the cold water on, letting it wake him properly. Then he mixed it with hot water to get to a comfortable temperature. But the scene with Franks returned again.

"Mark," said Franks who greeted him cordially, "take a seat. Are you okay?"

"I've had a few days to recover and I'm keen to get back to work."

"Unfortunately I have some news which you may like or you may not like." Franks assessed Hovein critically.

"What do you mean?" Hovein noted that Franks had an envelope to the right of his hands which were clasped together in a prayer like gesture.

"I'm afraid that the directors cannot have you associated with EIG anymore."

"Why? Haven't I done a good job over the time I've been here?"

"It's the lack of disclosure of the CDOs."

"But I advised you about that." He stopped himself from saying more. Franks had made up his mind, he could see that.

"I'm sorry." Franks handed Hovein the envelope. "What's this?"

Franks stood and nodded and suddenly two men from security stood beside Hovein. Franks said, "These men will accompany you to your desk. Please clean out your personal belongings and go."

And that was that. Hovein was dismissed like some junior who had been caught stealing the petty cash. It was humiliating.

These thoughts swirled around Hovein's head as he stepped out of the shower. He towelled down roughly, unable to keep his worries mounting. His life was falling apart. Daya who had been such a fine wife until her illness eighteen months ago was wasting away. His job had now perished. He had no friends because he spent all his time either working or investing his private funds and checking worldwide markets throughout the night. He had made some serious losses recently which had depleted most of his capital and he needed to work.

He continued brooding about this state of affairs whilst munching on toast and jam at breakfast. He asked the live-in nurse, Marie, to shift Daya to her day room, especially made for her to allow her a change of scenery. He then called Fred Harrison, one of the directors whom he knew well, and asked why the Board had taken the view he was no longer fit to run the Investment Division.

Harrison said, "I've no idea what you're talking about." Hovein explained what had happened and what Franks said.

Harrison said, "This is the first I've heard of it. Perhaps he wants to raise it at our next meeting."

"Can the decision be overturned then?" Hovein pleaded.

"It's unlikely. The Board usually takes into account what the CEO recommends."

After a few more words, Hovein hung up. He was furious. The one trait he most despised about Franks was his one eyed view when people fell out with him. He was unable to deal with people on merit. He either loved them, and they could do no wrong, or hated them and they could do no right. He had witnessed this at close quarters. When Franks was displeased he called in his PA to jot down a hastily thought through memo and sent it out without any further consideration. He had the reputation as a good manager in the corporate world but that was only because the company had been successful through good teamwork and he displayed a humble demeanour. And with the press he always appeared modest. Most of the words he spoke were developed by his team. He was the typical front man who spoke well but had few original ideas.

Hovein poured himself a whiskey and drank it straight. He then had another and another until the tears streamed. He had never experienced this previously. He had always been considered by his peers and former employers as a thinker, a man who could resolve problems. Now he was nothing and his wife was dying.

Suddenly Daya's nurse appeared. She looked oddly at Hovein for a moment then stammered, "Your wife needs to go to hospital."

Hovein stared at her for a second before it sunk in. He nodded and pointed to the telephone.

He wiped his eyes. He hoped she had not noticed he had been weeping.

The ambulance arrived not long afterwards and Hovein instructed the nurse to accompany his wife. He would catch up soon, he said. First he needed to carry out something which was urgent. He went to his dresser drawer and pulled out a pistol which he had kept in case of burglars years ago when he had been particularly security conscious.

Hovein was in no fit state to drive but he did anyway and drove cautiously so as not to attract attention. He entered the office by phoning a new employee who wouldn't yet realise he had been let go and advising him he had forgotten his security pass which provided basic access. He couldn't take the risk of asking his senior staff who may have been alerted somehow of his sudden demise. Office gossip often travelled faster than a bushfire.

Hovein then managed to get inside his office which had been locked by asking his personal assistant for the spare key. She believed him when he said Franks had summoned him and that an appointment for a possible consulting role had been scheduled for eleven o'clock. He waited. Soon Franks would enter the Group Investment Department after his early morning meetings had concluded. Hovein wondered how many people actually knew that he had been sacked. Would Franks call a meeting to brief Hovein's department, then circulate a memo to the rest of the company? That was normal practice. And he would bet that the man would follow normal practice.

CHAPTER 61

The street below was alive with ants, or so it seemed from the window on the 33rd level. Don Neilson turned back to Audrey, his personal assistant. She had just finished advising him of the meetings he had scheduled for the day. So soon after the kidnapping, Neilson was not interested in keeping all his appointments. He informed Audrey which meetings he would postpone to another time. His escape from harm during his ordeal in the confined area of a one bedroom flat made him appreciate the wider world and he was going to walk more and spend less time in stuffy rooms with stuffy people.

"What about Jordan Johnson who's due at 11 o'clock?" Audrey said.

Neilson regarded Audrey who had been his PA for only a few months. She was a tall brunette with a pleasant smile and long slim fingers. He wondered from time to time how magnificent they would be around his cock. He looked at his watch. It was already ten forty. "Show him in when he arrives. He won't stay long."

JJ was five minutes early for his appointment and he chatted to Audrey for a while until Neilson came out of his office and invited him in. They exchanged pleasantries.

Neilson's office was a large corner office facing the Quay and it had spectacular views of the harbour. JJ noted that he had personalised the room with a photo of his wife and dog on the desk, some pictures of family on the wall amongst prints from Salvador Dali. He had papers and reports to the right of his high backed ergonomic chair, leaving the left hand side of his desk for equipment such as telephone and laptop.

"You've made an appointment to see me?" said Neilson.

"That's right. I'm carrying out a review of how reports are set up on the system and what permission levels exit."

"Do you want a list of access levels for my staff?"

"Yes, that would be great. Also would you let me know when

these levels were set up and what review process you go through. And it would help to understand when changes to the different types of access occurred."

Neilson turned his chair to the right slightly. "I think Audrey may have a document detailing this but I'll give you an overview so..."

Audrey broke into the office and she spluttered, "There's been a murder...on level twelve..."

"Calm yourself," said Neilson, "Just take a deep breath and tell me what's happened."

Audrey stood still for a moment, heaving with several long breaths and said, "The Investment Division's receptionist called me and said that Mark Hovein shot John Franks."

Now calmness reigned. Don Neilson was stunned into silence. Audrey continued standing, staring at her boss. JJ downed his pen. The assignment was over. The case of the leaked report was over.

Donaldson and Morris arrived on the twelfth floor after uniformed police had made their way in to cordon off the crime scene. But they found two bodies. Hovein had also killed himself.

There was little else to do now except to note that the kidnapping case had ended. Donaldson wanted to continue to follow up on Jordan Johnson but was told by his superiors to let matters rest. The press, after discussions by police chiefs and the Commissioner, received a statement from City Central that Hovein was guilty of murder as well as kidnapping. He was believed to be the insider who had arranged the crime. The newspapers ran with the story.

Donaldson admitted to Morris, in private, that he didn't believe the press release but that was police politics in action. He took Morris and Braxton out for dinner one night after disbanding the remainder of the Strike Force but refused to discuss the kidnapping any further. He was tired of the nonsense he had to endure. He decided that he would retire at the end of the year. He genuinely liked Morris and Braxton and wanted to thank them for their work.

After the dinner, Morris accompanied Braxton to his place for a nightcap which lasted until the early hours of the morning.

Tennyson was extradited and put on trial in the United States. Neilson became the next Group CEO.

Waites was fired because he had withheld important information from the Board.

Other members who endured the kidnapping all resigned within months of the incident. New people were appointed to their positions. Only Neilson remained and he enjoyed the challenge but also, as the man in charge, decided to cut back on his hours.

EIG's share price eventually rebounded but never fully recovered. The balance sheet reported its true value which was twenty percent less than when Franks was in charge.

CHAPTER 62

The view over the Mediterranean was spectacular. The breeze was gentle and refreshing. He turned back to find his newly wedded wife fast asleep. They had had a wonderful evening enjoying a fine dinner and then a quiet stroll before retiring to a night of love making.

As he wandered back to bed, she stirred. She was a magnificent sight with her hair tousled, her legs tucked under her and her butt round and delicious. He didn't want to wake her so he eased himself back on his side of the bed and watched her. It was only seven o'clock and the sun did not have any effect on her sleeping.

He too soon dozed off. It was close to nine o'clock when they both seemed to wake simultaneously. They kissed good morning and without a word continued from where they had left off the night before. It was as if the lovemaking had been suspended in time.

Finally around eleven am, they wandered down to the breakfast room of the small secluded hotel which they had discovered by accident when driving through the countryside. The hotel was perched on the side of a cliff and overlooked yachts anchored nearby.

As they approached the dining room, a waiter who had served them the day before, said, "Good morning Mr Johnston." Then when Angela appeared he added, "Good morning Mrs Johnston, did you sleep well?"

Angela smiled but said nothing. "Bongiorno, Ricardo," said JJ.

Angela and JJ were shown to a window table and they ordered coffee before deciding whether to look at the menu or partake of the buffet.

Angela placed her hand over JJ's. "What a lovely spot. Can we stay a few more days?"

"However long you want," said JJ, "your father was very generous."

"What do you mean?"

"He doesn't want me to start work for him until we are ready." Angela smiled.

What JJ didn't reveal was that Nick had also deposited a tidy sum into JJ's bank account. JJ had quit EIG a month after Franks' death. It was interesting how things work out, he thought, once you put actions in motion and allow momentum to take over. His plan was merely to make the EIG executives face up to some hard truths. What happened was beyond any of his expectations.